LEGENDS II

Stories in Honour of
David Gemmell

LEGENDS II

Stories in Honour of
David Gemmell

Edited by Ian Whates

NEWCON
PRESS

NewCon Press
England

First edition, published in the UK August 2015
by NewCon Press
in association with The David Gemmell Legend Awards for Fantasy

NCP 081 (hardback)
NCP 082 (softback)

10 9 8 7 6 5 4 3 2 1

ISBN: 978-1-907069-81-9 (hardback)
978-1-907069-82-6 (softback)

Cover art © 2013 by Dominic Harman
Cover layout by Andy Bigwood
David Gemmell silhouette courtesy of the David Gemmell Legend
Awards

Interior layout by Storm Constantine

CONTENTS

LEGENDS II
AN INTRODUCTION

Stan Nicholls

Something interesting is happening in fantasy fiction. Other than the interest generated by inventive ideas and compelling storytelling to be found in the best of it, that is.

Science fiction, the genre to which fantasy has tended to be yoked – and which, make no mistake, this writer loves equally –was once the vessel for a certain kind of social commentary. I'm thinking of that often satiric, deflationary form summed up in a quote attributed (perhaps erroneously) to Ray Bradbury: "I don't want to predict the future. I want to prevent it."That strand of sf, if not gone, seems to have diminished a lot in recent times.

Is it possible that fantasy has inherited, or at least now shares, science fiction's mantle in this regard? Well, fantasy isn't science fiction, despite occasional overlaps, and goes about its business in its own way. Although it's maybe a generalisation that sf has majored in ideas while fantasy inclined to emotion, there is a grain of truth in that. But just as sf used to be weak on characterisation, for example, particularly in its depiction of women, and improved with maturity, fantasy is also coming of age. The truism that, whether set in the far future or on a distant planet, much science fiction is really about the here and now, just might be starting to apply to fantasy too. There certainly appears to be a growing engagement with 'the real world' as seen through fantasy's particular lens. In that respect the stories in this volume are a fascinating snapshot of the contemporary genre.

It's been said that whereas sf has fans, fantasy has readers. That's debatable, though it's undeniable that given science fiction's head start as a definable category there was time for a supportive community to develop. Fantasy, on the other hand, is a comparatively recent distinct form. But that could be changing too. Events centring on the genre, and increasing online activity, are building a discrete fan base. We like to think that the David Gemmell Awards for Fantasy are playing a small part in helping to foster it.

In their seventh year at time of writing, and consisting of the Legend Award (best novel), Morningstar Award (best debut) and Ravenheart Award (best cover art), all decided by an open vote, the Gemmells harness the energy of fantasy's emerging fandom. I suspect that's something David Gemmell, who placed a high premium on the sentiments of readers and championed their voice, would have been delighted about.

2016 will mark the tenth anniversary of Gemmell's passing. This anthology, ably edited by Ian Whates and made possible by the generosity of all the writers who have contributed to it, is a fine tribute to him and the genre as a whole, and helps support the awards bearing Gemmell's name. My hope is that *Legends II* will prove as popular as the preceding volume, and that we'll see a continuation of these showcases that, like fantasy fiction itself, will go from strength to strength.

Now that *would* be interesting.

Stan Nicholls
Chair, The David Gemmell Awards for Fantasy
April 2015
www.gemmellawards.com

The Blessed
and the Cursed

Gav Thorpe

"Just a bunch of priests, where's the danger?"

Words that had inspired confidence at daybreak were about to come back to haunt the brigands of the Scatha Vale. Calgallun shifted slightly in his hiding place within the undergrowth so that he could see Leopard, the band's leader. The tall, wiry bandit had not moved or shown the slightest inclination that all was not well. Calgallun glanced across to his left, to where Feranck was concealed from the caravan track behind a tree.

"Hsst! What in the Five Hells is Leopard doing?"

Feranck shot him an annoyed look and shrugged. "What're you talking about?"

"Look at them damn flags on the wagon," said Calgallun, wondering how Feranck, in his forties and almost twice Calgallun's age, had survived so long with such dull wits.

The 'wagon' coming along the muddy road was more like a huge strongbox on wheels, built from heavy timbers and banded with iron. It was pulled by four draft horses, Perastian Greys, each sturdy enough to drag a drayman's cart by itself. Two poles stuck out from the back, hung with a white banner displaying a scarlet fist design.

Feranck's look betrayed ignorance of the sigils' significance.

"Priests, all right," said Calgallun. "Monks from that shrine at Erod. Dedicated to the Creator as Avenger."

"Fighting priests?"

"You bloody plainsfolk are all the same. Don't know nothing important. Yeah, priest-soldiers of the Creator. Very dangerous."

The priests were just about visible now, six on each side of the wagon. At this distance one might have thought they were wearing silver robes, but Calgallun knew better. Their garb was the finest scale from the smiths of Erod, said to be lighter than steel mail but twice as resilient. Their hands were covered in gauntlets of the same. Their heads were protected by open-faced helms with cheek guards and scarlet crests, aventails of more scale guarding neck and throat. Each warrior carried a foot lance with long tapered head, blood-red streamers twirling in the wind that funnelled down the valley. At their waists they bore short stabbing blades.

It was hard to see features yet, but Calgallun could see that several were darker-skinned, natives of the southern lands, or descended from such people. He was just as surprised to see that some of the 'priests' were women. A female outlander rode on the wagon beside the driver, scanning the hills and cliffs to either side.

"We need to call off the attack," said Calgallun. "This is a bad idea."

"Afraid the Creator will strike us down?" sneered Feranck.

"No," Calgallun snapped back. "I'm afraid those priest-soldiers will. I better warn Leopard, it looks like he doesn't know what we're getting into."

"Move and you give us away," Feranck said sharply. "Calm down. There's a dozen of them and forty of us. We've got more bows than they've got men."

"From what I've heard that won't help," muttered Calgallun.

He looked again at Leopard, who was staring intently at the armoured cart and its escort. Even if the lowlander knew nothing about the Knights of Erod, Leopard could clearly see their military aspect. Calgallun tried to signal to his leader but Leopard never once glanced back in his direction.

"He won't call it off," said Feranck. "Not now. You know how he thinks. He said it was some chapel's tithe money for Lord Krieff, but with that sort of protection it's got to be something even more valuable. The bigger the guards..."

"...the more they're protecting," Calgallun finished one of Leopard's favourite sayings.

"Exactly. And I don't figure Leopard is the type that's easily intimidated. Do you want to go back to the camp tonight with an empty belly and purse? We didn't come to these accursed valleys for no reward."

"Better than not going back at all," countered Calgallun.

It was too late, they were definitely committed to the attack. The wagon was about two bow shots away now, moving at a brisk walking pace. The knights were alert to danger as the open valley closed in to the narrowing gorge occupied by the bandits. Stands of trees, scrubby bushes and scattered boulders provided the cover the brigands needed and the holy soldiers escorting the wagon had to know this. Scatha Vale had gained a notorious repute over the last few years due to the exploits of Leopard and his men. Pickings had been slim all summer; most merchants took the longer route to the south, which had forced Leopard to come into Bleak Valley.

From his hiding position only the southern edges of the dale were visible, but even within his restricted view Calgallun could see two sets of standing stones and a chill-inducing monolith atop the jagged hills. Ruins of an age passed long ago, but the tales still held that the spirits of those ancient heathens clung to this valley. Most folk avoided this area even more than the Scatha Vale, including Leopard's men.

Not so the priests, and so the bandits had crossed the Low Pass, acting on information from one of Leopard's spies at the Inn of the Crossed Roads.

Calgallun's instinct itched for him to back out now while he could, but he was too afraid; even more so than of the soldier-priests. If he pulled out of the attack and Leopard's gang survived, they would hunt Calgallun down for desertion. Promises had been made and brotherhood sworn. Honour, not to mention pride, would demand the life of any that broke faith with their fellow outlaws.

The trill of a mountain thrush – or the imitation of such by Leopard – signalled that the attack was about to start.

Calgallun licked dry lips and tested the string on his bow before nocking an arrow. He half-drew and sighted on one of the lead horses. Leopard had insisted that the first arrows were used to ensure the target could not gallop away.

"Creator spare me if this goes wrong," Calgallun muttered.

He pulled the bowstring to the full draw and waited for Leopard's next call.

Seven years at the monastery of Erod had taught Naldros much patience, but the continued belligerent ignorance of the wagon driver tested her sorely.

"The Creator brought everything into being," the Castigator

explained again, speaking slowly. "Dove and lion, rose petal and thorn, summer breeze and storm. Destruction and violence are nothing more than another part of the pattern the Creator wove into the fabric of the world. One can study war and know the Creator as well as finding the Creator's will through peace."

"But it's murder, right?" insisted Markwell. He picked a scab on his chin with his free hand, idly flicking away the tag of dried blood. "To kill is evil, right?"

"What if I were to kill an evil person to protect an innocent?" asked Naldros. "Besides, we of the Order of Erod do not believe in an afterlife. We think of the Creator as Avenger, not Judge."

"So we can do what we want while we live, is that it?" The driver looked dubious.

"Within the society and law we create and enforce ourselves. The Creator shaped us but he does not control us. It is only our fellow people and our own standards and conscience by which we are measured. At the point of death all that remains of us is the legacy of our decisions, whether barbaric, civilised or both."

"And you're civilised, right?" Markwell eyed the stocky priest with suspicion. "You get to decide which is which, right?"

"We all decide, each to his own morals," Naldros said with a sigh.

She gave up trying to explain and lowered herself down from the riding board. Gaitlin waited a few moments for her to catch up.

"So, Castigator, how goes the philosophical debate?"

"Discussing the cosmic order and inherent morality with Markwell is as rewarding as exchanging gastronomic advice with swine," replied Naldros.

"Forgive his ignorance, he has not had the benefit of our teachings and the time to contemplate and become one with the will of the Creator."

"Forgive him?" Naldros darted a look across to Skaios on the opposite side of the wagon. "You are mistaken, the Redeemer is over there. I am the Castigator."

"Very droll," said Gaitlin. He was about to add something but stopped.

Naldros felt it too. The teachings at Erod steered a warrior to finding communion with the Creator, able to sense the subtle ripples of energy and fate that continued to echo down through the ages from the moment of the world's birth. To be attuned to those waves was to touch upon senses beyond those of other folk, granting near-supernatural ability.

The call of a mountain thrush grated in her ear. To a lesser-trained warrior nothing would have been amiss, but to Naldros and his fellow priest-soldiers the artificial call was as obvious as a war shout. The moment Naldros detected it her conscious mind gave way to instinct. By the time the second bird-call sounded the knights of Erod were already responding to the coming ambush.

She turned and swung her foot-lance before the arrow left the shadow of the tree. Gaitlin moved as well, taking a step to one side, responding to the intent of his shrine-sister. The tip of Naldros' spear slashed through the space where Gaitlin had been a moment before. The razor-sharp edge caught the arrow mid-shaft and sliced it in two, sending the pieces tumbling harmlessly to the ground.

There were more arrows than shrine-warriors. Some of them deflected the missiles, but the horses were each pierced by several shafts. One survived the first attack, wounded and thrashing in the traces against the dead weight of its companions, whinnying in pain and terror. Markwell wrenched the brake with one hand while trying to rein in the bucking horse with the other. An arrow took the driver in the chest and he pitched from the riding board with a deathly croak.

Naldros blocked the noise and detected the crack of breaking twigs, the creak of bending bow and a pant of breath. She broke into a run even as her eyes picked out the stocky bandit crouching in the bushes to his right. Their eyes met and Naldros recognised dread in her foe's gaze; his hands were trembling and a fat tongue lolled over fear-dried lips.

Around Naldros the rest of the group was charging in silence towards the rocks and trees, drawing their short swords. Hastily loosed arrows whickered across the road, one of them finding Heiran's throat, sending her crashing to the ground with a spray of arterial blood.

Naldros focussed on the swaying point of the nocked arrow pointed at her and subtly adjusted her stride, leaning to the left. The brigand's shot passed by a sword's breadth to the right. The priestess was confident she would be upon the enemy before he had time to fit another shaft to the bowstring, but her attention was drawn to the left, where two muscle-bound bandits broke from cover, shields and swords at the ready.

Without breaking stride, Naldros turned her attention to these assailants as other bandits charged out to meet the oncoming warrior-priests. She ducked beneath the first sword thrust, slipping her sword from its sheath as her spear slashed across the bearded man's throat, parting hairs and windpipe with equal ease. The second man pulled his shield across to ward away Naldros' sword with a clang, but this exposed his leg. The priest's spear punched through the knee, sending the brigand crashing to his back.

Ripping her foot-lance free, Naldros parried the fallen man's sword and kicked aside his shield. The Castigator dropped to one knee as she plunged her sword through the man's chest. Straightening, flicking blood from the tips of both weapons, Naldros took a moment to judge the situation.

The spontaneous counter-attack had served the knights well, negating the archers hidden around the track. These bowmen rose from their hiding places, drawing knives and swords to help their companions embroiled in a melee along the edge of the road. However, not all of the archers had revealed themselves.

Naldros turned back to the brigand she had first seen, just in time to duck beneath another arrow. Breaking into a sprint, the priestess covered the intervening bare ground in moments. The brigand raised his bow to ward away Naldros' spear, the wood splintering as it met the hardened steel tip of the foot-lance.

A desperate dive carried the bandit away from Naldros' sword, but not far enough to escape completely. The tip passed through jerkin, shirt and flesh, leaving a clean cut through all three. The brigand cried out and rolled away, slithering through the undergrowth like a serpent as Naldros followed up.

A grunt of effort warned the priestess-knight to turn, a fraction of a heartbeat before a dagger rang from her right pauldron. Spinning, spear-tip a blur, she met the other bandit with a hand's span of steel, plunging the lance head through his heart.

Naldros was about to go after the wounded brigand but a cry from behind called her attention back to the main fight. She turned in time to see Gaitlin overpowered by three attackers, cut across the face and punctured in the chest by multiple spear and sword injuries. Suppressing a shout of anger, Naldros sprinted along the track to aid her beleaguered brothers and sisters.

The way of Erod turned fighting into an art, and when more or less equally matched in number there were none that could contest with the holy knights of the order. The brigands were far more numerous, though, and simply rushed the priests, ganging up on them in fours and fives, heedlessly battering and slashing, overcoming speed and finesse with numbers and raw aggression. Already three of the priests were down, though perhaps four times that number of bandits had also been slain.

A tall, lean man loomed over Karlia, battering a maul repeatedly into the knight's head, turning his flat features into a bloody mess. Naldros drove her sword between the shoulder blades of the brigand but it was too late, Karlia was beyond saving. Leaping over his body the Castigator cut the legs from under another attacker, coming face-to-face with the heavily scarred face of Skaios. The Redeemer's armour was splashed with crimson, some his own blood, some belonging to slain foes. The Redeemer's eyes widened in warning and Naldros dodged just in time to elude a spear thrust from behind.

She turned quickly, spear flashing out to open the man's throat. A last reflex of dying muscles slashed the brigand's spear toward Naldros' gut, forcing her back a pace. She stumbled, seeing Skaios' dead face as she fell backwards over the Redeemer's corpse.

Three outlaws converged on Naldros as she struggled to regain her feet, but not one of them made it to the priestess-soldier.

Emerging from the anarchy loomed a massive warrior with thick furs over studded leather armour, a bastard sword in his hands chopping down the priests' attackers. On his head was a simple basin helm, a row of spikes forming a crest along the top. Where the knight-monks had used guile and skill the newcomer ploughed a bloody furrow through the outlaws with raw strength and bullish determination.

Naldros rolled to her feet as another brigand tried to skewer her with the tip of a spear. She used her foot lance to puncture the woman's ankle. Tendons severed the bandit collapsed with a cry, the priestess' sword rising to meet her chest as she fell.

Without intent, the knight of Erod found herself by the side of the burly stranger, weapons at the ready. There were only a handful of outlaws left and a glance confirmed to Naldros what she had feared;

her priestly companions all lay dead upon the track. The brigands eyed the two surviving fighters warily and then, without any word of agreement, turned and fled, disappearing amongst the rocks and shrubs.

Stifling a cry of pain, the bandit Calgallun tried to get to his feet. He managed to roll sideways onto his knees and pulled himself up with the aid of a low branch. Panting heavily, he leaned against the tree. He could feel the warmth of blood slowly dribbling down his left leg from the wound in his side and as he tugged at his shirt the cloth stuck to his skin. Glancing down he saw a red stain spread from just under his lowest rib to above the hip and across his belly button.

"Not good," he muttered. He risked a glanced out to the road. There was one priestess still alive – the one that had come for him at the outset of the fight – and the unknown warrior. Everyone else was dead or had run away. The priestess looked towards the trees concealing Calgallun, head cocked to one side as if listening. "Not good at all."

The holy warrior started down the road towards him, the other man a step behind. The bandit pushed himself upright and tottered a few steps away from the road before his legs gave way, toppling him into the long grass. He crawled a few more paces until he felt a shadow fall over him.

The priestess stood over Calgallun with stabbing blade poised. A moment before the sword descended the stranger appeared at the knight's shoulder, one hand wrapping around her wrist.

"Wait on a moment," said the warrior. His voice was deep, with an accent from the northern provinces.

The priestess did not move except to turn her head towards the fighter.

"Wait?" There was a trace of an accent in the priestess' voice too, from somewhere much further afield – Vasria, perhaps, or maybe even further east. This was at odds with dark skin that spoke of a different heritage. A former slave, perhaps. "I am the Castigator, it is my right and my duty to punish this murderer."

"Murderer?" sputtered Calgallun. "You killed more people than I did today. What gives you the right to condemn me, sister?"

The priestess paused, eyes narrowing as she returned her attention to Calgallun.

"It was *you* that attacked *us*," she said. "This is vengeance for violence you initiated."

"I've surrendered!"

"You have been caught. There is a difference."

Calgallun looked into the priestess' face and saw no hint of mercy in her hard stare. The other warrior released his grip and stepped back.

"The certainty of tyrants," the stranger said, shaking his head. "I might expect better of a holy woman."

"He is already wounded, I would not expect him to survive the night," said the priestess-knight.

"So, a mercy, is it? If you might show such compassion to end his suffering, perhaps you might summon up enough to let him live."

"Why do you care so much about this filthy brigand? Your sword made short work of his companions."

"I recognise desperation, and I pity him. I spared those that ran away, and you can spare this one, surely."

"It doesn't really matter," said Calgallun. "You're right, I'll be dead afore nightfall unless someone stops this bleeding. And even then, we'll all be dead afore sunrise."

"Really?" The priestess lowered her blade and knelt beside Calgallun. "That is an odd threat to make."

"Not a threat. Look around. You see where we are? Bleak Valley. This place is cursed. Worse, it's haunted. Two travellers alone in these hills? You'll be dead not long after me. "

The priestess stood up, face twisted with a sour expression. "Myths, nothing more."

Calgallun grimaced as he sat up, feeling his shirt pulling at the dried blood scabbing on his wound. The priest's gaze moved between Calgallun's and the warrior, undecided.

The outlaw was not wholly misguided. There was something about the Bleak Valley that felt wrong to Naldros. Few birds and fewer animals broke the still with their presence. The air was hotter than it should be, oppressive and close, though the sun had not once pierced the clouds. It was as if a storm was permanently on the verge of breaking, full of pent-up destructive energy not quite ready to be released.

There was old power; what the heathens had called earth magic. There had been many sacrifices on those hilltop altars and the ground was steeped in the blood of those fallen in battle for control of the border passes.

Naldros had little time for campfire tales, but the brigand had a point. Centuries of myth surrounded this place, and only so much could be attributed to exaggeration and time.

"Three stand a better chance than two," said the warrior who had arrived so unexpectedly. He extended a hand. "Call me Keldrik."

Naldros ignored the proffered handshake. The stranger made her wary, his motives unknown.

"A timely intervention, for you to find us beset in such manner. What business brings a sword-wielder to the Bleak Valley? I might think that you are not such a lawful man yourself."

"I came across the tracks of the bandits this morning and thought I might be of service," said Keldrik. "I admit that had you not been a lady of faith I might have sided with your attackers for a share of the spoils. As it is, I call it luck or fate, you might call it the will of the Creator."

"Your sword, show it to me," said Naldros, sheathing her own and planting the butt of her spear in the dirt.

Keldrik did as asked, drawing the long-bladed sword over his shoulder. The silver grip was fashioned as two serpents entwining, spitting heads jutting out as the crosspiece with emeralds for eyes. Naldros could feel the keen edge of the blade cutting the air, latent with energy. She reached out but the stranger pulled the sword away from his grasp.

"A relic sword," Naldros said quietly, admiring the craftsmanship. There were delicate runes engraved along the blood channel of the blade, in a language so old even Naldros could not read them. It was obvious that the weapon was the source of Keldrik's ominous air.

"*Osdrik's Fang*," Keldrik told them. He turned the blade one way and then the other, catching the light along its length. "Gifted to me by my father, and passed to him through the generations, bearing several names as took their owners' fancy."

"Generations indeed," said Naldros. "Such weapons were forged by the heathen ironmasters."

A cough and a groan drew their attention back to the bandit. His face was ashen, one hand holding the wound in his side, his other fist clenched in pain. Naldros fixed him with a stare.

"Tell me, what brought you to a life of brigandage?" she asked.

"I was outlawed by Lord Krieff's marshal, DunFalcon. Just a labourer's son, aged fourteen. He wanted our lands. I would have died if Leopard hadn't taken me in. What did I know of hunting or surviving in the wilds?"

"Your parents? Siblings?"

The young man looked away. "Mother and father. They didn't make it as far as Leopard's salvation. My sisters, two of them, taken in service to the lord's estate. Service? Bondage more like."

"If we had not been armed, would you have killed us anyway?"

"No." The brigand looked earnest as he shook his head. "No blood spilled of the defenceless. Leopard was a hard man but not a cruel one."

"Very well," said Naldros, reaching a decision. "What is your name?"

"Calgallun."

The other members of the shrine were dead. She was the last of their small but influential order. Naldros was not only Castigator, but now Chancellor, Armourer and, most pertinently, Redeemer. Had she not been accepted by the Redeemer when he had been brought in chains to the shrine, the blood of innocents on her hands?

"I am Naldros." She nodded to Keldrik. "Help him to the wagon."

The priest unlocked the gate of the armoured cart and pulled open the door.

"See the treasures for which so many have given their lives," Naldros told them.

Held up by Keldrik, Calgallun peered inside the shadowed interior of the timbered frame. He thought to see strongboxes and chests, or perhaps ingots on shelves, but there were just a few sacks. Naldros used her spear to slit open one of the sacks. Red powder spilled forth, bringing with it a sweet fragrance.

"Incense for the chapels at Derith and Gabordon."

"Worth much?" asked Calgallun.

"Invaluable to us, as it has been blessed by the High Father at Cordoris. To the Unfaithful? Perhaps the same as its weight in grain."

The young bandit slumped in Keldrik's grip, feeling weak at the thought.

"Leopard had such big plans..." he moaned. "He told us there would be a lord's ransom in here. Tithes and collections from chapels and shrines across the region. He was going to feed a dozen villages with this."

"Your leader was poorly informed," said Naldros as she placed the spear to one side and pulled herself up into the wagon. She dug through a pile of smaller bags and boxes until she had retrieved a length of linen, a small box and a brown bottle. Jumping back to the track, she left the items just inside the door and retrieved her weapon.

"Cleansing lotion, needle and thread, and bandage." She looked at Keldrik. "You have the look of a man that has sewn a fair few wounds in his time."

"I can tend to him," the warrior confirmed. "What are you going to do?"

"I am going to give thanks," Naldros replied.

"For what?" Calgallun started to laugh but pain turned it into a harsh snarl.

"My shrine-kin are dead. I am not. I should be thankful."

The priestess turned away from them, head bowed, and headed to the side of the road. Keldrik lowered Calgallun against one of the cartwheels and started pulling at the wounded man's shirt.

"Let's have a look at this," he said, glancing up towards the hills. "As you said, we need to be somewhere else come nightfall."

They had been walking steadily north for some time. Naldros had insisted that she would continue her journey to Derith; the incense had been abandoned but the missives she carried in her pack still needed to be delivered. She had scoffed at Calgallun's talk of ghosts and haunted valleys and his pleas that they head south instead, and Keldrik had offered no argument.

Despite her scepticism about the supernatural, it seemed to Naldros that the sky was darkening earlier than he would have expected for the time of year. The arid air had not cooled in the slightest and it left an odd taste in his mouth, as of old blood. They had passed through the narrowest part of the valley, the steep-sided gorge Calgallun called the Snare, but the valley on the other side was even more devoid of life than to the south.

One thing had not changed. The hilltops were littered with ancient menhirs and the jagged remains of ruins. Naldros could feel the old power clinging to them, rising from the blood-soaked stoned as the sunlight waned.

Keldrik led the way, a dozen paces ahead, head bowed and shoulders hunched as though he was dragging a burden. His head constantly moved as he looked left and right.

"What do they claim haunts these hills?" the priestess asked.

"The shades of traitors," Calgallun replied. He limped along, one hand constantly holding his injury. He had relieved his former companions of bow and a quiver-full of arrows and these were now slung over his shoulder. "In the time afore the True Word came, the lands to the west belonged to King Naisar. The kingdom to the east was ruled by Osdrik."

"Osdrik?"

"Yes, the same as your saviour's sword is named after," said the bandit. His words took on the tone of a storyteller reciting a well-worn tale. "These were contested lands, ruled by thievery and raiding as much as laws and taxes. One of Osdrik's lieutenants betrayed his master to a general of Naisar's army, failing to arrive for a battle that saw Osdrik's banner fall and his rule shattered. The king survived the pursuit just long enough to call his curse-weavers and sorcerers together for one final bane-bringing. The traitors were cursed to guard these hills for all eternity. To this day revenants come out at night and fall upon any traveller caught in the wilds between Norfurn and Derith."

"And your leader, Leopard, he did not believe these tales?"

"He believed them all right!" Calgallun said with a laugh. "He didn't plan on there being a fight though, and said we'd be back in the woods above Norfurn by sunset. I'm surprised you came this way at all, with all your learning and that."

"The Chancellor was dismissive of ghost stories, and we agreed with him," explained Naldros. "We were spared the speculation and details."

"You don't think the dead can come back?"

"I believe many strange things are possible by the grace of the Creator, I just don't think this valley is haunted," said Naldros. "More likely it is just a tale told by your leader's predecessors to sow fear in the minds of any that might scour the Scatha Vale for hideouts. How is it that you thought we were protecting riches sufficient to lure you into such benighted lands?"

"Leopard was always good to spread the spoils far and wide. We take what we need but the rest goes to people suffering from Lord Krieff's abuses. That brings favours from every hamlet, ale pit and store station in the Scatha Vale. Eyes and ears everywhere. Your wagon drew much speculation. I suppose Leopard got carried away with imagining what was inside."

"I do not understand. You describe Lord Krieff as some kind of tyrant, but that has not been my experience of the man."

"That and worse. His attack dog, DunFalcon, does all the dirty work, stopping farmers getting their produce to market, locking up the storehouses, starving people into submission. Nothing gets bought or sold 'cept by his say. And then Krieff puts taxes on top."

"And the people you kill, that is justified? Rebellion against your lawful ruler makes it right?"

Calgallun gave her a long look and after a while the priestess thought he understood his intent.

"The good of the many outweighing the good of the few?" ventured Naldros.

"Not as such. Though we'd sooner leave throats intact, it's just a few lowlanders in return for hundreds of hillfolk. This is justice, not rebellion. You've killed afore. What do you tell yourself to make it all right?"

Naldros had no easy answer to that – what would be the point explaining that her morality was derived from understanding the deeper nature of the Creator – and was spared the attempt by a call from Keldrik.

"Less talking, more walking," the bear-like warrior shouted back to them.

His pointing finger swept along the hilltops to either side. An odd mist was coagulating about the standing stones – against all experience and nature it gathered on the summits not in the valley. There was an ochre tinge to the thickening fog and Naldros did not need honed senses to detect the energies being slowly set free by the rune-carved megaliths.

"Oh sweet Creator, we're doomed," wailed Calgallun, stumbling to his knees. He stared up at the sky, now a dark purple of twilight. "The dark'll catch us and Osdrik's Cursed'll take us back to their tombs and barrows for all the life of the Creator."

Keldrik looked south and Naldros followed his gaze. Calgallun's words suddenly took on a literal meaning. An unnatural night was sweeping up the valley from the Snare, blanketing everything with darkness. The priestess grabbed Calgallun's arm and pulled him to his feet.

"We can outpace the darkness," Naldros snapped. "We must run."

"I can't," Calgallun sobbed, clutching a hand to his injury as he tried to pull from the priestess' grasp.

"He tells the truth," said Keldrik. "More exertion will open the stitches. He has lost a lot of blood already, he can't afford to lose more."

"Then it seems my mercy was wasted after all."

Calgallun looked over his shoulder at the encroaching darkness. He felt Naldros let go of his arm and walk away.

"We can move faster without him," Naldros told Keldrik. "It is senseless for three to die when two might save themselves."

"It is too late to escape the valley," said Keldrik. "See how the darkness quickens?"

Calgallun saw that this was true. Already the line that marked the coming night was moving at a brisk walking pace.

"I am not prepared to surrender my life so lightly," said Naldros. She turned north with long strides, but as she stepped past Keldrik the man held out an arm to stop her.

"We cannot run, we must fight," said the northerner. "There is a place nearby we can defend."

"Where?" said Calgallun, casting her gaze across the forbidding landscape.

Keldrik pointed north-west to an outcrop of rock that looked like a headland jutting into the sea of the valley. At its outermost point stood several broken towers and the remnants of a wall.

"Fordrik's Keep?" Calgallun bared his teeth in horror. "That was home to the chieftain who led the traitors. You want to make a stand in the heart of this madness?"

"Yes, I do. The old stones remember his treachery and will aid us against their shades. Trust me, there is nowhere else in this valley where we will have any chance."

"A defensive position sounds better than the open," declared Naldros. She eased aside Keldrik's arm with a glare at the warrior. "What have we to lose?"

"Our souls?" suggested Calgallun.

"Speak for your own," said Naldros. "Mine shall become one with the Creator."

"And what about yours?" Calgallun asked the other man.

Keldrik shrugged and turned away.

The climb up to Fordrik's Keep became steeper and the failing light made the ascent even more treacherous. There was not a glimmer of moon or starlight above; the valley was infused with an altogether more dreadful illumination. The fog from the standing stones and barrows followed the three travellers, gathering into a low bank a few hundred yards behind, catching up with every pace they took.

Calgallun frequently glanced back, convinced he could see something else in the sickly glow of the mist. It looked like silhouettes of men and women; gaunt, armoured figures with spears and shields.

"The shades of the treacherous dead are coming for us," he moaned, almost losing his balance as he hastened forward in his panic. "I hear their groans and laments."

"Nonsense," snarled Naldros. "There is no sound but the wind in the bushes."

The priestess reached a flat outcropping where Keldrik waited for them. Naldros turned back to look down into the valley and her eyes widened with shock. "But perhaps there is something to what you say."

Calgallun scrambled up to his companions, panting heavily, though neither of them seemed the least out of breath. He looked up and saw a forbidding cliff face that formed the foundations of the tumbled fortress. Another glance towards the encroaching fog confirmed that the denizens of the Bleak Valley were no more than two hundred paces behind them.

"Rocks and sheer walls'll be no obstacle to these spectres," the brigand said, shoulders drooping in resignation. "There's no way we can reach the tower afore they are on us, not with such a climb."

"Good for us that we don't have to climb any more rocks," said Keldrik. He stepped along the ledge and seemed to disappear into the cliff. Calgallun hurried after, and found that in the gloom he had missed an opening, obscured by the roots of a tree above.

The gap had a lintel overhead and two pillars a little thicker than his legs to either side. There was an inscription on the lintel and he felt Naldros behind him pause to look at them.

"A very old language," said the priestess.

"What's it say?" Calgallun feared some dread warning to those that would enter, and looked past Naldros at the approaching bank of luminous fog. There were ragged banners amongst the ranks of warriors pursuing them.

"I do not know," confessed the priestess, pushing past. "Not at a glance and far from my books."

The luminescence of the valley faded as they moved into a square-hewn corridor. In the last glow of light they saw Keldrik waiting at the bottom of spiralling stone stairs.

"This was a sally port for the defenders," the warrior told them. His fur-clad shoulders almost filled the passageway from wall to wall and the spiked crest of his helm scraped the ceiling. "To send messengers and raid a besieging foe. It leads into the east tower."

"You know a lot about Bleak Valley," said Calgallun as they followed Keldrik up the steps. Within moments they were in total darkness. The brigand was forced to use fingertips on the wall and a cautious step to keep his footing on the uneven stone stairway. "How come? Nobody lives here, surely?"

"I've spent much time here," Keldrik replied, "but Bleak Valley belongs to the dead."

After ascending in silence for a while, they emerged into a semi-circular chamber of bare stone. Part of the outer wall had collapsed, the timbers and planks of the upper floors long since rotted away to reveal the night sky. Here on the summit, Calgallun could just about see the stars as though through a wispy smoke.

"This way, quickly," Keldrik said, moving to the breach in the wall. The other two followed into a courtyard of cracked flags, the paving covered with weeds, grasses growing between. A twisted mountain ash blocked the collapsed remains of a gateway, but there was just about room to squeeze past and into the square surrounding the central keep.

Calgallun saw steps on the inner wall and quickly ran up them to get a view of what was happening. He could see the length of the valley all the way to the Snare, but it was the phosphorescent glow of the undead host around the castle walls that drew his attention. He thought he heard reedy, distant horns, the skirl of mournful pipes and the soft thump of drums. There were no gates left at the main wall and the glowing horde surged through the gatehouse, a pale aura emanating from the column of skeletal warriors.

"They're here!" he yelled, bounding back down the steps three at a time.

"The keep gate," snapped Keldrik, drawing his sword. "We'll hold them there."

"How do you kill the dead?" Calgallun asked as the three of them retreated under the faint shadow of the keep's gatehouse.

"Allow me," said Naldros.

Laying down her foot lance, she placed her hand upon the quiver of arrows hanging on Calgallun's back and another close to the sheaths at his waist. The brigand could not see wholly what she was doing, but the priestess whispered swiftly in a language Calgallun did not understand. A warmth touched the nape of the outlaw's neck and seeped into his hips.

"Your arrows are blessed by the energy of the Creator," Naldros told him. She picked up her spear. "Mine already possess such power. Keldrik, hand me your blade."

"No need," said the other man. Calgallun could see that there was a sheen to the blade of the great two-hander and the serpents' emerald eyes glowed with jade sparks. "Power older than your prayers lingers within *Osdrik's Fang*."

There was no more time for talk. The ghosts of the traitors were now at the extent of the inner courtyard, massing around the ash tree and slipping over the rampart. Calgallun nocked an arrow and noticed a tiny white flame burning at its tip. He gritted his teeth as the effort of drawing the bow pulled free the stitches in his side. Fresh blood seeped into his crimson-stained shirt. He took aim at a warrior advancing from the gateway. The wretched thing had half a face, scraps of cloth and mail still clung to its body and in its hands it held a splintered shield and crooked spear.

"Creator, guide my shaft," the outlaw whispered, letting loose the string.

The arrow seemed to pass through the dead warrior's ribcage but at its touch the spectral figure evaporated into smoke, a hint of fire consuming it from within. Slicing through four more ghosts behind, the arrow slew them all likewise, leaving a trail of glittering silver vapour.

Now understanding the power of Naldros' blessing, Calgallun took his time with his next shot, lining up more than half a dozen targets before he released the bowstring. As before the arrow cut through them as easily as it parted the fog that surrounded the dead, burning each apparition to nothing.

"Praise the Creator," laughed Calgallun as he readied another arrow.

"Not yet," replied Naldros, pointing with her spear to the right. Dozens of spectres were passing over the wall. She flicked the foot lance to the left where the scene was repeated. The scrape of ancient war harness and creak of bones echoed from the weather-beaten stones. "Arrows alone will not win this battle."

"What will?" said Calgallun his hope suddenly punctured. "There must be thousands of them."

"Sunrise," Keldrik said quietly. "Hope for daybreak."

"That's impossible..." Calgallun loosed his arrow and looked up. The stars flickered as though behind a veil and there was no sign of the moon. He returned his attention to the army closing on the keep. "Too long. Too many."

"Less time than you think," said Keldrik. "If we can hold the doorway, their numbers mean nothing."

Calgallun did as much as he could, slaying the apparitions by the half-dozen and more, until there were no arrows left in his quiver. He threw it away, and his bow, and drew the two long knives that hung at his belt. They felt light in his hands, the sheen of Naldros' blessing dancing along the blades. He winced as pain flared in his side.

"I think this is where you two'll be handier," he said, taking a step back towards the empty doorway so that the priest and warrior had room to swing their weapons.

The dead came on without a word of challenge or shout of battle, eye sockets gleaming with magic, jaws hanging slack but weapons raised.

Naldros moved first, stepping out to decapitate the closest spectre with her spear before retaking her place at the threshold. Keldrik swept his sword in a wide arc, the blade passing through upraised shields and rusted blades without pause, cleaving undead spirits to dust.

Soon the press of the dead was such that the weapons of both were in constant motion; on Calgallun's right the white-fire trails of spear and short sword and on the left the emerald flicker of Keldrik's relic sword. Between them they wove what seemed to be an impassable barrier to the shades of the ancient traitors, through which not a rusted blade nor rotted speartip could penetrate. Beyond, the yellowish light of the dead grew to a haze that illuminated the surrounding walls and towers, throwing flickering shadows of skeletal warriors and skull faces into nightmarish portraitures on the wind-scoured fortifications.

Calgallun would not allow hope to rise again; he could not. His wound was aching and the exertions of the day were returning to drag him down into unconsciousness. It took all his effort simply to remain standing and alert, fighting the mesmerising effect of the whirling blades before him.

He felt a touch of cold on his neck and turned, worried that the breeze came through some breach in the keep walls. The ground floor of the fort was mostly one large hall, with rooms to the left and right through square archways. All sign of furnishing and decoration had long mouldered away, but the stones of the walls seemed intact.

At the far end of the hall, beyond a cold firepit, the floor gave way to a set of narrow stairs leading down. To dungeons or cellars or perhaps another sally port, Calgallun did not know. His blood froze as he saw faint yellowish light licking up the stairs.

"Keldrik! Where do these steps lead?" he shouted, not daring to turn his head as the light grew stronger.

"The tombs, why?" the warrior bellowed back, not pausing in his sword swings.

"The dead, they're coming from below!"

"Fight in my place," growled the warrior. He turned and strode back across the threshold leaving Calgallun no choice but to step forward.

For a moment Naldros held the doorway alone, a bright figure at the centre of a white star that seemed to melt the undead at its touch. Calgallun yelled wordlessly and threw himself into the gap left by

Keldrik, the glowing slender blade of the dagger in his left hand plunging into a spectre's chest, dissipating it like ochre-coloured steam.

Calgallun risked a look over his shoulder just long enough to see more of the dead spilling up the interior stair, stumbling into Keldrik's blade as he threw himself at them. Parting two more spirits, Calgallun looked back again to see Keldrik hacking his way to the top of the stairs. A moment later he had disappeared from view down the steps.

At outset the battle had seemed to Calgallun to be a lucid dream, devoid of the usual clamour, smells and emotions of combat. He had been detached, without the scent of blood and steel in his nostrils, no war cries or shouts of pain to jar his conscience. Now that he was close to the spectral enemy he realised that this was not wholly true. His assailants' features – those that had them – were twisted in grimaces of pain and terror, as though it was not they but the living that were dread-inspiring creatures. He could hear harsh, whispered voices as if from a great distance, and the cries of the dying from afar whenever his glittering knives banished another soul.

'*Absolve us...*' they clamoured.

'*We repent.*'

'*Have mercy.*'

'*We were betrayed also.*'

Again and again with every ghost dissipated by his daggers or Naldros' weapons he heard a last plaintive wail.

'*Forgive...*'

He knew not how he could understand the words of warriors three thousand years dead. And perhaps he didn't but merely conjured speech from meaningless sound. Maybe it was his own guilt that gave voice to the horde of the dead, for it seemed to him that amongst the throng he would spy a familiar face; familiar in that they belonged to merchants and soldiers killed by his arrows over the years of outlawry. The same faces that haunted his dreams on occasion now manifested in the features of the damned host of Bleak Valley.

He glanced back to see if Keldrik had returned but there was no sight of the huge fighter. In the moment of distraction, Calgallun failed to see a ghostly bronze spear thrust from the melee. Just as his weapons passed through the apparition, so the spectral speartip slid into him without splitting skin or shedding blood.

That was not to say the blow did not cause any pain. Agony flared in Calgallun's left shoulder like the sting of a hundred wasps, burrowing into the deepest bone and nerves.

With a cry he floundered back, losing the knife in his hand as his fingers spasmed. He almost tripped on the threshold flags and had to take another step in retreat to avoid the spear coming at him again.

He rallied, slashing his remaining knife through the insubstantial throat of his attacker, but the dead had already pressed up to the door's boundary, almost surrounding Naldros.

The moment Calgallun had been forced back Naldros knew what would happen. She needed no divine sight to see that the brigand's stamina was failing him, nor did she harbour any illusions of the likelihood she could hold the portal alone.

Naldros gritted her teeth against the burning of the muscles in her arms and cut through a dozen spirits with a flurry of sweeps and stabs, giving herself time to leap back within the keep itself.

She felt a shock of transition as she passed over the threshold. Keldrik had been right, there was ancient energy still buried here, akin to the power of the old menhirs but subtly different. The two sprang from the same source but were opposed to one another, like the poles of a lodestone.

For a moment Naldros thought the spectres would be baulked at the gate by this old energy but it did not come to deter them. The ghosts stepped into the keep without any resistance and it fell to her spear and blade to keep them back. Just behind her, Calgallun was snarling like a wounded animal, occasionally lashing out with his knife at a foe that eluded the warrior-priestess' attacks.

"Shut up! Shut up!" yelled the brigand, becoming wilder with each passing moment. "Die, cursed traitors!"

Naldros thought the young man had gone mad but after a moment's concentration heard the voices too. They were not natural sounds, like the wind across the hills or the brush of leaves on the stone, but came from someplace else; a place of mind and spirit alone.

'*He damned us.*'

'*We were tricked.*'

'*We swore no oaths.*'

'*The treachery was his.*'

'*Forgive...*'

Dead faces suddenly came to life, wracked with tortured expressions, voices rasping with regret and bitterness.

'Hate and fear they left us.'

'No love, no friends, no hope.'

'Forgive...'

"We're going to die," cried Calgallun, desperately lunging, his knife dissipating another dead warrior. "They're going to take us to the realm of the damned.'

"Where is Keldrik?" Naldros demanded.

"Below, somewhere."

At any moment Calgallun's last strength would fail. When that happened Naldros would be surrounded. She managed a look toward the stair where her other companion had gone, judging the distance. She was not convinced she would be able to make the run before the spectres were upon her. Even if she reached the sanctuary of the narrow steps there was no guarantee Keldrik continued to hold the attack from below.

Her anger flared, fuelling a blistering series of attacks that cleared the area around the gate, allowing the holy knight to push forward to the threshold again. It was so stupid that she had ended up here. She should have left the brigand and the barbarian to their own devices and trusted to her own instincts and abilities.

Naldros spat a curse at her attackers and the words seemed to form a ripple in the fog, sending the spectres reeling. She swore by the Creator to end their miserable existence and this too sent eddies of power roiling through the fray.

But it was still too little against the monotonous, determined assault.

Misery.

It flowed around her as a tangible wind, suffusing Osdrik's Cursed. They had been damned to haunt these hills until they atoned for their betrayal, never knowing one spark of mercy or gratitude or love ever since. Their damnation was utter, a torment of the soul that outweighed any physical malady a thousandfold. Looking into the glowing eyes of the dead, Naldros could see they were not mindless but fully aware of their horrific fate. In the face of such hopelessness her anger couldn't be sustained.

She felt a moment of pity for them.

The closest spectres reeled back as if struck, but did not disappear. They stumbled and staggered, flowing into and around each other. Naldros thought she heard a sob of relief.

She definitely heard Calgallun fall to his knees with a last gasp of effort, knife clattering from his exhausted grasp.

The spirits were in disarray, reaching out with clawed fingers, not in threat but entreaty.

'*Forgive...*' they rasped. '*Forgive...*'

She glanced down at the fallen brigand and remembered the thought that had caused her to spare the outlaw. Naldros was Redeemer as well as Castigator. As a deadly warrior she had the power to end life, to mete out punishment and bring vengeance to those that deserved it. But the power of the Redeemer was to withhold such ability, to spare life, to value it above everything else. It took a lifetime of hardening heart and self-discipline to be Castigator, but it took only a heartbeat of compassion to be Redeemer.

The dead were recovering, their plaintive looks turning to anger and hatred. They massed a few paces from the doorway, glaring at Naldros as though to dare her to step out. It would be easy to match their scorn with her own, to lift spear and short sword once more.

"I forgive you," he said.

She felt the stones around her lurch as she tapped into the power kept within the keep. She recognised it now, counter to the despair that fuelled the spectral host. It was hope. Like the last candle in the night, the ancient fort, citadel of their treacherous chieftain, held the last shreds of hope for the army of the damned.

"I forgive you," she said again, casting aside her weapons and lifting his hands with palms held towards the Cursed.

"Are you mad?" shouted Calgallun, grasping at the hem of Naldros' scale robe.

"I forgive you." Naldros spoke loudly, feeling the sentiment strengthening in her soul. The words reinforced the feeling, lending power to her mercy, drawing the old energy from the ground beneath until it flowed out from her like light from the sun. "By the Creator, be damned no more."

Calgallun was not sure what happened. One moment he was almost blacking out, the next he saw the priestess-soldier dropping her weapons and holding up her hands as though to give a blessing.

A white flame burst forth from Naldros, expanding out through the spectral host, lapping up the broken stones of the ancient keep. Where the fire touched it seemed to Calgallun that all was repaired. In the near-blinding flicker of the light he saw battlements raised as they had been three thousand years ago. There was an oak gate within the towers and banners of black and red fluttered from poles atop the walls and outer defences.

And the traitorous dead were alive again; men and women and children, of flesh and blood, going about their lives without care, not knowing the doom about to be laid upon them. In that instant Fordrik's Keep was a place of toil and hardship but also laughter and love, family and companionship.

Surrounded by armoured warriors, their chieftain rode back through the gates, a bear of a man in thick furs and studded leather, a spiked helm upon his head. His coming brought consternation; Calgallun could feel the unease of the people at their master's untimely return.

The fires flickered away and the scene faded, leaving nothing but starlight and moonlight shining on pale stone and grey moss.

Calgallun looked at Naldros, mouth agape. The priestess lowered her arms and turned, a calm smile on her lips, eyes moist with tears.

The army of the damned had disappeared.

"Look," said Naldros, pointing to the east. The first glow of dawn smudged the sky with purple. "A new day comes."

"What did you do?" asked Calgallun as Naldros helped him to his feet. "I thought you'd lost your mind."

"I gave them that which they had craved these last three thousand years. I remembered what it was like to live in misery and hopelessness and I gave them what no other has been able to give for three millennia, the gift I received from the order. I gave them forgiveness and love."

"You lifted the curse," said Calgallun, still not sure he believed he was still alive. "But why? It was a desperate gamble. If daybreak was so close, we could've lasted a little longer."

Naldros looked east and her smile faded.

"The Bleak Valley was cursed, my friend. There would have been no dawn while the undead remained. Only the acknowledgement of their suffering and atonement could break the hex placed upon these

33

hills."

"Keldrik seemed certain." Calgallun had almost forgotten the other warrior. He looked across the hall towards the steps but there was no sight or sound of the other man. "Do you think he survived?"

They moved to the steps, calling the warrior's name but no response came up from the lower levels. Naldros led the way down the steps, taking them into a corridor lined with cellars for stores. At the far end was another stair, narrow and straight. Calgallun fetched a simple rushlight from his belt and by its dim glow they continued into the depths.

The level beneath the cellars was more roughly fashioned, with archways sealed with unkempt stonework and plaster, and upon each lintel a heavy inscription.

"Tombs," said Naldros, running a hand over the runes carved into the grave markers to either side of the nearest barrow door. She looked along the tunnel. "Seven generations, from Fordrik who raised this keep to the chieftain that betrayed Osdrik."

At the end of the passage they came to an open barrow, and looking within they saw a body laid out for burial on a stone slab. There was no coffin here and no marks upon the clay plates at threshold. Stepping inside, Calgallun could see that the skeleton was of a large man – the chieftain he had seen in the moment of vision. His furs had mouldered to nothing and only scraps of his armour remained, but in bony fingers he clasped a weapon.

A long relic sword, with hilt and crosspiece of entwined serpents, their eyes fashioned from faceted emeralds.

"I don't understand," said Calgallun, moving aside so that Naldros could see. "Did this revenant slay Keldrik and take his sword? Where's his body?"

"You are a simpleton, Calgallun," replied the priestess, her smile returning. "The name on this tomb... Keldrik. Our companion was no more flesh and blood than the spectres we fought at the gate. He brought us to this place in the hope that I would free his people. That is why he rescued me, and saved you. An act of contrition and another of mercy."

Calgallun looked with astonishment at the old bones, and only then recognised the similarity between the warrior who had interrupted the ambush and the chieftain in his vision.

"The name should have alerted us to his nature," said Naldros. "And the accent."

"A northerner? Why?"

"Not from the north, though that is where the last of the original people of the Scatha Vale now remain. Even you are not a true highlander, but a descendant of the plainsfolk that moved into these parts after Osdrik and his kin were driven out. Come, let us leave these remains in peace."

Calgallun lingered a moment longer, not sure if he believed any of what had happened in the last day. Perhaps, he wondered, he was in a fever dream, dying on the road in Bleak Valley, and all of this was unreal.

A call from Naldros snapped him from his thoughts and he realised he was alone in the tomb with the chieftain's corpse.

He hurried after Naldros, and the two of them ascended to the main hall. The priestess did not stop but walked straight for the doors.

"What about your weapons?" Calgallun asked, pausing beside the priest's foot lance and sword. "Won't you need them?"

"In time the order of Erod will grow again, and I will bear the spear and sword, but those belonged to the bearer of a title I no longer desire," Naldros replied, not looking back. "Each order is founded not by the Castigator, but by the Redeemer."

The priestess stopped outside and turned, one hand outstretched to Calgallun.

"We all need to seek forgiveness for something. Will you join me?"

Rescue

Mark Lawrence

"I spent a year hunting down the men who burned my home. I followed them across three nations."

"I see." The old man laid down his quill and looked up across the desk at Makin.

Makin returned the stare. The king's man had a long white beard, no wider than his narrow chin and reaching down across his chest to coil on the desk before him. He'd asked no question but Makin felt the need to answer.

"I wanted them to pay for the lives of my wife and my child." Even now the anger rose in him, a sharpness twitching his hands towards violence, a yammering in his ears that made him want to shout.

"And did it help?" Lundist studied him with dark eyes. The guards told Makin the man journeyed from the Utter East and King Olidan had hired him to tutor his children, but it seemed his duties extended further than that.

"Did it help?" Makin tried to keep the snarl from his voice.

"Yes." Lundist set his hands before him, the tips of his long fingers meeting before his chest. "Did taking your revenge ease your pain?"

"No." When he took to his bed, when he closed his eyes, it was blue sky Makin saw, the blue line of sky he had watched from the ditch he had lain in, run through, bleeding out his lifeblood. A line of china blue fringed with grass and weeds, black against the brightness of the day. The voices would return to him – the harsh cries of the footmen set to chase down his household. The crackle as the fire found the roof. Cerys hid from the fire as her mother had told her to. A brave girl, three years in the world. She hid well and no one found her, save the smoke, strangling her beneath her bed before the flames began their feast.

"…your father."

"Your pardon?" Makin became aware that Lundist was speaking

again.

"The captain of the guard accepted you for wall duty because I know your father has ties with the Ancrath family," Lundist said.

"I thought the test…"

"It was important to know that you can fight – and your sword skills are very impressive – but to serve within the castle there must be trust, and that means family. You are the third son of Arkland Bortha, Lord of Trent, a region that one might cover a fair portion of with the king's tablecloth. You yourself are landless. A widower at one and twenty."

"I see." Makin nodded. He had disarmed four of Sir Grehem's men when they came at him. Several sported large bruises the next day although the swords had been wooden.

"The men don't like you, Makin. Did you know that?" Lundist peered up from the notes before him. "It is said that you are not an easy man to get along with."

Makin forced the scowl from his face. "I used to be good at making friends."

"You are…" Lundist traced the passage with his finger. "A difficult man, given to black moods, prone to violence."

Makin shrugged. It wasn't untrue. He wondered where he would go when Lundist dismissed him from the guard.

"Fortunately," Lundist continued. "King Olidan considers such qualities to be a price worth paying to have in his employ men who excel at taking lives when he commands it, or in defence of what he owns. You're to be put on general castle duty on a permanent basis."

Makin pursed his lips, unsure of how he felt. Taking service with the king had seemed to be what he needed after his long and bloody year. Setting down roots again. Service, duty, renewed purpose after his losses had set him adrift for so long. But when he had thought himself cut loose once more, bound for the loneliness of the road, he had, for a moment, welcomed it.

Makin stood, pushing back the chair that Lundist had directed him to. "I will attempt to live up to the trust that's been placed in me." Makin thought of the ditch. Cerys had faith in him, a child's blind faith. Nessa had faith, in him, in his word, in God, in justice… and her trust had seen her pinned to the ground by a spear in the cornfield behind her home. He saw again the blue strip of sky.

Lundist bent to his ledger, quill scratching across parchment.

As Makin turned to go, the tutor spoke again. "The need for vengeance feels like a hunger, but there is no sating it. Instead it consumes the man that feeds it. Vengeance is taking from the world. The only cure is to give."

Makin didn't trust himself to speak and instead kept his jaw locked tight. What did a dried up old scribe know of the hurts he'd suffered?

"There's a gap between youth and age that words can't cross," Lundist said. He sounded sad. "Go in peace, Makin. Serve your king."

"The Healing Hall is on fire!" A guardsman burst through the door into the barracks.

"What?" Makin rolled to his feet from the bunk, sword in his hand. He'd heard the man's words. Saying 'what' was just a reflex, buying time to process the information. He glanced at the blade in his grasp. An edge will rarely help you when fighting flames. "Are we under attack?" No one would be mad enough to attack the Tall Castle, but on the other hand the queen and her two sons had been ambushed just a day from the capital. Only the older boy survived, and barely.

"The Healing Hall is on fire!" The man repeated, looking around wildly. Makin recognised him as Aubrek, a new recruit, a big lad, second son of a landed knight and more used to village life than castles."Fire!" All along the barracks room men were tumbling from their beds, reaching for weapons.

Makin pushed past Aubrek and gazed out into the night. An orange glow lit the courtyard and on the far side tongues of flame flickered from the arched windows of the Healing Hall, licking the stonework above.

Castle dwellers scurried in the shadows, shouts of alarm rang out, but the siege bell held its peace.

"Fire!" Makin roared. "Get buckets! Get to the East Well!"

Ignoring his own orders Makin ran straight for the hall. It had once been the House of Or's family church. When the Ancraths took the Tall castle a hundred and twenty years previously they had built a second church, bigger and better, leaving the original for the treatment of the sick and injured. Or more accurately, to repair their soldiers.

The heat brought Makin up short yards from the wall.

39

"The devil's work!" Friar Glenn's voice just behind him.

Makin turned to see the squat friar, halted a few yards shy of his position, the firelight glaring on the baldness of his tonsure. "Is the boy in there?"

Friar Glenn stood, mesmerised by the flames. "Cleansed by fire…"

Makin grabbed him, taking two handfuls of his brown robe and heaving him to his toes. "The boy! Is Prince Jorg still in there?" Last Makin heard the child had still been recuperating from the attack that killed his mother and brother.

A wince of annoyance crossed the friar's beatific expression. "He… may be."

"We need to get in there!" The young prince had hidden in a hook-briar when the enemy came for him, more than a week earlier. He sustained scores of deep wounds from the thorns and they had soured despite Friar Glenn's frequent purging in the Healing Hall. He wouldn't be getting out on his own.

"The Devil's in him – my prayers have made no impression on his fevers." The friar sank to his knees, hands clasped before him. "If God delivers Prince Jorg from the fire then –"

Makin took off, skirting around the building toward the small door at the rear that would once have given access to the choir loft. A nine-year-old boy in the grip of delirium would need more than prayers to escape the conflagration.

Cries rang out behind him but with the roar of the fire at the windows no meaning accompanied the shouts. Makin reached the door and took the iron handle, finding it hot in his grasp. At first it seemed that he was locked out, but with a roar of his own he heaved and found some give. The air sucked in through the gap he'd made, the flames within hungry for it. The door gave suddenly and a wind rushed past him into the old church. Smoke swirled in its wake, filling the corridor beyond.

Every animal fears fire. There are no exceptions. It's death incarnate. Pain and death. And fear held Makin in the doorway, trapped there beneath the weight of it as the wind died around him. He didn't know the boy. In the years Makin had served in King Olidan's castle guard he had seen the young princes on maybe three occasions. It wasn't his part to speak to them – merely to secure the perimeter. Yet here he stood now, at the hot heart of the matter.

Makin drew a breath and choked. No part of him wanted to venture inside. No one would condemn him for stepping back – and even if they did he had no friends within the castle, none whose opinion he cared about. Nothing bound him to his service but an empty promise and a vague sense of duty.

Makin took a step back. For a moment in place of swirling smoke he saw a line of brittle blue sky. Come morning this place would be blackened spars, fallen walls. Years ago, when they had lifted him from that ditch, more dead than alive, they had carried him past the ruins of his home. He hadn't known then that Cerys lay within, beneath soot-black stones and stinking char.

Somehow Makin found himself inside the building, the air hot, suffocating, and thick with smoke around him. He couldn't remember deciding to enter. Bent double he found he could just about breathe beneath the worst of the smoke, and with stinging, streaming eyes he staggered on.

A short corridor brought him to the great hall. Here the belly of the smoke lay higher, a dark and roiling ceiling that he would have to reach up to touch. Flames scaled the walls wherever a tapestry or panelling gave them a path. The crackling roar deafened him, the heat taking the tears from his eyes. A tapestry behind him, that had been smouldering when he passed it, burst into bright flames all along its length.

A number of pallets for the sick lined the room, many askew or overturned. Makin tried to draw breath to call for the prince but the air scorched his lungs and left him gasping. A moment later he was on his knees, though he had no intention to fall. "Prince Jorg…" a whisper.

The heat pressed him to the flagstones like a great hand, sapping the strength from him, leaving each muscle limp. Makin knew that he would die there. "Cerys." His lips framed her name and he saw her, running through the meadow, blonde, mischievous, beautiful beyond any words at his disposal. For the first time in forever the vision wasn't razor edged with sorrow.

With his cheek pressed to the stone floor Makin saw the prince, also on the ground. Over by the great hearth one of the heaps of bedding from the fallen pallets had a face among its folds.

Makin crawled, the hands he put before him blistered and red.

One bundle, missed in the smoke, proved to be a man, the friar's muscular orderly, a fellow named Inch. A burning timber had fallen from above and blazed across his arm. The boy looked no more alive: white faced, eyes closed, but the fire had no part of him. Makin snagged his leg and hauled him back across the hall.

Pulling the nine year old felt harder than dragging a fallen stallion. Makin gasped and scrambled for purchase on the stones. The smoke ceiling now held just a few feet above the floor, dark and hot and murderous.

"I". Makin heaved the boy and himself another yard. "Can't." He slumped, boneless against the floor. Even the roar of the fire seemed distant now. If only the heat would let up he could sleep.

He felt them rather than saw them. Their presence to either side of him, luminous through the smoke. Nessa and Cerys, hands joined above him. He felt them as he had not since the day they died. Both were absent from the burial. Cerys wasn't there as her little casket of ash and bone was lowered, lily-covered into the cold ground. Nessa didn't hear the choir sing for her, though Makin had paid their passage from Everan and selected her favourite hymns. Neither of them watched when he killed the men who had led the assault. Those killings left him dirty, further away from the lives he'd sought revenge for. Now though, both Nessa and Cerys stood beside him, silent, but watching, lending him strength.

"They tell me you were black and smoking when you crawled from the Healing Hall." King Olidan watched Makin from his throne, eyes wintery beneath an iron crown.

"I have no memory of it, Highness." Makin's first memory was of coughing his guts up in the barracks, with the burns across his back an agony beyond believing. The prince had been taken into Friar Glen's care once more, hours earlier.

"My son has no memory of it either," the King said. "He escaped the friar's watch and ran for the woods, still delirious. Father Gomst says the prince's fever broke some days after his recapture."

"I'm glad of it, Highness." Makin tried not to move his shoulders despite the ache of his scars, only now ceasing to weep after weeks of healing.

"It is my wish that Prince Jorg remain ignorant of your role,

Makin."

"Yes, Highness." Makin nodded.

"I should say, Sir Makin." The king rose from his throne and descended the dais, footsteps echoing beneath the low ceiling of his throne room. "You are to be one of my table knights. Recognition of the risks you took in saving my son."

"My thanks, Highness." Makin bowed his head.

"Sir Grehem tells me you are a changed man, Sir Makin. The castle guard have taken you to their hearts. He says that you have many friends among them…" The king stood behind him, footsteps silent for a moment. "My son does not need friends, Sir Makin. He does not need to think he will be saved should ill befall him. He does not need debts." The king walked around Makin, his steps slow and even. They were of a height, both tall, both strong, the king a decade older. "Young Jorg burns around the hurt he has taken. He burns for revenge. It's this singularity of purpose that a king requires, that my house has always nurtured. Thrones are not won by the weak. They are not kept except by men who are hard, cold, focused." King Olidan came front and centre once more, holding Makin's gaze – and in his eyes Makin found more to fear than he had in the jaws of the fire. "Do we understand each other, Sir Makin?"

"Yes, Highness." Makin looked away.

"You may go. See Sir Grehem about your new duties."

"Yes, Highness." And Makin turned on his heel, starting the long walk to the great doors.

He walked the whole way with the weight of the king's regard upon him. Once the doors were closed behind him, once he had walked to the grand stair, only then did Makin speak the words he couldn't say to Olidan, words the king would never hear, however loud.

"I didn't save your son. He saved me."

Returning to his duties Makin knew that however long the child pursued his vengeance it would never fill him, never heal the wounds he had taken. The prince might grow to be as cold and dangerous as his father, but Makin would guard him, give him the time he needed, because in the end nothing would save the boy except his own moment in the doorway, with his own fire ahead and his own cowardice behind. Makin could tell him that of course – but there are many gaps in this world… and there are some that words can't cross.

THE LOWEST PLACE

Edward Cox

The beast's scream shattered the icy air. Jurin's spear slid through its body, pinning it to the rotting wall of a lean-to. Jurin twisted the spear, encouraging the beast's wails to echo across the ruins of the village.

"There are two such creatures guarding that place," the magician had said, back at the meeting. "I suppose you could call them *mates*."

No one refused a summons from a magician. Unless you happened to be a person powerful enough to refuse, the type of person which Jurin was most certainly not. What Jurin *did* possess was peculiar knowledge of great interest to a magician; and so, without choice or defence, she had been transported to a dank and gloomy lair, forced to attend an incongruous meeting, which had, in turn, delivered her to this grim place...

The beast thrashed against the agony, clawing the air wildly, talons unable to reach its attacker. The screams had subsided to a sad mewling, somehow as questioning as it was pitiful.

"Why didn't I see them before?" Jurin had asked, to which the magician replied, "Because when you last visited the village, the village wanted you there, Jurin. Next time, it will not."

Now, beneath a sky the colour of bruised skin, devoid of sun or moons or stars, Jurin listened for sounds in the thin mist that crawled between broken buildings. The beast had ceased to struggle and its steaming breath came in short, sharp pants. Clawed hands gripped the shaft penetrating its body, weakly attempting to pull the spear free.

Jurin kept her weight pressed against the spear, locking gazes with her captive. Large eyes, yellow and black-veined, full of aguish, stared back at her. A hideous merging of human and dog, pale and hairless, the beast bared teeth like jagged icicles in the cave of its mouth.

Jurin felt no pity, and she waited.

"Where you find one beast, the other will never be far away," the magician had said.

One did not ask for a magician's name. It had been a bloated spider of a woman who had summoned Jurin to her lair. Nameless, ancient, poisoned by centuries of magic addiction. She sat in her *nest*: a sharp-walled cavern, perhaps far underground, perhaps in the heart of a mountain, but where no natural light shone. Her swollen mass concealed within a leather cloak, a patchwork of animal skins – probably including humans' – she had been attended by corrupted acolytes, soulless apparitions with one foot already in Otherside.

"I'm a solider," Jurin had told her. "I know how to deal with *beasts*."

"What, like you did last time?" The magician's voice had carried the distant undertone of breaking glass. "To kill the guardians, you will need more than the cunning and steel of a solider."

In the village, from somewhere close, a mournful voice – almost a howl – drifted through the mist. Hearing its mate, the beast stirred, growling, and Jurin twisted the spear again. This time, the anguished screams were answered by bellows of fury that headed towards them.

"You will need a touch of magic," the magician had told Jurin; and from the shadows of the lair an ungainly acolyte had appeared, blind, naked and sexless, carrying a spear which was laid at Jurin's feet. It had a simple wooden shaft, but the head was made of clear crystal, shaped like a teardrop, the facets and point wickedly sharp. Inside the crystal, supernatural energy glowed.

"This is more than a weapon to defend yourself with," the magician had said. "Keep it close, Jurin, and use it well."

When the second beast emerged from the mist, it came fast, rounding a dilapidated residential dwelling, bounding on all fours through the mud, snarling, slavering, desperately racing to save its mate. Yellow eyes shone like torch fire in the gloom. The first beast screeched. Jurin held her nerve, heart thumping in her ears, holding her captive's struggling weight against the rotting lean-to wall.

She waited until the second beast was within ten feet of her, and then she yanked the spear from the body of the first. Even as the crystal head released a sting of magic that reduced the human-dog to a pile of hot ash, Jurin spun and faced the second beast as it leapt for her.

With a howl, the creature impaled itself on the spear. The glowing teardrop slid through its body as easily as a hot blade through soft cheese and burst from its back. Jurin dodged a clumsy swipe from clawed fingers, and knocked the beast to the ground. Stamping a boot down on its stomach, she wrenched the spear free, and watched as the magic again reduced her foe to burning ashes that settled in the mud, hissing.

"I've been watching you for a long time... waiting." That had been the first thing the magician had said to Jurin. The second had been: "We are of mutual benefit to each other."

As the embers in the ashes died, the spear felt warm in Jurin's hands, its weight perfect.

"Your friends need you, Jurin."

She looked around at the village. Abandoned. Ruined. Unwelcoming. She looked up at the strange, bruised sky, neither knowing nor caring if it was day or night.

"You remember your friends, don't you...?"

Yes, she remembered. She never forgot.

When Jurin had first happened upon the village, she had been travelling home after fighting for gold in someone else's war. Three other soldiers travelled with her; the survivors from a company of mercenaries that had headed north several months before. Balia was the eldest by some years; she had led the group. Honn, taciturn and mostly humourless, he had been a mountain of a warrior, content to follow. Lastly, the youngest of them: Taalij, none too bright and the butt of many jokes, but a good soldier to stand beside in battle. They all were.

The group had thought to buy supplies at the village, perhaps spend the night in the soft beds of a tavern, before conducting the last leg of their journey home. The horror was supposed to be behind them. It had all seemed so simple. At first.

With mud squelching beneath her boots, the spearhead glowing like a torch, Jurin headed towards the village square. She knew how to get there; a map of this place had being haunting her dreams for more than a year.

"I know you have seen the monster that dwells in that village, Jurin," the poisonous old magician had said. "You might be the only living person who has."

Old Balia had always joked that she had survived so many wars because demons watched over her. She had been the monster's first victim. Taalij had pissed his trousers, dropped his weapon, and wept in the mud before his death. Honn, that fearless mountain of a warrior, had tried to fight the monster, but he hadn't stood a chance. As for

Jurin...She had been the only one to make it out of the village alive.

Pushing her fear down into the lowest depths of her being, Jurin trudged on.

"That monster is a rare sort of creature, and it has piqued my interest." Like some perverted virgin bride, the magician's face had been hidden behind a veil of dusty cobweb that barely moved as she spoke with her broken-glass-voice. "But it has an innate fear of magicians, and would disappear if I came anywhere close to that village. The monster will, however, be drawn to your despair and shame, Jurin."

Despair: a reference to the knife that Jurin had been holding in her hand when the magician first transported her to the lair; the knife she had intended to use on her wrists to end the nightmares, and the shame. Jurin remembered dropping the knife to the lair floor, and the magician's laugh still chittered like a nest of spiders in her memory.

"Why would I agree to help you?" Jurin had demanded.

"Ah, now *that* is the question." Although the magician had never once revealed her face, Jurin had known that her eyes were fixed on the knife on the floor. "You have given up, and that makes you valuable to me."

For over a year Jurin had tried to rediscover the village, driven by thoughts of vengeance, a desperate need to slay the monster that had slaughtered her friends. To make amends. But the magician had waited until Jurin finally conceded that she would never find the village again; waited until she had lost all hope, succumbing to her torment, before offering revelations and an alternative.

"Jurin, you believe the spirits of your friends *drifted off* to paradise after they were killed, and from that place their spectral eyes watch you, always, heavy with judgement and wrath. You suppose that killing the monster will appease your friends, and banish your guilt. But you are wrong."

The magician could have added that Jurin had no choice but to do her bidding, but she hadn't. Instead, she had told the truth in a cold, matter-of-fact tone. "The monster is more than you think it to be. It is a collector. Of ghosts. Of spirits or souls – whatever your preference."

Jurin remembered the spark of intrigue that had invaded her hopelessness. The first hint that not all was lost. "The monster has *collected* the souls of my friends?"

"Along with the countless others that have been lured to the village over time. As I said, it is a rare sort of creature." The magician had sounded admiring, perhaps desiring. "What I'm offering you, Jurin, is the chance to save the ghosts of your friends. Help me, and I will return you to that village and show you how to end your nightmares."

Of course Jurin had agreed. What other choice did she have? And she had asked the magician if she planned to kill the monster. Why did it interest her?

"Actually, I'm more interested in the bigger fish for whom the monster is collecting ghosts. But that's really none of your concern, Jurin. Now, here's what I need you to do..."

There were no signs of life in the village now the guardians were dead. Jurin's footprints were lonely tracks in the mud; the clouds of her breath fleeting moments of warmth in the dead air; the magical light of the spearhead the closest this place would get to sunshine.

When Jurin, along with Balia, Taalij and Honn, had first seen the village, it appeared normal, welcoming, peaceful. The only oddity had been the lack of villagers and animals, as though the village were a stage waiting for its players. But not until the mercenaries had reached the square did the village reveal its true visage. A site of rotting buildings, crumbling ruins, where nothing lived – at least, nothing until the monster came.

"You will have to go looking for the monster, entice it out of hiding," the magician had said, as if this were an act of simplicity itself. "Please understand, the village is a façade. It conceals a gateway to Otherside."

Otherside, the dark mirror image of the real world, where demons and the damned dwelt, where no one sane would venture, where despair gained true meaning...

"You will recognise the gateway when it reveals itself to you, Jurin."

Reaching the village square, Jurin discovered something that had not been there before. An impossible building rose from the centre of the square. A bizarre parody of a house, of many houses, piled one on top of the other, twisting upwards, rising so far into the beaten sky that Jurin could not see where the structure ended. The building's wooden beams creaked as it swayed; loose stonework rustled and clacked, tumbling down its length. There were windows – more windows than

Jurin could count – and each appeared broken. Yellow tongues of silent fire licked out of them. Strange how the flames danced almost majestically without the menacing sounds of crackling and burning.

At the base of the impossible building, more fire spilled from the windows on either side of the wooden entrance door. But there was something almost homely about the yellow glow that glinted upon the wet and muddy ground. It was accompanied by a faint, cheery sound: the clinks of glasses, the clangs of tankards, and comradely voices laughing and jeering. The ambience of a friendly inn.

Jurin used the luminous crystal spearhead to push the door open. Leading with the weapon, tense and alert, she entered the impossible building.

It was as though the interior were an inverted version of the exterior. A single room, as rotting and broken as the rest of the village. The ceiling and roof were missing, showing a clear, star-filled sky, magical, very different from the dreary emptiness of the sky outside. But most of the floor was also missing. The old wooden boards had been crudely broken away, leaving a gaping pit filled with silent, heatless fire, sinking who knew how far into the ground. The remaining rim of floor was less than three feet wide around the pit, and didn't feel too stable beneath Jurin's feet.

"Hello, Miss."

The voice startled Jurin, clearer and louder than the faint whisper of patrons.

She hadn't noticed the man standing on the opposite side of the pit. He was elderly, grey-looking, worn and weary, his eyes hollow, but with amiable enough expression. He wore threadbare clothes – shirt and trousers, and an old woollen waistcoat. Behind him was a closed door.

Once again, Jurin remembered the words of the magician. "To find the monster, you must step into Otherside. To do that, you must first pass the gatekeeper."

And the gatekeeper said, "I wasn't expecting anyone else in tonight." His tone was perfect for a kindly grandfather. "As you can see, we're a little busy."

He didn't seem to know where he was as he gestured to the empty room and what remained of the rotting floorboards around the fiery pit. He did so as though the echo of revelry was accompanied by the presence of tables and customers, and the smells of roasting meat, tobacco smoke and ale.

Jurin fancied she heard a distant sigh of laugher, and then, with an apologetic air, the gatekeeper added, "I'm sorry, Miss, but I haven't got any rooms left."

When Jurin said nothing, he ran his fingers through thinning hair to scratch the bald spot on his crown. "Let me have a quick word with the missus, see if we can rustle something up for you," and he turned to the closed door behind him.

Of this man, the magician had said, "You must think of the gatekeeper as a lost spirit, a *wisp*, addicted to the memory of the life he once led. He is harmless, Jurin, but if you let him leave, you will be stuck in that room forever... or until madness drives you into its pit of fire."

As the gatekeeper's hand closed around the doorknob, Jurin's arm flashed forwards. The spear flew across the room, over the pit, hitting the old man square in the back, slicing through him. The magic in the spearhead sparked as it thudded into the door. Without so much as one yell of pain, the gatekeeper faded, his spirit swirling to nothing.

The room began to change. The remains of the walls collapsed; the brittle beams crumbled to tinder. Jurin tried to back away, but behind her the entrance had been replaced by a viscous fluid as thick as pitch but fog-grey in colour. It spread, cracking and creaking, replacing the walls and floor. It was slippery beneath Jurin's feet, and she watched as the substance poured into the gaping, fiery hole, dousing the flames, until the void was filled and Jurin stood in a cavern that looked to be formed from hard, dirty ice.

"Once you have dealt with the gatekeeper," the magician had explained, "the real fun can begin."

On the opposite side of the cavern, where the second door had been, a tunnel led into darkness. The magical spear lay on the floor before its mouth. Jurin's footsteps echoed as she crossed the cavern and retrieved her weapon. She stared into the dark tunnel, and someone spoke.

Jurin...

There was no mistaking old Balia's voice. Jurin's leader, her captain, spoke directly into her mind.

Jurin... why?

51

Her teeth gritted, the way illuminated by magic contained in a crystal teardrop, Jurin stepped into the tunnel.

"In Otherside you will face your shame," the magician had warned. "In Otherside your nightmares are real."

Jurin felt pressure in her ears. Her breath, hot and steaming, murmured around the tunnel. By the light of the spearhead she saw movement, people behind the dirty-ice walls. Or were they trapped within the grey substance? Fleeting glimpses of suffering: mouths opened in screams; fingers clawing to be free; fists smashing. Noiseless. Desperate. Stolen ghosts. Jurin ignored them and her fear, willing her feet to keep walking forwards.

"You hid like a coward," the magician had said. There had been no accusation in her voice, no judgement. Only the truth. "You hid, and when the monster set about your friends, you spied your chance to escape. While they died, you ran and you ran until the village let you go." The magician had chuckled. "I wonder, Jurin – how soon after your escape did guilt begin to poison your mind?"

Jurin began running, her knuckles white as she gripped the spear and charged down the tunnel. The voice of the magician scurried through her memory.

"I'm rather glad of your cowardice, Jurin. By abandoning your friends, you have grown a desire for atonement at any cost. This is our strongest weapon against the monster."

Jurin shouted her defiance, her anger, her shame. The end of the tunnel came into view, a disc of sterile light, and she quickened her pace. A wind of dead men's breath buffeted her, trying to push her back, but her step didn't falter. She heard voices, cries and bellows of pain and rage; and a smell, sour, toxic, dangerous... the smell of a monster.

The way ahead blurred. A sudden pain seared through her head. A starburst of light blinded her eyes. And Jurin leapt into Otherside.

She was back in the village square. Above, the sky was again coloured with the purple and green hues of bruised skin. Broken buildings formed a wide box around the square, but the impossible, bizarre inn was gone. In its place, the remnants of a well; a well that Jurin remembered. It looked exactly as it had over a year ago: the hiding place that had saved the life of a coward. And standing beside it was Balia.

Jurin's heart skipped a beat to see her old captain. But Balia was not pleased to see her.

The aging soldier backed away from Jurin, hastily removing her traveling cloak. She drew her sword, and held it threateningly, defensively. Her hand shook.

Confused, Jurin called to Balia with words of camaraderie, but the voice that came out of her mouth was a roar, vicious as thunder. Balia prepared to attack. Jurin raised a hand in a calming gesture, but the hand that rose before her was that of a giant. Nails black, skin the colour of corpses, puckered and thick like the hide of an ox. She no longer held the spear but a huge hammer, its head a block of chipped and cracked stone. The weapon of a monster.

Balia attacked. Jurin rumbled a laugh and forgot who she was.

The monster's hammer met the sword, stone clashing against metal, and sent it spinning away, along with the hand that held it. Screaming, Balia clutched her bleeding stump and sank to her knees. The monster's next blow removed her head from her shoulders with a spray of blood and bone. Even as Balia's body toppled to the mud, her ghost rose from her remains, a thorny tangle of silver wisps. The monster hungered, calling to the spirit. As though drawn to the blood covering the hammer, the spirit raced towards the monster in many streaks of silver, each one absorbed into the weapon's stone head.

Stepping over Balia's body, the monster moved on to the weeping wretch that was Taalij. The youngster crouched in the mud, covering his head with his hands. The sound of his whimpering was as irritating to the monster as a volley of arrows stabbing its leathery hide. A jab from the hammer punched Taalij onto his back. A downward strike crushed his ribcage. Taalij coughed blood, choked once, and then died. The monster collected his ghost.

A blow came from behind. The monster stumbled slightly and turned.

In life, Honn the Warrior had towered over most people, as grizzly as a mountain bear, but the monster looked down on him. So puny and weak. Honn's mighty battle axe seemed no more threatening than a whittling knife. His forest of beard was split by clenched and broken teeth. He raised his axe with two hands, but before he could strike, the monster's hammer smashed down on him, over and over, again and again, until Honn was reduced to a steaming mound of red pulp. The silver strands of his spirit flowed into the chipped and blocky head of the hammer like slow streaks of lightning.

"No."

The woman's voice surprised the monster. It sounded small.

"You cannot keep them."

Turning to the well at the centre of the square, the monster watched as a woman climbed up and over the remnants of its stonework. She carried a spear. Its head was made of crystal and shaped like a teardrop. Magical energy glowed inside the head, but not just any kind of magic. The monster could taste what the teardrop held. Something it wanted so very, terribly much... a starburst of light filled its vision, searing pain erupted in its head.

"How far would you go to save your friends?" the magician had asked, a lifetime ago in the stale gloom of her lair. "What would you give?"

"Anything. Everything."

And the magician, addicted to her own power, poisoned by eldritch secrets, longer lived than most humans were supposed to, had found joy in torment, success in misery. "Self-sacrificed is worth more than a hundred ghosts taken by force..."

And Jurin remembered who she was.

The monster, every inch as terrible as she remembered, stood watching as she climbed from the well. Its hair was an unruly mass of thick moss, through which pale antlers sprouted like small trees of bone. The monster's beard, a nest of roots and vines, reached down to a heavy breastplate of dark wood. Gnarly, lichen-covered bark served as guards for powerful arms and legs. Its exposed skin was ashen and lifeless, sullied by dirt and scars.

Huge, twice the size of most humans, the monster tilted its head to one side, regarding Jurin and the spear with eyes as big as bucklers, filled with a livid, moving green like a forest canopy in a gale. Jurin stared at the massive hammer in its hands and swallowed her fear. Beneath the blood, the stone head carried the silvery sheen of ghosts.

"Never could you hope to stand against the monster, Jurin," the magician had said. "And while the stars still shine in the sky, you never will."

The monster made no move. Its forest eyes stared at the glowing spearhead. Its root and vine beard split, revealing a cavernous mouth. A black tongue licked across stalactite teeth obscenely. Slowly, Jurin began to unscrew the teardrop from the spear's shaft.

"Strike a bargain." The magician's words had been filled with dark certainty. "To appease your shame, to end your torment, you must offer the monster what it cannot refuse."

Jurin dropped the shaft and held the teardrop in both hands. The sterile light of its magic brightened. A groan of desire rumbled from the monster's mouth.

"My ghost, my spirit," Jurin shouted, holding the teardrop forward. Her gaze flittered briefly on the bloody remains of her fellow soldiers lying in the mud. "If you release my friends," she told the monster, "I will give it to you willingly."

The monster's grin was a hideous stone-toothed grimace that at once threatened Jurin and acquiesced to her terms.

Balia, Honn, Taalij, Jurin prayed silently. She held the glowing teardrop above her head. *Your coward friend brings you peace.*

She hurled the teardrop towards the monster. It arced through the air, a tail of light following it. With a howl of triumph, the monster raised the hammer and met the crystal spearhead with a fearsome blow, shattering it with the sound of a thousand damned souls screaming. Freed magic blazed with super nature, blinding Jurin, sending her reeling away with a cry.

And the last thing the magician had said to Jurin rustled through her mind: "The final trick you will play on the monster will be that you have no ghost to give away." The ancient, poisonous spider had practically delighted in her own cleverness. "I will cut the ghost out of you, Jurin, and replace it with a surprise of my own."

As the slashes and spots of magical energy cleared from Jurin's vision, she heard the monster roaring – first with rage, then with panic. The spell the teardrop had released surrounded the giant abomination in a great orb comprised of a thousand lines of white fire. The skin of the monster's hand hissed and smoked as it touched the burning lines, and it gave a bellow of pain. The hammer sent sparks of energy fountaining to the ground with a series of blows, but try as it might, the monster could not escape the trap. Before long, the hammer shattered and crumbled to powder as fine as stardust.

The orb began to shrink, and the monster with it. Its voice became quieter and quieter until no more than a sigh in the icy air, and the orb, the trap, the prison that tasted like Jurin's ghost, was once again a crystal teardrop filled with glowing magic.

All around, the strange and treacherous village remained as lifeless and ruined as always; but now a darkness had invaded the stillness, hanging in the air, misshapen and jagged like the shadows between two mountain boulders. A smell assailed Jurin's nostrils, something ancient, poisonous: the stench of a magician's lair.

A figure stepped from the darkness. Naked, crippled, blind, one of the magician's acolytes dragged its feet through the mud, pausing only to pluck the teardrop from the ground before returning to the strange doorway from which it had appeared. As the acolyte carried the teardrop into the darkness, Jurin heard a distant voice like broken glass: "Farewell." And the wound in the air closed.

All strength fled from Jurin. Her legs buckled and she fell facedown into the mud. With supreme effort, she managed to roll onto her back and gaze up at the sky. Gone was the thick and ugly umbrella the colour of bruised skin. The splendour of the night now greeted her eyes. The moon, a fat silver-blue disc, glared down at her with clean light. The stars, countless pinpricks in a black canvas, winked and glimmered across the sky with majestic messages that only oracles could divine.

This was like seeing music, Jurin decided, a song sung just for her. An alien sensation arose within her and crawled over her body; something she hadn't felt for so long she barely recognised it at first: peace. The shame, the nightmares, the inner turmoil – they ended here.

Jurin turned her head until her cheek lay flat against the mud. Her eyes filled with tears as she gazed upon the broken bodies of her comrades, her friends, the fellow soldiers with whom she had survived the horrors of war, but not the terror of this village. Jurin's tears did not come with remorse, though; they fell from her eyes with relief to see thorny tangles of silver wisps rising from their shells.

"I'm sorry I left you here," Jurin whispered. The ghosts detached from the flesh, hovering in the air as though bearing witness to the soldier lying in the mud. Jurin smiled at them. "I didn't run this time. I didn't run..."

Darkness was descending. The last sleep beckoned, and Jurin saw her friends rise towards the glory of the heavens, free and at peace. And then Jurin saw nothing more.

The Giant's Lady

Rowena Cory Daniells

As we entered the white-walled courtyard, the music stopped and every islander turned.

Wyrd, they whispered.

My lady stood tall, her pale hair glinting in the hot noonday sun. A full-blood T'En throwback, she did not try to hide her hair or her six-fingered hands, and her distinctive wine-dark eyes held quiet defiance. As for me, I was not a Wyrd, not even a half-blood, just a freakishly big True-man, and an ugly one at that.

My lady headed for two seats at the end of a trestle table. By the time we reached it, the table was empty. She sat, turning her long legs to the side. Dropping our travelling bags, I took the opposite seat, where I could watch the courtyard gate.

Wyrd they whispered, and... *Plague Bringer.*

By chance last spring we'd arrived on Sundowner Isle just as the rose-plague broke out. My lady did what she could but the distinctive rose shaped rash travelled so fast that even a T'En healer could not hold back the tide. Trying to save everyone would have killed her.

On Sundowner Isle she'd advised the king to close the port. He'd refused because the island had been about to host a religious festival. Now, every second trading vessel carried plague across the Lagoons of Perpetual Summer.

The mandolin player began a tune and conversation gradually resumed. No one came to take our order, meanwhile several people slipped away discretely.

My lady sent me a wry smile. "Shouldn't be long."

I loved her.

Had loved her from the day she'd rescued me. As tall as a man at twelve, all I had ever known was cruelty and hunger. I could have grown bitter and hard, instead I'd tried to understand how those who had been physically blessed could find amusement in my humiliation.

The day she'd found them baiting me in a village square she could have walked away, instead she'd offered my master a healing in exchange for me. He'd driven a hard bargain, then reneged on it and tried to capture her for his travelling freak show.

In the past, no matter how he'd beaten me I'd never fought back. That night I held him down while my lady used her gift on him. From then on, whenever he tried to force himself on a woman, his cock would shrivel.

My lady, dispenser of justice. How could I not love her?

Now, ten years later, I had followed her to the end of the world, to King Vonanjiro's troubled island empire. I'd argued against coming here. War was brewing in the Lagoons of Perpetual Summer. There were too many island kingdoms ruled by ambitious, petty princelings, and they had too many hungry subjects with too little arable land. But when my lady had heard that King Vonanjiro's only surviving heir was deathly ill, she'd booked passage and, whether she realised it or not, Pinnacle Isle had always been her life's destination.

"Note the palace, Gyf."

I'd already done so. To please her, I glanced over the tavern's red-tiled roof to the grand white building on the island's only high ground. There were screened verandahs to keep the interiors cool, but other than that it was identical to T'En buildings in the north.

"Pinnacle Palace proves the old stories are true." In her excitement, my lady clasped my forearm and I felt her gift stir. My heart raced.

According to the stories, T'En power repulsed honest True-people but I loved it. The overflow of her gift made my life more intense, colours richer and scents sharper.

Her wine-dark eyes gleamed. "They say that when my people arrived there was nothing around the pinnacle but marshy tidal flats. Now look at it."

Between the port wall and the palace were houses three and four storeys high, packed with True-men, women and children. The southerners were small of stature, with golden-skin, sleek dark hair and darting black eyes. And they were clearly uncomfortable with my lady, legend given life.

A pilgrimage to the last home of the Wandering Wyrds, I could understand but I did not see what my lady hoped...

"My price for saving the King's heir will be access to the palace records."

She'd skimmed my mind again. I looked down to her pale fingers curling around my forearm. Touch enhanced her gift. I used to resent her casual mental intrusion, until I realised that forbidding her this intimacy would be like asking a sighted person not to look.

"Surely you understand, Gyf?" She searched my face. "I've always wanted to learn where my people went."

"The Wandering Wyrds sailed west into the Endless Ocean and were never seen again."

She sent me a slanting look. "Only the ignorant believe they sailed off edge of the world. My people must have had a destination. They wouldn't have risked their children."

"They had no choice. The locals rose up against them."

"They were great ship builders and sailors."

"True…" But it was over six hundred years since the Wandering Wyrds had set sail and in all that time no one, not T'En or True-man, had arrived from beyond the setting sun. I feared my lady's search would bring her only sorrow.

Wordlessly, she squeezed my arm.

"You there, Wyrd!" a man bellowed.

I tensed and went to rise but my lady shook her head and it was she who straightened slowly, making him come to her as the locals watched.

He wore the island king's colours, cerulean blue and silver. His chain of office was bright against the sun-bronzed skin of his broad shoulders and his sarong sat low on his hips. From his waist hung a nasty scimitar. As he strode across the tavern courtyard, he kicked a foolish fowl aside.

A big man, indeed.

But he had to lift his chin to meet my lady's eyes and this made him grimace. "They say you can heal when all else has failed. Is this true?"

"If I can heal, I do."

"None of your Wyrd riddles. I want a straight answer."

She lifted her hands, palm up. "How do I know if I can heal until I see what's wrong with the person?"

"You'll see soon enough. The King commands your presence."

Despite his bluster, his words had the ring of a request. Few True-people could meet my lady's eyes and fewer still could hold them and remember what they'd meant to say.

I grabbed our travel bags and stood, turning to reveal the deformed side of my face. My head looked as if it had been squeezed while the dough of my skull was still soft, causing my right cheekbone and eye to bulge.

The kingsman made the sign to ward off evil, before leading us out onto the street where half a dozen men formed an escort. Despite the whispers of war, people thronged the market place. Spicy scents made my mouth water. The locals stood aside as we passed and our escort's swift rhythmic jingle filled the growing silence.

A small boy darted out, face alive with curiosity. The very next moment, a butcher cuffed him over the ear and dragged him off muttering, "Lazy blood-eye."

Blood-eye... slang for half-blood Wyrd. My lady cast me a troubled look. Slavery was common in the lagoons. If parents became indebted, they indentured their children. But this boy had been unlucky twice over. He combined the southerners' golden skin with a half-blood's mulberry eyes and copper hair so dark it was almost black. More proof, if needed, that Wyrds had lived here and interbred with the locals.

So much for King Charald the Conqueror's attempt to eradicate Wyrds. Banishment had only sent them out into the world, and it hadn't rid his kingdom of their impure blood. Even now his subjects still produced half-blood babies and, despite the royal edict, not every tainted babe was exposed at birth.

With their vivid colouring the half-bloods were pretty creatures. What's more, they didn't have the dangerous gifts of the full-bloods. To this day there was a trade in half-blood infants. Sold as exotic slaves, they were scattered across the mainland. My lady's own parents had been runaways. They'd sacrificed their lives so she could escape capture when she was fifteen. The following winter, she'd rescued me and I'd been her devoted servant ever since.

She was mine to adore and protect but I could not protect her from herself. I cursed the Lagoons of Perpetual Summer with their hollow legends of Lost T'En.

Just before we reached the palace gate a shout went up as our party met a group of wounded kingsmen. There was talk of

Sundowners attacking. I tried to catch my lady's eye but her mouth was set.

Passing through a beautifully proportioned archway, we entered another white-walled courtyard. As people hurried to help the injured men, my lady hesitated and I knew she was fighting the urge to heal. Such was the power of her gift. Sometimes, it laid her low with mysterious seizures. It was my honour to guard her until she escaped the nightmares.

Our escort led us through a rabbit warren of little rooms where True-people had divided the once grand T'En chambers. At last we came to a tiled ante-chamber and were told to wait. I went straight to the window. It was a long way to the port -wall and freedom but I memorised several paths just in case.

"His Majesty," a servant announced. "King Vonanjiro, ruler of the Seven Islands. Saviour of Pinnacle Isle. Greatest King in all the Myriad Isles."

Vonanjiro swaggered in. White haired and heavily overweight, he had to be seventy yet he wore elaborate armour. According to the stories, he was an iron-willed empire builder. At his age, he should have been a grandfather but both his marriages had been cursed with stillbirths. Only three sons had survived to adulthood and they'd died leading armies to serve his ambition. When the last one fell without issue eight years ago, the King had married for the third time and produced another son, a last precious male heir.

My lady and I bowed then I introduced her. "Last of the Legendary T'En, the Lady Shen is blessed with the Gift of Healing."

"You claim to be a healer, Lady Shen." The King gestured to me. "Yet you haven't corrected your manservant's deformity."

"Ask him why."

The King looked at me.

"I wear the face I was born with because the only friends I want are those who can see past it." If people dared to ask, they usually approved of my answer but I swear the King's lips twitched.

He turned to my lady. "They say you brought plague to Sundowner Isle. If so, I thank you for killing my enemies."

"Plague is everyone's enemy, sire. If you wish to save your people, you'll isolate every new ship for ten days. Then, only if the crew and passengers are healthy, let them disembark."

He eyed her thoughtfully. "You are a long way from home."

"I am a student of history. Is it true your family has ruled in an unbroken line from father to son for over six hundred years?"

"It will be true if you can save my son. He languishes with a mystery illness no medicine man can cure."

"I will do my best, but –"

"You want gold. No matter." The King was dismissive. "I rule more islands than any other King of the Myriad Isles."

"I was going to say that I can make no promises and my price is not gold. It is access to the palace records. I'm writing a treatise on your illustrious kingdom." My lady held out her hand. "Done?"

"Done." The King grasped her hand briefly. "Come."

A servant met him at the bed chamber door, reporting on the Prince's health as they both approached the bed.

Under cover of their conversation, I whispered, "What did you sense, my lady?"

"He's not long for this world. He has the sugar sickness."

"Not that. Can he be trusted?"

"His mind is multi-layered. The deepest part hides behind a wall of stone."

I was not surprised. Some True-people had the innate ability to shut her out.

We entered a dimly lit, sumptuous bedchamber. It was stiflingly hot. Despite the season, a fire burned in a brazier and heavy brocade curtains shrouded the windows. Semi-precious gems glinted in the candlelight but my gaze was drawn to the small figure on the huge bed.

Whatever I might think of King Vonanjiro, I felt for his son. The boy was about six. Slender and pale, he fought to hold his eyes open.

The senior servant joined three lower servants.

"This is Crown Prince Vonanjiro," the King told my lady. "The medicine men tried everything, even an elixir of crushed pearls and gold dust dissolved in…" He frowned at the corner, where a woman stood in the shadows. "What's *she* doing here?"

The senior servant glanced to the child.

"Please, Father," the boy whispered. "Don't send her away."

The King grimaced. "If she must stay, she's to keep back and remain silent."

"Tronanova…" the senior servant muttered. It sounded like an insult but it could have been her name.

There was a knock at the door and a kingsman peered in. "Forgive the interruption sire, there's been an attack on –"

The King swore and strode out, calling over his shoulder, "Bring the healer what she needs."

The door no sooner closed than my lady turned to the senior servant. "Let in light and fresh air."

He did not approve but he ordered the curtains opened, which revealed a lattice-shrouded verandah. I beckoned a servant and we went to open the lattice.

"Who is Tronanova?" I asked softly.

"Not who, what," the servant said. "A Tronanova is an unacknowledged royal child."

"She's the boy's sister?"

"Half-sister."

I glanced through the archway to the unfortunate woman, seeing only dark hair and eyes. "She is…" I searched their language for the word that meant illegitimate. "She was born outside of the royal bed?"

The senior servant barked an order and my informant hurried off.

I returned to find my lady examining the young Prince. On seeing the painful bruises on his inner arms where the medicine men had bled him, my lady's lips tightened with anger and a rush of power swept through the room. To me it felt like a fresh breeze, but the boy's unfortunate sister gasped and the servants looked askance.

"There, that's better." My lady sounded pleased.

The boy's unblemished skin made the servants mutter. *Fools, what did they expect of a renowned T'En healer?*

"You have been very brave, little man." My lady's voice was like honey on a warm day, rich and sweet. "You will sleep and when you wake you will be well. You understand?"

He nodded.

Smiling, she pressed the sixth finger of her left hand to his forehead. At her touch, he fell into a deep slumber.

Then she stood abruptly, eyes glittering. "All of you out. You, too." She gestured to the unfortunate sister. The senior servant protested but my lady overrode him. "My giant will watch the boy. Go."

I waited until they were gone. "What's wrong?"

"Poison." Her voice shook with anger. "Someone has been poisoning the Prince. Who has the most to gain?"

"His sister?" I gestured to where the unfortunate woman had stood. "If he is the last of the King's sons, she would be next in line."

"Tronanova is his sister?"

"The word means unacknowledged royal."

My lady frowned. "If she's illegitimate then she can't inherit."

I shrugged. "Maybe she wants revenge after being passed over in favour of her brothers."

"The boy loves her."

"That makes it easier to slip him poison."

"Perhaps... But I heard rumours of an ambitious nephew. I must warn the King. Meanwhile, don't let anyone in."

I caught her arm. Someone in this palace was willing to poison an innocent boy and she was a hated Wyrd. "My lady –"

"Don't worry. Vonanjiro needs my gift."

So I sat by the bed to wait. As the afternoon wore on, I heard people in the courtyard. They spoke as if war was inevitable. At least the boy was on the mend, already his colour had improved.

I could not bear the thought of my lady alone and in danger. Coming to my feet, I found my hand on the hilt of my knife and prowled the chamber. In one way, war was good. If the islanders were distracted we could slip away.

Eventually, the sun set across the sea. Night came quickly this far south. My stomach rumbled, and still my lady did not come back.

I'd just returned to the chair by the bed, when a soft click drew my eye to the fire place. In the dim light I saw a panel shift. Was this how the poisoner had reached the prince?

Feigning sleep, I snored softly as someone approached cautiously. Judging the moment right, I grabbed the intruder only to find the unfortunate sister struggling in my arms.

"You!" And to think, the boy had defended her. Disgusted, I lifted her off her feet, carried her out to the balcony and I swung her legs over the rail.

She gasped, clutching me.

"How could you? The Prince loves you."

"And I love him."

"Not as much as revenge. Your father doesn't acknowledge you, so you poisoned his son to punish him."

A wild laugh escaped her. Was she mad?

I shook her. "Do you deny that you poisoned him?"

"My brother was never in danger. I needed to lure Lady Shen here."

"If harm has befallen her, I swear –"

"I would never hurt your lady. My own son is a full-blood Wyrd."

"I don't believe it!"

"Why not?" Thrusting her hand in front of my face, she splayed her fingers.

For a heartbeat I saw nothing wrong, then I understood. "Six fingers. You're a half-blood."

"Exactly, a Tronanova. So the last thing I would do is hurt your lady."

The moment I released her, she scrambled back over the rail. In the moonlight, her dark-copper hair and mulberry eyes looked black. It was hard to pick her age. Around thirty, perhaps.

"I am not your enemy, Lord Giant. I need Lady Shen to save my son. The King keeps him locked in the dungeon, poor boy."

Behind a stone wall… Vonanjiro hadn't been blocking my lady's gift as much as hiding his secret.

The unfortunate sister took my hand. "Unless you trust me, Lord Giant, your lady will never leave the palace. My father will imprison her to keep her healing gift for himself."

"Others have tried."

"The King is not like other men. Where they have hearts, he has only hunger for power."

"He might imprison my lady but she would never –"

"She would agree to protect you, just as he kept me prisoner by –"

"Threatening your son. And the boy's father too, I'll warrant." A thought occurred to me. "Was he a half-blood slave?"

"No." She flinched. "My own brother."

I was aghast.

She shuddered. "Wyrd blood has always run strong in our line. My father locked away his Tronanova sons, claiming they'd been stillborn."

"But… why would the King want a throwback?"

"Power. He wants to harness the Wyrd gifts." She grimaced and her chin trembled. "It was too much for my brother. He took his own life. I was going to smother the baby at birth, but he was so helpless…"

I reached out to her.

She shook her head, every bit as determined as her father. "The King's gamble paid off, my son has visions."

"I'm sorry." I hated to destroy her illusions. "They're not visions, only hallucinations caused by gift-induced seizures. My lady suffers from them too."

"My boy saw you. He told me to trust the philosopher with the ruined face."

I was still trying to make sense of this, when she took my hand, leading me inside. "We must go."

"I can't leave the Prince. I promised my –"

"He's safe. And it is not your lady who is in danger." The unfortunate sister drew me across the bed chamber. "The King has sent men to –"

Voices came from the adjoining room and the connecting door started to open. We ran for the fireplace. I had to bend double to get through the opening but once inside the secret passage I could stand normally. The panel closed just in time then I felt her turn towards me in the dusty dark.

In silence we listened, as around half a dozen men entered. Unable to find me, they feared the King's wrath and went to search further afield.

"I must warn my lady."

"Do you love her?"

How could she ask? "I'd do anything for her."

"Then come with me." The unfortunate sister pressed a candle stub into my hand. "This place is riddled with secret passages. They'll get us as far as the palace wall. I've made hooded cloaks but I've never been outside the palace." She struck a spark and her mulberry eyes gleamed with fanatical determination. "You must promise to take my boy with you."

"Of course." With a little boy to love, my lady would have what she'd been searching for. "I won't fail you or her."

Voices reached us as more people entered the chamber. The unfortunate sister snuffed the candle.

"…see for yourself, sire," my lady said. "Your son is sleeping safely."

"The poison?"

"Will be gone by tomorrow." A pause. "That's odd. I told Gyfron to watch –"

"I have your giant locked in my dungeon," the King said. "Do you think me a fool, She-Wyrd? You come here calling yourself a student of history but I know you're here for revenge. It was my ancestor, Vonanjiro the First, who led the rebellion against your people. He was going to murder them in their beds but someone sounded the alarm and the Wyrds fought their way to their ships. We executed those left behind, put their heads on pikes along the port wall. The only good Wyrd is a tame Wyrd, I say. And that's what you'll be, now that I have your giant."

There was silence, then… "What do you want from me?"

"I must live long enough for my son to grow up. By the time I die, he will rule the Myriad Isles."

"I want to see Gyf. If your men have hurt him –"

"You will heal him. Come."

As soon as they left the chamber I whispered, "But I'm not chained up in his dungeon."

"It is enough that she believes you are." The unfortunate sister lit the candle again. "Now we must rescue your lady as well as my boy."

We hurried along the secret passage until we came to narrow stairs, built for long-legged Wyrds. Down and down we went, between walls of sheer rock.

"We must be below sea level by now."

"Yes. Pity my poor boy, he's never seen the sun."

"He will, I promise."

She cast me a swift look. "He said you would have to make a decision and that we could only hope you would make the right one."

"What kind of decision?"

"He couldn't say. His visions are only glimpses. There's been no one to teach him how to use his gift."

"Same as my lady. Learning on the job, you might say."

She nodded and kept going. "Not far now."

A moment later she came to another secret panel. "We'll free your lady first."

We were about to step into a stone corridor, when the jingle of armour told us kingsmen strode past. Once it was safe, we left the secret passage and at the very next bend we heard the King gloating over my lady.

"Stay here." I darted around the corner.

A guard stood in the doorway, with his back to me. Covering the distance in two strides, I caught him in a choke-hold.

His muffled struggles were enough to alert the King who turned, reaching for his sword. My lady was quicker. She touched his neck and I felt the overflow of her power as the King collapsed slowly, fighting every step of the way until he lay on the floor, glaring up at us.

I put the unconscious guard aside.

The unfortunate sister came up behind me. "What's going –" Her nose wrinkled with distaste. "The Lady's gift is strong this close."

Strange. She should have been used to T'En power. "Why –" I broke off as voices echoed up the corridor, along with the jingle of approaching kingsmen. "I'll go."

"No, I'll go," the unfortunate sister said. "They're used to seeing me down here."

Even as she slipped out my lady told me, "Watch the King."

"Wait…"

But she didn't listen. A moment later I heard the unfortunate sister chatting to the kingsmen. Her tone was casual and I had to admire her. She didn't know my lady was waiting around the corner to help her. I should be with my lady, not here with the King.

He watched me, black eyes calculating. "She's using you."

I drew my knife. "Yell and I'll slit your throat."

"Lady Shen is using you, just like the boy uses his mother. She's addicted to his gift, you know. Would do anything for him."

"She's his mother." And not a bit like my mother, who'd sold me for a quart of ale.

"Lady Shen –"

"Rescued me."

"Of course she did. Look at you. Big as a Wyrd and devoted to her. But all you are is a means to an end. All Wyrds are eventually corrupted by their own power. That's why my ancestor revolted. We True-men must stick together. She trusts you. You can get close enough to –"

"Don't listen to him." The unfortunate sister returned. "His words are poison."

"I'm no fool."

The King caught my arm. "You're a fool if you trust –"

"Stand back, Gyf," my lady said. "I must finish what I began."

The King eyes filled with furious terror.

My lady crouched over him. "If you were really smart, you would have realised that if I can reach inside a body to heal, I can also reach inside to cripple."

"Why not kill him?" the unfortunate sister asked. "He would not hesitate to kill you."

"Death is not justice," my lady said then touched the King's temple.

Power built as she overcame the King's resistance. I had to steady the unfortunate sister.

"There." My lady stood, wiping her hands on her thighs. "Today I have delivered justice for all the half-blood sons and daughters that the King and his forefathers locked up. I've locked him inside his own body."

Vonanjiro glared up at her, all impotent fury. I laughed.

"Get the guard's keys," my lady told the unfortunate sister. "Set the other half-bloods free."

"Too late," she said, voice tight with grief. "Two of my older brothers were killed while trying to escape and the last one killed himself."

"I'm sorry." My lady frowned. "Then who did the King lock behind a stone wall?"

"My boy. He's a full-blood throwback like you."

"Another throwback…" My lady's face lit with hope and she looked to me. An answering joy filled my heart.

"We must go." The unfortunate sister retrieved the keys then ushered us out, locking the door on the paralysed King without a second glance.

She retraced our path, past the entrance to the secret passage then up three steps, where she signalled us to wait. Before I could ask why, she stepped around the corner.

"It *is* you, Kurdon," she said. "He told me you would be on duty the day it happened."

"What happened?"

"This. Lord Giant?"

As I stepped around the corner, the man's eyes widened.

"You've been kind to me and my boy, Kurdon. He told me you would have to make a choice. A Wyrd philosopher once said, we are the sum of our life choices. The King could have honoured his bargain with Lady Shen but he reneged on it and paid for his treachery."

"The King is dead?" The guard sounded hopeful.

"He won't be ordering anyone's execution," my lady said, joining us.

The guard stiffened with fear.

I didn't blame him. Even without touch, I could feel her gift surging like the incoming tide, rising higher each time she forced it down.

My lady reached out to Kurdon. He jerked back, hit his head and passed out. The unfortunate sister opened the door so I could drag him inside.

At first glance the sumptuous chamber appeared empty. Was the unfortunate sister mad after all? More likely the poor boy was afraid of me, most people were.

I turned my hands palm up. "We mean no harm, lad. We're here to free you."

The unfortunate sister stared into the darkest corner. "Ardonyx, it's time."

Still he did not come out. I strode towards that corner. "We must..."

The words dried in my mouth as I sensed danger hiding in the darkness. Trapped and desperate, the power was rank like a caged predator.

"Gyf." My lady's voice came from a great distance. "Put the knife away."

I looked down to see the blade in my hand. Did not remember drawing it. Did not want to sheathe it. "There's dangerous power, here. Evil."

"Not evil. Different. His gift doesn't feel like mine." My lady took my free hand. "See through my senses."

She found his power rich and enticing but, even as she welcomed the sensation, my instincts screamed a warning.

"Gyfron, please," she whispered. "Put the knife away."

The unfortunate sister stepped in front of me. "Ardonyx, your grandfather is paralysed. His new wife will claim the throne for her son, or his nephew will take it. Either way, we'll be executed. We must go. Drop the illusion."

The intensity of the threat dissipated and, just like that, I could see him standing in the dark corner. This was no sweet little boy. He was almost as tall as me and, from his smooth chin, had more growing to do. It wouldn't be long before this throwback outmatched me physically.

No wonder the True-men of old had feared Wyrds.

As the throwback's wary wine-dark eyes studied me, I was reminded of the legends of dangerous, deceiving T'En. What if he was as power-hungry and conniving as his grandfather, King Vonanjiro? Was I about to unleash the Wyrd of nightmare on True-men?

The King had been right. The unfortunate sister was addicted to her son's gift and blinded by love. His power was already strong enough to entice my lady. Power corrupted. He would steal her love and I would be alone again.

I had to protect my lady from herself.

Tension gathered in the Wyrd's shoulders but I could take him. Then I felt his gift rise again. If I wanted to come out of this alive, I had to kill him from a distance.

"Lord Giant won't hurt you, Ardonyx," the unfortunate sister said. "Get your things, we must leave now."

"No." His gaze flicked to her. "I had another vision. They will recognise you as we try to escape."

She laughed. "Do you think I care? As long as you're free, nothing matters!"

"Don't say that." He dashed across the chamber and dropped to his knees, hugging her around the waist. "Please don't make me do this, Ma."

And just like that, I no longer saw him as a threat. He was the boy, his mother loved. Maybe one day, he would be the kind of man my lady could love, but right now, he was a half-grown lad who needed our help.

Shame filled me.

Although the boy's gift still grated on my senses, I refused to be blinded by prejudices. I sheathed my knife. "Your mother's right, lad. We should go."

"I'll fetch the cloaks and travelling packs," the unfortunate sister said.

We made it to the secret panel then out of the palace without mishap. In the confusion of a city preparing for war no one looked twice at our hooded party. The streets were packed with mustering kingsmen and hurrying crowds. Many people carried belongings as they headed for the wharves, others had come to stay with relatives and were welcomed into homes where the owners were busy boarding up the ground floors.

On the port wall, we spotted a ship taking on passengers. We were almost at the gangplank when half a dozen kingsmen came towards us.

"Keep your heads down," the unfortunate sister warned.

But one of the kingsmen pointed. "It's the Tronanova." He lunged to grab her arm.

I shouldered her aside, pulled his own sword from his waist and shoved him back into his companions. "Go."

The unfortunate sister urged her son towards the gangplank.

"Gyf…" my lady whispered, grief stricken.

"Go. I'll hold them while you board."

"Sweet Gyfron…" She kissed my ruined cheek.

And I felt the searing power of her gift. My heart raced. Everything slowed. There was plenty of time to turn and catch the first attacker's blade, sending him off the port wall into the sea. Two more fell off the other side, onto the crowd below.

A roaring filled my head as more kingsmen arrived, carrying torches. As soon as the ship's gang plank was drawn up, I edged around so that a pile of bales protected my back.

The ship's sails unfurled.

Two more kingsmen fell under my blows. I could feel the rush of my lady's gift drain away. There were too many attackers. I wasn't getting out of this alive but at least my lady was free and she was no longer alone.

My borrowed blade shattered deflecting a strike. Another blow tore the hilt from my bloody fingers and sliced my thigh. I went down on one knee.

So this was how it ended.

The kingsmen held their torches high. As they jostled for the honour of the killing blow, I turned my maimed face towards them and waited. The True-men stared horrified.

One pointed. "He has the rose-rash."

"Plague! Plague Bringer!"

I had the plague? Impossible.

But they backed off. Word spread and people fled.

I slumped against the bales, with my hand pressed to my thigh. Blood oozed between my fingers as I tried to make sense of what had just happened.

At least I could see my lady's ship negotiating the harbour.

Word of the plague spread along the port wall. People ran back into the city, carrying the contagion with them.

My lady had promised I wouldn't get the plague. How could...

The scales fell from my eyes.

King Vonanjiro had been right. My lady had come here to dispense justice. Long ago, these islanders had turned on her people, stolen their home and murdered those left behind. To avenge that dark day, she had used me to carry the plague, activating the contagion with a kiss.

My heart broke as I sank to the planks.

I wanted to die.

But I did not bleed out and, as the night passed, I saw fires spring up across the city. There was fighting on the palace wall. Men fell screaming to their death. The Prince's mother and the nephew were battling for the throne.

I did not care. My lady had betrayed me.

Towards dawn the fighting subsided, although several fires still burned. I shivered, wracked with fever, as I waited for the plague to kill me.

"Gyf?"

"My lady?" I must be delirious.

She came up the sea steps of the port wall, with a storm-lantern and the lad, Ardonyx.

As her cool hand cupped my cheek, a wave of power settled my fever and sealed my thigh.

"It *is* you." Tears burned my eyes. "You came back."

"Of course."

"I thought..." Shame filled me. "*They* thought I had the plague."

"That was my doing." Her thumb brushed my cheek where she'd

kissed me. "I branded your skin. They took it for sign of the rose plague."

I blinked, confused.

She laughed softly. "My kiss made them think you had the plague. It was all I could do to protect you." She came to her feet. "And now we've come back for you. Help him up, Ardonyx."

The lad offered his hand and I took it. King Vonanjiro had been right, power could corrupt. But we had a choice.

An Oath Given

John Gwynne

Maquin was first to see the rider approaching.

It was close to the end of his watch, night's chill gnawing deep in his bones as he viewed the sun clawing its way over the bulk of Forn Forest. He was standing upon a timber walkway that ringed Aenor's Hold, last settlement before the wild of Forn. As he turned his eyes away from the forest he saw a glint on the north road, sunlight catching on iron. The blade of a spear.

He raised a horn to his lips and blew, one short blast. Feet drummed on the walkway, warriors gathering above the closed gates. They were always shut – you never knew what could wander out of Forn, but it was usually predatory, and hungry.

The rider swayed in his saddle as he drew close, a warrior clothed for battle, his shield rent, helm dented. The gates remained closed and he reined his mount in. From this distance Maquin could see the white streaks of salt stains in the horse's dun coat.

"Name yourself," Maquin called down.

"I am Ulfilas of Tancred's Hold. We were attacked." He sucked in a breath, grimaced. "Attacked by the Hunen." The warrior swayed in his saddle, then slipped to the floor like a sack of grain.

Maquin shifted in his saddle, sweating beneath his woollen tunic and coat of mail. His war helm was strapped upon his head, narrowing his vision, making each breath sound like distant thunder. A heavy spear rested in the crook of his arm, its butt sat in a leather cup stitched onto his saddle. He had ridden hard for half a day with three-score warriors, his lord Aenor at their head. It was not often that Aenor rode out these days, brooding younger brother of the King, but the warrior at the gate had come from Tancred's Hold. And Tancred was wed to Rosamund, Aenor's sister.

They passed through rolling hills and meadows. To the east Maquin could see the fringes of Forn, clusters of red fern and twisted hawthorn standing like a vanguard before the wall of thick-trunked oak and ash that loomed tall and solid, stretching into the distance as far as his eye could see. Maquin rode immediately behind Aenor. He was well thought of by his lord, had proven himself, standing as Aenor's shield during an ambush by brigands where others had broken and run.

Loyalty is of more value than gold, Aenor had said to him afterwards, and Maquin's da had beamed with pride.

My da. He felt a fist close around his heart just at the memory of the man, dead half a year, now. Slain by a pack of wolven come ranging out of Forn in the heart of winter. Maquin's hand drifted to the hilt of his sword, the iron pommel worn smooth – his da's sword.

"You all right, lad?" a voice said to his right. Radulf, Aenor's first-sword. Radulf always called Maquin *lad*, even though Maquin had seen more than thirty summers go by.

"Aye," Maquin grunted. In truth he was tense, felt that mixture of excitement and fear that preceded imminent violence. He was no stranger to combat, their first years at Aenor's Hold spent clearing the land of bands of lawless men, and there was always something to hunt and fight within the fringes of Forn – packs of wolven, bears, even a rogue bull draig last spring, but the warrior that had ridden to their gates had said *Hunen.*

Giants. Remnant of one of the giant clans, ancient enemy of mankind in these Banished Lands, the Hunen were said to be the most vicious. Legend spoke of their fortress deep within Forn, protected by both glamour and snare, and men told tales around campfires of the rare times the Hunen would stray from their forest stronghold. Those tales said they always left blood in their wake. Maquin had seen a giant's war hammer hanging in the fortress of Mikil, and his da told of a giant raid that his grand-da had witnessed, but other than that for all Maquin could prove the giants were a tale told to keep bairns in their cots at night.

"Have you ever seen one of the Hunen?" he asked Radulf.

"No, lad, though I've met some that have." He regarded Maquin with his steady gaze. "The Hunen are no faery tale."

"Who do you know that's seen them?" Maquin tried to keep the scepticism from his voice.

"There's a brotherhood of warriors that call themselves the Gadrai, giant-killers they are. Live in a crumbling tower in Forn somewhere close to the river." Radulf was as steady as they come, a fine balance for his Lord Aenor's hot-headedness. He was not one to be taken in by fanciful tales.

"I've heard of them," Maquin said begrudgingly.

"I've drunk with some of them, and they'll tell you the Hunen are real enough. But I don't think it was the Hunen that attacked Tancred's Hold. I think our survivor has had one too many blows to the head. It would take a warband of the Hunen to overrun Tancred's Hold, and I've never heard of the giants coming out in those kind of numbers. More likely it was a band of lawless men. Attacking at night the enemy is always bigger, more fearsome." He shrugged. "We'll find out soon enough."

Columns of black smoke became visible, billowing into the sky a few leagues ahead, birds circling lazily.

Never a good sign.

They rode in silence now, the clatter of hooves, the jingle of harness and chainmail the only sounds marking their passing. Tancred's Hold appeared before them, a palisaded wall sitting upon the crest of a low hill. Its gates were open, one hanging from its hinges. Maquin searched the walls for movement, but he saw only the flutter of wings, heard only the raucous cawing of crows. Aenor led their column of warriors up the hill, the white horsehair plume of his helmet flowing out behind him. He lifted his spear from its cup, dipped it a little, ready. Maquin and three-score warriors did the same.

Aenor passed through the gates, Maquin and Radulf close behind. The smell hit Maquin first: blood, decay, charred flesh. They rode into a wide courtyard, a timber feast-hall at its far end, doors blackened from fire, still smoking. Bodies were everywhere, some still in one piece, many eviscerated, dismembered, limbs scattered. Swarms of flies buzzed in great clouds. A horse slipped in a pile of intestines, the rider dragging on his reins to stay seated.

Aenor dismounted and strode ahead. Maquin and Radulf were close behind, moving either side of their lord. They shared a look.

Stay close, don't let him get ahead, the look said. Aenor was known for his temper. It had led him into dangerous situations before now.

Within heartbeats a dozen more warriors had formed up around them, the rest fanning out through the courtyard. Aenor climbed the steps to the feast hall. He stopped and waved his spear at a daring crow.

It sat upon a mound before the feast-hall's open doors and squawked angrily as it took to the air, red beak dripping droplets of gore.

It took a moment for Maquin to realize what the bird had been feasting upon. A huge warrior lay across the entrance, considerably taller than a grown man, though shorter than two, Maquin guessed. The figure was thick-muscled, dark haired, clothed in leather and mail. The crow had taken its eyes. A great wound stretched across its throat, blood pooling black about the body. Maquin spied a swirling tattoo spiraling up one bare arm, a vine thick with thorns. The warrior still clutched a war hammer in its death grip.

"The Hunen," Aenor muttered.

"The rider spoke true, then," Radulf said.

Maquin felt a spike of fear, cold and sharp in his belly. He took a deep, slow breath, controlling it.

Other bodies lay beyond the giant: men, heaped and twisted in death. Aenor knelt beside one, fair-haired beneath the matted blood.

"Tancred," he said, wiping crusted blood from the man's face.

Where is Rosamund, my lord's sister? thought Maquin.

Aenor rose and stepped through the doors.

Maquin followed, shield gripped tight, spear ready. He blinked in the twilight of the hall. Shafts of light dissected the room, cutting down from holes in the roof where the thatch had burnt away. Thick flakes of ash drifted on the air like black, corrupted leaves. Tables and benches were strewn about the hall, smashed, heaped together. They passed another Hunen, this one fallen in the fire pit, a spear in his belly. His face was twisted in a snarl, pain or rage Maquin could not tell. Charred fingers still gripped the pit's edge.

At the far end of the hall there were three more dead giants, before them a mound of warriors, piled in a half-circle like bags of grain against a flood.

Their last stand.

Beyond them, draped upon the few steps that led to the high table, lay another body. A woman, judging by her clothing. Aenor let out a great sob and knelt beside her.

Rosamund.

A huge wound spanned her chest, flesh and bone cleaved in one great stroke. Aenor cradled her body.

Radulf signalled to warriors, motioning towards a door at the far end of the hall.

The Hunen are gone from here, thought Maquin.

There was a scraping sound, an overturned table shifting, and every warrior in the room was instantly poised, spears levelled.

A face poked out from the ruin, blackened with ash, eyes wide with fear, cheeks tear stained.

Maquin raised his spear, then paused. *It is a bairn. Only a bairn.*

The child they had discovered was Rosamund's and Tancred's son, Jael. He was seven summers old and sat before Maquin now, both hands gripping the high saddle pommel. He had whimpered when they set off, the first sounds he'd made since they pulled him from the rubble of broken furniture in the feast-hall.

"Nothing to fear, lad," Maquin had whispered to him, feeling immediately like a fool. *He has plenty to fear, and will probably be having nightmares for the rest of his life.*

After discovering Jael they had searched the rest of the Hold. In total nine Hunen corpses were found. There were no more survivors and so they set to caring for the dead, Aenor sending scouts to search for signs of the giants. As the last stones were laid upon the cairns of the dead the scouts returned, telling of tracks coming from and then returning to Forn Forest.

Aenor had gone to where the giant dead had been laid out, upon a bed of rushes. He raised his sword and with a great cry cut the head from one of them. It took three swings. He tied it to his saddle and then set a torch to the rushes. In moments a fire roared, great tongues of flame caressing the giant corpses.

They rode from the Hold in grim silence.

The sun was dipping into the horizon, their shadows stretching along the road far ahead, when home came into view. Maquin breathed a sigh of relief, the gnawing dread that Aenor's Hold had been attacked while they were away evaporating with the sight of the Hold's timber walls. Far beyond them Forn spread, a brooding shadow swallowing the horizon.

Horn blasts announced their return, a crowd gathering to greet them as they cantered through the gates into a wide courtyard. Cheers stuttered and died when Aenor reined in his horse and raised from his saddle the giant's head, holding it high for all to see.

"Our ancient foe has returned," he cried, "striking from out of Forn to slay my kin." He called to old Erengar, one of the Hold's smiths, asking for a hammer and long nails. Erengar hurried away and returned quickly. Aenor rode to the gates, stood in his saddle and hammered the long nail through the giant's skull into the timber frame. When he was done he dropped the hammer and stared in silence, breathing hard.

"Let none forget," he shouted, then kicked his mount on to the stables.

Maquin and the warband followed, and for a while all was chaos as horses were tended and stabled. Maquin lifted Jael and stood him in a corner while he stripped saddle and blanket from his horse, going through the ritual of checking hooves and rubbing down.

Radulf came to him as he finished and was standing looking at Jael, wondering what to do with the lad.

"Take the bairn for some food, then bring him to Aenor's chambers," Radulf said.

"Food? Me?"

"Aye. Aenor's orders. Until later, then." Radulf left.

"Right lad, let's find you something to eat," Maquin said as he held out a hand. Jael took it and they set off for the feast-hall. Maquin took Jael through the hall, a great boar turning on a spit above the fire pit, then through a door and into the kitchens. The smell of baking bread and a dozen other aromas set his mouth watering. His eyes searched out Odilia. She was two years widowed from a shieldman of Aenor's, and Maquin had a mind to court her. *Two years grieving is long enough. Long enough to not give her a bad name.* Aenor's Hold was large by any standards – over a hundred warriors, three times that in women and bairns, as well as all the traders needed to keep a Hold running – smiths and farriers, tanners, weavers, horsemen, crofters, but really it was like a huge extended family, a small village where everyone new everyone. There was a closeness amongst those that lived here, that bound them together, almost as if they were kin.

Odilia smiled at Maquin when she saw him, and he thought her eyes sparkled a little. In return for a whispered telling of what had happened at Tancred's Hold he was given two bowls of venison stew and bread still warm from the oven. Jael ate every drop and crumb.

"Do you want some more?" Maquin asked.

Jael shook his head.

Maquin stared at Jael. *What do you say to a boy who's just lost everything?*

"Come on," he said, and with a grateful nod to Odilia led Jael from the kitchens and made his way to Aenor's rooms. It was dark now, stars bright in a cloudless sky. He nodded to his swordbrothers standing guard outside Aenor's chambers and was ushered in, Jael following silently behind.

Maquin saw Irma first, Aenor's wife. She was tall, elegant, her face fine featured, hard if not for the smile she was directing at her husband. Aenor sat in a fur-covered chair, bouncing a child upon his knee. Kastell, his son. The lad was laughing hard, fighting for breath, his face almost as red as his hair. Aenor was smiling, creases around his eyes softening the usual stern lines of his face. He saw Jael first and stopped bouncing Kastell, the boy protesting. Aenor placed Kastell on the ground.

"Kastell, this is Jael, your cousin."

"Hello," Kastell said, suddenly serious, his face still red from laughing.

Irma crouched down and held out her hands to Jael.

The boy looked at the floor and shuffled his feet.

"Come here, Jael," Aenor said and Jael walked forward.

"You are safe now," Aenor said. He took Jael's hand and looked into the boy's eyes. "It is early yet, but I want you to know, you are welcome here. You are kin, my sister's son, and if you wish it you will have a home here, always."

Jael chewed his lip. "Can you see the forest from here?" he asked, his voice little more than a whisper.

"Forn. Aye, you can," Aenor said.

"I don't want to stay here," Jael said, louder.

"If you prefer I can send you to my brother, King Romar." A string of emotions twisted Aenor's face for a moment: sadness, shame, finally anger. "I think you would be better off staying with me. No harm will come to you while you're here. You're safe," Aenor said.

"That's what my da said."

Maquin woke to a knocking on his door. He pulled his boots on and opened it wide, blinking blearily in the morning sunlight. Aenor stood there, the bulk of Radulf looming over his shoulder. Another figure pushed into view, squeezing a head around Aenor's legs. Kastell, Aenor's son.

"Walk with me," his lord said, then turned and strode away.

Maquin chased after them, quickly pulling on a tunic and grabbing his scabbarded sword and belt, which he slung over a shoulder. He cursed as he stabbed himself with the pin of his cloak brooch. Aenor led him to the Hold's wall, then climbed stairs, finally stopping on the walkway above the eastern gate. The air was cold, damp, a thin mist still in the air. Dark clouds gathered on the horizon.

There's a storm coming.

Radulf walked on a few steps, taking Kastell with him. He lifted the boy to his chest and pointed into the distance.

"I have something to ask you," Aenor said to Maquin, looking out at the vastness of Forn Forest, a dark stain that consumed the horizon.

"Anything, my lord."

"No. Wait until you have heard what I am asking."

Maquin frowned. Aenor was larger than life, quick to anger, and once upon a time quick to laugh, although that had changed since he had argued with his brother, the King. Since then he had become silent and brooding, had left the court at Mikil for a life in the wilderness, his family and retainers following him into his self-imposed exile. But one thing that Maquin had never seen him appear was scared. Until today.

"I am troubled, Maquin. I grieve for my sister Rosamund, and more. The Hunen striking out of Forn in such numbers as to destroy a Hold, over seventy shieldmen slain..." He shook his head. "Something is wrong. Something is happening."

"It won't happen here," Maquin growled, but he felt a spike of doubt. Seeing the carnage left behind by the Hunen had troubled him, and fear was in the air; he had heard the talk spreading through the Hold like a rolling mist.

"Perhaps," Aenor shrugged. He gripped the timber wall and squeezed, his knuckles white. "I have a mind to ride out and see if I can find these giants." His expression darkened into something Maquin had seen before. It usually ended with blades drawn and blood spilt. He felt a thrill at the thought of riding out after the Hunen, part excitement, part fear.

"Whatever I decide, we must be prepared," Aenor continued. "You have been part of my Hold a long time. Fourteen years have passed us by since your sixteenth nameday, since you sat your Long Night and became a man. You have served me well, risen through my ranks, become a man that I trust."

Maquin blinked, did not know what to say. "Thank you, my lord," he mumbled.

"You swore an oath to me, to be my sword and shield."

"I did." Maquin looked at the scar on his palm, where he had spilt his blood to seal his oath to Aenor.

"I would ask you to make that oath to another."

"What, you mean... leave you...?"

"No. I am speaking of Kastell. I want you to become my son's shieldman. I want you to swear your oath to him. To protect him above all others – even before me. Unto death."

"Kastell." Maquin looked past Aenor at the lad, still held in Radulf's arms, staring out enraptured at Forn as Radulf whispered tales of sharp-toothed wolven or mighty draigs.

"Aye, Kastell," Aenor said. "This would be no small undertaking, no light words. You would be binding yourself to him for life, and I hope that he has a long one to live."

Maquin blew out a long breath. He was happy with his life, content living at Aenor's Hold, with the position he held. He was born to be a warrior, it was all he knew. Other than the growing presence of Odilia in his mind he had no real thoughts of change for the future, just more of the same. *Would being Kastell's shieldman change that?* In real terms, probably not. Or at least, not until Kastell came of age. The boy was six summers old, would grow to inherit all that Aenor was building now. But Maquin new that Aenor was asking, and offering, a great deal. To become shieldman to the lord's son, that was a great honour indeed. It spoke of trust, not only in martial skill, but in practical judgement and wisdom. *Am I wise? Not particularly. Though I don't count myself amongst the stupid, either.*

"What is wrong?" Aenor asked him.

"I do not feel worthy, my lord. It is a great honour that you offer me."

"Aye, it is. And a great responsibility. My son is precious to me, and I cannot be at his side always. I would rest easier knowing that someone I trust is with him. You are my obvious choice, Maquin. Skilled, brave, loyal." He paused and held Maquin's gaze. "If you would rather think on it."

"No, my lord, I know my answer. I would be proud to be Kastell's shieldman."

"You are sure. I would not think less of you – and there would be no consequences. Nothing would change between us."

"I am sure, my lord. There is no doubt in my heart." All that Maquin felt was an overwhelming sense of pride. *I wish my da were here to see this.*

"Let us do it now, then. Kastell, come here."

"Now?"

"Aye. We will have a feast tonight to celebrate, and I will drink to you." He clapped his hand on Maquin's shoulder and grinned, a rare sight these days. "But I want it done now. It is on my mind, and I will rest easier once the deed is done."

Radulf set the lad down and he ran to Aenor. Maquin saw Kastell had a wooden sword in his hand. He stabbed Aenor in the leg with it.

"You know Maquin, Kastell." The boy nodded, suddenly serious. "He is one of my bravest warriors –"

"As brave as you and Radulf?" Kastell asked him.

"Aye, Kastell, as brave as both of us, and more than that. He is loyal, which is of greater value than gold. Maquin is going to watch over you from now on. He is to be your shieldman. That is a sacred role, between lord and warrior –"

"I am his lord, then?"

"Yes." Aenor smiled and ruffled his son's red hair. Maquin smiled too at the mischievous sparkle in the boy's eyes.

"That does not mean you can order him about," Aenor added. "Maybe one day, after your Long Night. But not yet."

Maquin was glad that Aenor had made that clear.

Kastell looked disappointed, but still nodded.

"You would accept Maquin as your shieldman, then?"

Kastell looked Maquin up and down. "If you choose him for me. I trust you, da."

"Good. There is also something that you must do. You have seen men swear their oaths to me."

"Do I have to cut my hand?"

"Yes, you do."

"Why?"

"Because you are both making a promise to each other. To do all that you can, unto death, to protect one another. Making the cut says that you are prepared to spill blood for that oath; your own blood, or someone else's."

"Will it hurt?"

"Aye."

Kastell dropped his wooden sword and looked at his open palm, as if imagining it bleeding. Then he looked up at his da.

"All right, then."

"Your sword, Maquin," Aenor said.

Maquin drew his sword and rested the blade's tip between them.

"Maquin, will you bind yourself to my son, Kastell ben Aenor, become his sword and shield, the defender of his flesh, his blood, his honour, unto death?"

"I will," Maquin said, a swell of emotion making his voice raw. He gripped his sword's blade, cut his palm, then held a fist above it, blood dripping onto the smooth iron pommel, running down the hilt and cross-guard.

"Kastell, will you bind yourself to Maquin ben Calon, accept his fealty, swear to provide and protect him to your utmost ability, unto your dying breath?"

"I will," Kastell said, and without prompting he gripped the sword blade and squeezed. When a droplet of blood ran down the blade Kastell lifted his hand and clenched a fist, waiting as Maquin had until blood dripped onto the hilt, mixing with Maquin's.

"It is done," Aenor said.

They all stood there for long moments, Maquin's world contracted to the pulsing throb of the cut on his palm. Kastell stared at him, big hazel eyes in a freckled face. Maquin grinned and dipped his head.

"My lord," he said.

Kastell copied him. "My shieldman," he replied. Aenor barked a laugh and Radulf slapped Maquin on the shoulder.

"Your da would have been proud to see this," Radulf whispered to him.

Footsteps sounded behind and Maquin turned to see a warrior and child climbing the stairs towards them – Jael and Ulfilas, the warrior that had brought word of the giant attack at Tancred's Hold.

Aenor greeted them both, and Maquin nodded to Ulfilas. His arm was bandaged, a young man no more than twenty summers.

"I have told Jael that he is welcome to stay here with me and become a part of my Hold. I would make the same offer to you, Ulfilas," said Aenor.

"I thank you, my Lord. I would like to stay here – your people have made me welcome. But I must go where Jael goes – I swore an oath to Tancred." He dropped his head. "I could not keep my lord Tancred safe, but Jael..."

"I understand," Aenor said, glancing at Maquin.

While the men were talking, Jael and Kastell eyed each other. Kastell hefted his wooden sword, then offered it to Jael.

"No. It is a toy for bairns," said Jael.

"How old are you?"

"Seven summers."

"Then you are a bairn, too."

Jael looked away. Kastell scowled.

"Jael, have you thought more on where you would live?" Aenor asked.

Jael had turned to look out over the timber walls. He was just tall enough to see the land beyond. Green meadows rolled towards Forn Forest. He let out a whimper.

"There's no need to be scared," Kastell said, his tone helpful. "Forn's only made out of trees, and trees aren't scary. My mam told me that."

Jael gave Kastell a dark look. "Your mam doesn't know what she's talking about."

Even though Jael was only seven Maquin bridled at the insult to Aenor's wife. By the look on his face, so did Kastell.

"Don't talk about my mam like that," Kastell said.

"It's the truth, and you don't tell me what to do," Jael snapped.

Kastell dropped his wooden sword and bunched his fists.

Oh dear, thought Maquin. Before he could act Kastell was moving. He shoved Jael hard into the wall, leaving a smear of blood as Jael's nose crunched. Jael fell over, then launched himself at Kastell, hissing like a cat.

The two lads crashed about on the walkway, kicking and biting, rolling perilously close to the edge. Maquin was the first to move, the other men staring wide-eyed. Maquin grabbed two belts and hoisted the boys into the air, holding them as wide apart as he could. They fought to get at each other.

"Enough!" roared Aenor and the two boys stilled.

Radulf leaned close to Maquin. "In case you didn't know, Kastell has a rare temper on him."

Maquin sat in the feast hall, wiping rain from his eyes. A storm had rolled in and the short walk from his chambers had served to soak him and almost blown him into a wall. He unclasped his cloak and shook it. Beneath it he was wearing his best tunic, over it a gleaming leather jerkin. He had spent half the day polishing his sword and warrior torc, and he wore the silver arm ring that Aenor had given him after the brigands' ambush. In other words he was wearing almost all of his warrior finery. All that he'd left behind in his chambers was his coat of mail and his helm. Aenor was announcing him Kastell's shieldman tonight.

What have I got myself into? he thought, remembering Kastell's brief fight with Jael. He smiled to himself. *Kastell's got spirit. He's like his da, has a temper – should keep me on my toes, long as he's not still picking fights after he's sat his Long Night.*

After his altercation with Kastell Jael had stated that he had no desire to live at Aenor's Hold. He had gone as far as to demand that he be sent to live with King Romar. Aenor had not liked that, it had been plain to see, but he had held his temper. Jael and Ulfilas had left by highsun. Aenor had sent a dozen warriors with them as a guard. *Probably for the best that Jael's gone. Don't think he and Kastell got off to the best of starts.*

The hall was busy, the fire pit blazing as fat dripped and sizzled. Smoke rose thick in the air, pooling amidst the rafters around the roof's smokehole. People ate and drank. It was not as full as usual for a celebration, though. Aenor had doubled the guards on the walls in light of the attack on Tancred's Hold. The mood was more subdued than usual, talk of giants out of Forn still on most people's tongues. Hounds snapped at one another under the benches as scraps came their way.

A figure sat on the bench beside Maquin.

Odilia. He knew it was her by the faint smell of cinnamon that always surrounded her.

"What're you all dressed up for?" she asked, eying the warrior torc around his neck and squeezing his arm ring.

He tapped his nose and smiled at her.

"Don't be so mysterious," she said. "I'll give you an extra spoonful of cream with your oatcakes and honey..."

"I'd tell you anything you want to know for that." He grinned. Odilia made good oatcakes.

The hall quietened as Aenor and Irma entered, Kastell following at her side.

Radulf went to the quartered auroch turning on the spit and sliced Aenor the first cut of meat, then waited a moment for any willing to challenge his right, as was the custom. There was no challenge and he returned to his seat.

Aenor banged his cup with his knife and the room grew silent.

One of the hounds at Maquin's feet growled, low and deep. Maquin put a hand on it and felt its hackles up.

"Easy boy," he murmured, his attention mostly on Aenor.

The hound half rose, snarling at the closed doors of the feast-hall. Maquin realised other hounds about the room were doing the same. He frowned. Outside Maquin could hear the storm raging.

A horn call rang out, distant and swirling. It sent a shiver of ice through Maquin's veins.

The call to arms.

Something crashed against the feast-hall's doors, a booming impact that sent a cloud of dust roiling inwards.

"To arms," Radulf yelled.

Maquin rose, drawing his sword.

"What is it?" Odilia gasped, gripping Maquin's wrist.

The doors boomed, cracked, burst open.

"Nothing good," Maquin said.

A gust of wind howled through the open doors, hurling rain into the room like a swarm of flies. Sounds filtered in, rising and falling: screams, the clash of iron. Something solid filled the doorway, blotting all else out. A huge figure silhouetted by flame. Tall, wide, a war hammer raised high.

Maquin froze for a dozen heartbeats, open-mouthed. He had seen a giant's corpse only a day gone by, but that had still not prepared him for this. Dead, the giant had appeared as a sail with no wind in it,

88

crumpled, empty. This creature that stood in the doorway radiated strength and menace. It stood a man and a half tall, wrapped in leather and fur, thick cords of muscle writhing. A long drooping moustache was bound with leather cord, its face all sharp angles and jutting brows.

"*Sinn gabh cuidich ciod bha caillte,*" it bellowed, spittle flying.

"The Hunen," yelled Maquin, moving forward. Odilia cried out behind him, clutched at his arm. He paused, looking between her and the open doorway. The giant surged into the feast-hall, war hammer swinging, smashing into the chest of a warrior. Maquin heard the crunch of bones over all other noise, the warrior hurled through the air. More giants crowded behind the first. In a heartbeat everything turned to chaos, people standing, running, benches overturning.

"To me," he heard Radulf shouting.

"Stay behind me," Maquin said to Odilia. Gripping her hand he threaded his way through the hall towards Radulf. A table hurtled past him, landing in the fire pit, sending sparks swirling. Flames caught quickly, a bank of heat making Maquin swerve. Odilia staggered but Maquin steadied her and dragged her on. Everywhere screams filled the hall, punctuated by the guttural yells of the Hunen. The wet sound of iron cleaving flesh. Panic spread faster than smoke. Maquin kept on moving, his eyes on Radulf. Behind the first-sword he glimpsed Aenor standing with blade drawn, one hand on Irma. Kastell held on to her leg.

"What do we do?" Maquin yelled as he reached Radulf. The warrior stood a dozen paces before Aenor, eyes scanning the hall. A score of warriors were with Radulf now, more emerging from the chaos of the hall.

"We must get Aenor out of here," Radulf grunted. "We'll not make the same mistake Tancred did, getting cornered in here like rats in a trap. We need space. See to Kastell, we're heading out the back door."

"What about..." Maquin glanced about the hall. Bodies were scattered everywhere, a handful of giants wading through the hall swinging war hammers and axes at anything that moved. *It's like terriers in a barrel of rats.* He saw faces he'd lived with, laughed with. Shadow and flame contorted everything, banks of smoke rolling across his vision.

"Remember your oath," Radulf snapped. "Aenor, Irma and Kastell are our charge. Go." He pushed Maquin towards their lord, warriors sweeping about them like a closing fist.

"Stay close to Irma," Maquin said to Odilia. Aenor was staring beyond him at the carnage in the hall. "This way, my lord," Maquin said, pulling at Aenor's cloak.

They all moved together, Maquin hardly pausing as he kicked open the door to the kitchens, a wave of heat from the ovens hitting him. He turned to check Aenor and the others were following, saw a huge figure appear out of a billowing cloud of smoke. Maquin had a moment to yell a warning, then the Hunen's war hammer was sweeping down.

It crashed into Irma, fragments of flesh and bone exploding where her head had been. People screamed – Aenor, Kastell – Odilia flew through the air, caught by the hammer as it followed the arc of its swing. She crunched into a wall and slid down, a trail of blood smearing the stone.

Maquin stared at Irma's ruined form.

He moved, his feet carrying him before he had time to think. The force of its blow had swung the giant away and Maquin darted close – don't give it room to swing that hammer – and cut two-handed at the giant's waist. Blood sprayed as his blade sliced through fur and leather, bit into flesh. The giant grunted. Maquin yanked his sword free as he spun behind the giant, back-swung at a leg to leave a red gash, then the giant was turning, much faster than Maquin thought possible for something of its bulk. It saw him, snarled and lashed out, fist connecting with Maquin's shoulder, sending him sprawling. Pain bloomed. He rolled, glimpsed the giant following him, saw it lurch and drop to one knee. Ignoring the pain he pushed himself upright, found his sword, charged at the giant, swung overhead at its neck.

The giant reached out, grabbed his arm in one big hand, stopping him dead. He writhed in its grip but could not pull free.

On its knee the giant was at eye level with Maquin. They stared at each other for a moment, the giant's eyes small and black beneath its jutting brow. Then Maquin's other hand found his knife and he drew, punched it into the giant's armpit, twisting as he felt the blade grate on bone. The giant bellowed, hurled Maquin to the ground. He cracked his head, white lights exploding in his vision. The giant rose unsteadily and raised its war hammer.

A spearpoint burst from its throat, blood jetting in a fountain, and it collapsed to its knees. The spear blade was yanked back, Radulf appearing from behind the giant. Then Aenor was there, other warriors, all stabbing, hacking. The giant toppled to the side, crashed to the ground.

Radulf pulled Maquin to his feet.

"With me," Aenor yelled, his face twisted with rage. He led a dozen men into the hall. Maquin glimpsed them attacking another giant. It swung a two-bladed axe, roaring as spears pierced it.

"Aenor is grief-mad," Radulf said, "there's no stopping him. Take Kastell and get out."

"You'll need my sword arm."

Radulf gripped his shoulder and shook him. "Remember your oath, lad. Get him out, keep him safe." His face softened, just for a moment. "I'll see you again, this side or the other." Then he was gone, running after Aenor.

Maquin went to Odilia. Her neck was twisted at an impossible angle, eyes staring sightlessly. Kastell was sitting beside his mam's corpse. He was holding her hand. Maquin crouched beside him and gently pried their hands apart, then swept Kastell up into his arms and he was running. Through the kitchens, along a corridor and out into the night.

Rain splattered his face, wind tugging at his warrior braid. It was dark, his vision blurred. No giants loomed nearby, the sound of combat faint.

"I feel sick," Kastell said.

Maquin put him down and Kastell bent over and vomited.

Maquin patted his back, Kastell retching long after his stomach was empty. Eventually he looked up at Maquin, bile and spittle on his chin.

"Where's my da?" Kastell asked him.

"That way," Maquin gestured towards the swirling sounds of combat. "Don't worry lad, Radulf is with him. He'll be back with you soon enough."

Maquin hesitated. *Fight or flight?* He knew his duty was to protect Kastell, but the thought of walking away from his lord and his shield-brothers felt so wrong it bordered on cowardice. *I could hide him, then go fight.* While he was still deliberating Kastell made the decision for him, sprinting past him into the darkness. Maquin tried to grab him but the lad swerved and then he was gone, heading back towards the battle.

Damn it, Maquin cursed and chased after him.

They ran along the side of the feast-hall, with every step the sounds of battle growing louder. Maquin caught up with Kastell just as he stumbled into the courtyard in front of the feast-hall. They both skidded to a halt and stood staring.

It was a scene from the Otherworld.

Buildings around the courtyard were in flames, huge tongues of fire curling into the sky, rain hissing and spitting as it turned to steam. The courtyard seethed with bodies, giants swinging their war hammers and axes, warriors rallying, small knots trying to bring down the Hunen, like hounds around a boar. Bodies lay everywhere, the stench of blood and faeces hitting Maquin, clawing with insistent fingers into his throat.

There must be fifty giants out here.

In a glance he knew the Hold was lost.

In the centre of the courtyard a giant roared and toppled to the ground. Maquin knew he should be doing something – *running, fighting* – but he caught a glimpse of Aenor and Radulf highlighted by flames, stabbing at the fallen giant. He stood transfixed. Only a few warriors were with Radulf and Aenor now. Two giants fell upon them, howling as they came. One warrior's head spun through the air. Another was crushed by a war hammer. Radulf deflected a blow somehow, caused the giant's axe to crash into the ground, an explosion of earth. Radulf's sword swung and severed the giant's arm at the elbow. Aenor retreated before another giant, who held a war hammer two handed, like a staff. The butt end snaked out, slammed into Aenor's chest. He staggered and dropped, the war hammer rising and falling, a sickening crunch audible to Maquin.

Radulf yelled something incoherent, threw himself at the giant standing over Aenor.

"Da," Kastell screamed and set off running, weaving through the yard. Maquin followed, stooping to snatch up a spear.

Kastell ran between a giant's legs, swerved around an overturned wain and then he was standing before his da's broken body, Maquin a heartbeat behind him. Radulf was swinging his sword two-handed at the giant that had slain Aenor, for a moment his ferocity driving the huge warrior back. Then the giant was setting his feet, catching Radulf's sword on his hammer-haft, jabbing the butt out as it had against Aenor.

Radulf's only got moments before he's down. Maquin hurled his spear, caught the giant in the shoulder, staggering it. Radulf darted in, left a diagonal cut along its thigh as Maquin circled it. The giant pulled the spear from its shoulder, hurled it at Maquin. He ducked and surged in, cut at the giant's forearm. Radulf struck, the giant bellowing in frustration as the two men stepped in and out, striking and moving out of range, like hounds worrying at a bull.

The giant stumbled over a body and Maquin chopped at its knee, sending it crashing to the ground, then the two men were hacking at it, blood spraying, the giant trying to rise. Maquin chopped fingers from a hand, then he had one foot on its chest and drove his sword into its throat. It twitched and was still. Maquin leaned on his sword, breathing heavily.

Radulf was stood over Aenor's corpse.

Maquin grabbed Kastell by the wrist. "There'll be no more running from me, lad." He turned to Radulf, saw a bleak, grim look in his eyes. "Nothing left for us here."

"Get the bairn out of here," Radulf said, hefting his sword. "I'll watch your back."

Maquin had seen the deathwish before, and it was writ upon Radulf's face now.

"You'll come with us," Maquin, said. "I need you. He needs you."

"No," Radulf shook his head, eyes fixed on Aenor's body. Tears streaked his cheeks.

"Kastell is Aenor's kin. Remember your oath," Maquin snarled, knowing kindness would not keep Radulf alive. Then he was moving, picking up Kastell and running. There was a pause and then he heard Radulf's feet pounding close behind him.

People were running in all directions, a few knots of combat still ringing out. The feast-hall was in flames now, a wall of heat rolling into the yard, the flames sending shadows rippling, dancing like some mad Midsummer's Eve celebration. All was confusion, screaming, death. Maquin headed for the stables that ringed the courtyard, tripped over a corpse, slipped in blood, righted himself and threw himself into the shadows of the stables. Smoke churned in here, flames crackling in the roof overhead, horses neighing.

"Help me," Maquin snapped at Kastell as he opened a stable door, the horse inside white-eyed, stamping its hooves. Radulf was behind him and the three of them set to saddling up their mounts.

Taking too long, Maquin thought, the sounds from the courtyard quietening. He hoisted Kastell onto his horse's back, saw Radulf moving through the stable, opening doors, untying horses, slapping flanks, sending over a score of them charging for the doors.

Radulf leapt onto his own mount's back. "Now," the old warrior yelled over the wild neighing and thunder of hooves. They followed the stampeding horses out into the courtyard, saw a giant trampled beneath a tide of hooves, others leaping out of the way. The horses headed for the widest road through the Hold, leading to the eastern gates and Maquin and Radulf followed, leaning low over their horses' backs.

The gates appeared, open, broken, one hanging from its hinges. The rush of horses swept through them, Maquin close behind. A figure flew from the shadows of a building, a giant grasping at him. It crashed into his mount's flank, sending them staggering, Kastell crying out. Maquin looked back, saw the giant raising its axe, then a sword hacked into its neck and it was collapsing, Radulf wrenching his blade free.

Other Hunen appeared from the shadows, bellowing warcries.

"Ride on," Radulf yelled.

Maquin dragged on his reins, trying to turn his mount. Giants closed about Radulf. His horse reared, hooves lashing out, sending a giant crashing, face a bloody ruin. Then an axe swung, cleaved through Radulf's shoulder and chest, a spray of blood and bone.

Maquin yelled, raw and deep, rage and pain mixed.

The giants about Radulf turned to face him, swept forward, their feet drumming upon the ground. Maquin spurred his horse away, galloped through the gates and out into the night, thundering along the flagstones of the old road.

"Are we safe?" he heard Kastell's voice, whipped by the wind.

Maquin risked a glance back over his shoulder, saw the broken gates of the Hold highlighted by flames. The silhouette of a Hunen stood outlined there. It raised its war hammer at them.

"It's all right, lad, we're away. It's you and me, now. I'll keep you safe. I gave you my oath, remember." Maquin blinked away his tears and rode into the night.

THE SINGER

Stella Gemmell

Amy lay in the darkness listening to the small voice singing, fraying her nerve-ends, just above the threshold of her hearing. In the depths of the night, full of incoherent dread, she dug her husband in the ribs once, twice, and at last Rob rolled over.

"What?" he mumbled. Then, "Lord, not again!"

"I wish he'd stop," she whispered, trying to sound merely worried rather than breathless with fear.

They both listened. It was a wild night outside. Gusts of wind rocked the old cottage and rain sluiced down the window above their heads. At times, for a while, they could hope he had stopped. But then the din of the storm would die a little and they would hear the boy's piping, relentless voice.

"He keeps singing the same words," Rob said.

Amy sat up. "Of course he does!" she told him angrily, a part of her glad to crack the tension. "He has to go back to the beginning if he gets something wrong. How did you not *know* that? This has been going on for weeks now!"

But there was nothing but silence from the other side of the bed and after a while she lay down again. Rob always refused to get into an argument.

"Does he ever get to the end?" he asked her after a while.

She shook her head. Then, because he could not see her, she said, "No. He gets tired and makes mistakes, or he falls asleep."

"What would happen if he did?"

The pitiless sun burned down on the dead and the dying. The parched desert soaked up the blood, *all* the blood shed that day, and thirsted for more. Bodies blanketed the gritty sand in bright shades of red and green and blue, and more red. By the end of the day the colours would have turned to brown and grey and black.

Cuchlain the Battle King threw himself from his horse and

ordered a boy to give the beast some water. Most of the horses were dead now, but a king could not walk into battle and this last mount would have to live at least as long as he did.

"How many?" he asked his brother, Agrain, his inevitable question. He was not asking how many had died that day, just how many lived to fight again tomorrow.

"Five hundred and forty seven," his brother replied promptly. Cuchlain glared at him, daring him to lie, but Agrain's face was invisible, hooded against the fierce sun. There was no breeze, there had not been the breath of a breeze for more than a hundred days. They ducked together into the tent which was, if anything, hotter than outside. Cuchlain tore off his helm and snatched up the jug of water and drained it, letting some splash over his face and down his neck.

Then the other question he asked each day. "Is the boy still singing?"

Agrain nodded and Cuchlain felt the clutch of dread in his belly and a random, treacherous thought: *How could I ever think I could conquer this place?*

"What happens when he stops?" he asked.

Days dragged past, each one a torment. Inside the fortress conditions were as bad as those outside. Food had long since run out, the dogs and cats had vanished and even brown rats were scarcely seen. Most of the wells were dry and all the water, for a thousand-odd people, came from the last and deepest of the wells, which was guarded and its water carefully rationed. Daily it turned darker and muddier and all knew that when it ran out they would soon die. But inside there was at least shade within the ancient walls, and coolness deep in its dungeons where today's prisoners were there of their own choosing; they were the women and children and old folk, existing each day in the dark waiting for death by thirst or under the invaders' swords.

Among them was Aska, who had been daughter, wife, mother, grandmother and great-grandmother and in her hundred-some years had seen all her family die of disease or in childbirth or war. She was the oldest person within the walls. She was quite alone in the world, but as her body shrank to skin and ropey sinew and bone so the hot gleam in her eyes became brighter. She claimed to remember the last time the fortress was under siege, a century before, when the boy singer had first appeared. He had sung then until the siege ended.

"When the boy stops singing the fortress will fall," she said to her captive audience, her voice bone-dry and sharp with prescience.

"When the boy stops singing the siege will end," the shaman accompanying the invading forces had told the Battle King.

Cuchlain had nodded briskly, as if that was what he anticipated. It seemed to satisfy him, and not one among his knights dare point out the ambiguity of the prediction.

"Then kill him," he had ordered.

But it seemed the singer could not be killed, for though his voice was heard throughout the fort and among the invading forces beyond, he was seldom seen, and only then as a slender, insubstantial figure glimpsed on turret or crenellation. Men murmured that they had seen him walk through the warriors' camp at night, stepping among the sleepers, his feet barely touching the ground. They said he was heard amid the crash and clash of battle, and in the cries of dying men, and in the songs of the stars.

He is a ghost; a ghost cannot be killed, the knights whispered among themselves. Our arrows will fly right through him. He is a dream, some said, and we will only awaken from it when we are dying.

He has a throat, a thing of flesh and sinew, to sing with, rational Agrain argued. He can be killed.

But the best of bowmen – and these were not the best, for their eyes were parched gritty and their arms weak from hunger and thirst – could not have hit the distant, indistinct shape, even when they could spot him. In his fury the Battle King ordered them all killed and only his brother's cool-headedness saw the order reversed at the last moment. The shaman had already been put to death many days before.

"Let's wake him up," said Rob a few days, and long nights, later. "Perhaps he'll go to sleep again and forget his dream."

"He's not asleep," Amy repeated tiredly. "I've been in there a dozen times and he's wide awake and I tell him to snuggle down and sleep. I tell him he's keeping us awake. I tell him he'll make himself ill. He says he has to get the words right, then he can go to sleep, but he never does. He's very upset."

"I'll talk to him," Rob said, swinging his legs out of bed.

"You won't stop him. He'll just sing more quietly."

"Good enough," he said.

On the last morning the sun did not show its face. Dawn was an eerie lightening of the sky, green and yellow streaks staining the horizon. Clouds hung low over the land, clouds heavy with fate. The Battle King's remaining soldiers had not the strength to climb the siege ladders, far less fight. The defenders, all of them injured, most of them dying, propped themselves up on the walls, weapons to hand, and looked up into the lowering sky.

The boy sang on.

"We must do something! We're getting no sleep. He's getting no sleep. We can't go on like this!"

"He sleeps during the day," Amy said, but she knew her husband was right. The boy was pale and gaunt, his eyes dark with pain. Wherever he went to at night, it was draining the life from him.

"We could sing it for him," Rob suggested. "We know the words well enough, for Christ's sake."

"We don't know all of them. We don't know how the song ends."

They looked at each other.

"Do you know the words?" they asked him. "Do you know the end? Tell us the words and we'll sing it for you tonight. Then you can get some sleep."

The boy was tearful, weighed down with his burden. He shook his head. "It has to be me. I have to be there."

Cuchlain the Battle King crawled up the wall at dead of night, his knife in his teeth. His once-burly frame carved to a spectre, his eyes hot and hungry, he climbed like a black spider up the high wall of the southernmost turret. No sane man would attempt it, but he was no longer sane. His knights were all dead. The only man left alive was his brother, who clung to life alone in the tent surrounded by blood-encrusted weapons.

The stones of the wall were each the size of a fist and they were crumbling and treacherous, but Cuchlain managed to cling on, to keep climbing on this, his last attack, for attack was all he knew.

He grasped the top of the wall and heaved himself up. For a long while he lay there, gasping, hurting, reckless of the enemy. And there were no defenders now; the few who remained no longer expected a night attack and many of them feared the boy singer more than they feared the forces of the Battle King. Most were lying deep in the cool dungeons with their kinfolk.

The singing was loud and clear up here and Cuchlain lifted his head and looked about him. Mist swirled along the tops of the walls and around the turrets, and through it he could see another turret, a taller one, the tallest of all and the figure standing at its top, in plain view, his head lifted to the darkness, his voice clear as water.

Cuchlain struggled to his feet, paused for breath then stalked along the wall, eyes feverishly fixed on the boy. He stepped into the darkness of the turret and saw stairs spiralling upward. He climbed them, his heart lifting with hope. At the top he walked out into the mist and saw the small boy standing on the low turret wall. He was hardly a dozen paces away and perched high above the lethal drop on to the stones below. Cuchlain took his knife in his hand and moved toward him.

The boy turned and saw him and his voice paused for a heartbeat. The king grinned.

Then the boy opened his mouth. "The valiant warrior scaled the wall, his trusted blade his only friend," he sang, his clear young voice sharp as silver.

Cuchlain, lifting his knife to strike, hesitated.

"Unarmoured, he braved the demon's eye and fell to his doom upon the sword."

The Battle King lunged forward but the figure of the boy drifted like mist and the knife thrust through nothing but darkness. Cuchlain lost his balance and stumbled, falling forward over the low wall and plunging down to smash on the stones below.

When Agrain struggled from his tent in the dawn, weak and half-maddened by blood-loss and by thirst, he found his brother lying broken on a gentle slope of green grass which led down to a lazy, sunlit river. Of the fortress and all its people there was no sign.

The boy never again sang at night, indeed he showed no interest in singing for the rest of his life. He soon forgot about those strange experiences and his father did too, but Amy kept them close to her heart and sometimes, after midnight when she thought she heard a distant voice raised in song, she would shudder.

Sandrunners

Anthony Ryan

Blue for the mind. Green for the body. Red for the fire. Black for the push… And white. She paused in the recitation to issue a giggle, so shrill and barely controlled she could scarcely credit it came from her own mouth. *White for the madness.*

The sand gave way beneath her feet, tipping her face first into the dune she had been climbing, rust stinging her lips and invading her mouth. She choked and gagged, finding she had no spit to clear the metallic tang and scraping at her mouth with feverish fingers. "The Red Sands," Wittler had said when they first caught sight of the crimson dunes three days gone. He had shouldered his long-rifle and crouched to scoop up a handful of the red dust. "Except it ain't sand, Miss Ethy. See?" He held out his hand and she peered at the tiny flakes in his palm. "Rusted," Wittler said, holding his hand up to let the wind take the flakes away. "All that's left of whatever stood here before the Crater."

The crater… She stifled a sob, closing her eyes against the memory. *Only a day ago, when Wittler had still been kind. Big and scary, but also kind…*

The bullet gave a soft whine as it careered past her ear and buried itself in the dune barely an inch from her head. She gave a hoarse shout and jerked to her feet, reeling to the right, then the left, scrambling up the dune in a cloud of dust, hoping to confuse his aim. *Six seconds to reload a long-rifle. Never saw him miss before.*

The second shot came as he crested the dune, plucking the sleeve of her duster, leaving her arm numb but unbloodied as she tumbled down the far side in a tangle. She reached the bottom with a pained yelp, lying spent but forcing herself to wait for the dust to settle before drawing breath.

Must've been at full range, she decided when her babbling thoughts calmed enough to draw a conclusion. *Puts him a mile behind me, less if he's out of Green.* Green or not, the two missed shots told another story, even at full range Wittler wouldn't have missed twice. *He's truly as mad as a*

Blue-soaked dog.

Blue... She sat up, trembling hands exploring the felt-cushioned box on her belt, sighing in explosive relief on finding her vials unbroken. She held them up to the light one by one. All the Red had gone back at the Crater, when the night grew so cold they thought they'd freeze before morning. The Green was still two thirds full, but still best kept for direst need. The Black was reduced to just a smear at the base of the vial, and the Blue... *Enough for only one more taste.*

She resisted the impulse to gulp it down there and then. *She won't be expecting me yet,* she knew, recalling a deeply instilled mantra. *When the sun's half-set. Not before. Not after.*

She returned the vials to the box and reached for her pack, feeling what was inside roll a little. Checking it for cracks was redundant. *They never break.* But still she undid the straps and peered down at the pale, round shape, fingers tracing over the marble-like surface and finding it cold. They were always chilled to the touch, waiting for the waking fire.

She closed the pack and got to her feet, eyes scanning the surrounding dunes for the most likely course. Getting clear of this desert was her first priority, back to the badlands where at least there was cover. Out here she risked Wittler's eye every time she climbed a dune and what were the odds he'd miss three times?

She unslung the canteen from her shoulder, still half full thanks to the company's strict water discipline, and washed the iron from her mouth before taking a drink. *Only as much as you need,* Wittler had said every time they filled the canteens. *Never as much as you want. Indulgence kills out here.* He had smiled his kind smile, big hand resting on her shoulder for a second, eyes warm, so different from the wild, terrorised stare she saw back at the Crater. And his voice, hissing, thick with accusation: "Miss Ethy... You know what I saw..."

She started for a low series of dunes to the north, hoping he'd stick to the higher ground, and moved on at a half-run, fighting memories.

They had set out from Carvenport near two months before, five seasoned members of the Honourable Contractor Company of Sandrunners and their newest recruit. Ethelynne Drystone, recently granted employee status in the Ironship Trading Syndicate, officially contracted Blood-blessed to the Sandrunners. She was the youngest

Academy graduate to ever accept such a position, and not without opposition.

"I had hoped sanity might prevail," Madame Bondersil had said with a faint sigh of exasperation as Ethelynne stood before her desk. "Clearly twelve years of my tutelage was insufficient to imbue you with basic common sense."

There had been no real venom in the words, Ethelynne knew, just a maternal sense of concern and a well-concealed pride. "I want to see…" she began but Madame Bondersil waved her to silence with a flick of her elegant hand.

"What's out there, yes. As you have told me many times. Too many books, that's the problem. Filling your head with adventurous notions." She fell quiet, regarding Ethelynne with a steady eye and a grim smile. "I have agreed to act as your liaison for this little jaunt, with the Syndicate's blessing. naturally."

Ethelynne had stopped herself reaching for Madame Bondersil's hand, knowing displays of affection were never very welcome in her office. "Thank you, Madame. An honour."

The tutor's smile faded and she went to the window, gazing out at the fine view it afforded. The Academy stood on one of the ten hills across which Carvenport had sprawled since their people came to this land two centuries before, seeking riches and finding more. Out in the harbour an iron-hulled ship ploughed its way towards the sea, great paddles turning and stacks trailing smoke as the Blood-blessed in her engine room drank Red to stoke her fires. Her hold would be filled with barrel upon barrel of all colours, mostly Red and Green, with a small and heavily guarded stock of Blue and an even smaller stock of Black. But nowhere on that great ship nor any of her sisters, would you find a single barrel, or even a vial, of White.

"This man," Madame Bondersil said. "The captain of these Sandrunners."

"They call him Wittler, Madame."

"Yes, Wittler. He's truly convinced he can find it?"

"He has a map, Madame. Very old, showing a route through the badlands to the Iron Sands… and the Crater. Last season they made it as far as the Sands. He believes he can make it to the Crater with the assistance of a Blood-blessed."

"The Crater," Mrs Bondersil repeated with a soft laugh. "Where the Whites are said to still soar."

"Yes, Madame."

"It's a myth, Ethelynne. Just another hopeless search for a long dead legend."

"The Whites are real, or at least they were. We know that from the records left by the first colonists."

"And none have been seen for a century and a half."

"All the more reward to be reaped when we find them."

She saw Madame Bondersil shake of her head before stepping back from the window, going to her desk to extract a box from one of the drawers. "Finest quality," she said, opening it to reveal the four vials inside. "Wild blood, not bred stock. It cost a tidy sum, I must say."

Ethelynne approached to peer at the vials, the contents all a different shade of crimson. Light and almost clear for the Blue. Opaque with a faintly amber hue for the Green. The Red dark and the most viscous, clinging to the glass like oil. The Black was little more than slightly reddened pitch. The colours were not natural but the product of the harvesters' art, a result of the various chemical additions to stop the contents spoiling and prevent the effects of imbibing undiluted product, effects that would be dangerous for a Blood-blessed but fatal for others.

"When the sun's half-set," Mrs Bondersil said, extracting the Blue and tapping it lightly against Ethelynne's nose. "Not before. Not after. I do have a schedule to keep."

The Badlands remained stubbornly beyond the horizon as the sun began to dip, heralding the fast descending chill that made traversing these wastes such a trial. This sea of iron would retain heat for only a short while, becoming sheened in frost by the time the sky grew dark, and cold enough to strip skin from unwary hands as the night wore on. Ethelynne closed the duster and tightened her belt before pulling on her gloves, green-leather like the duster and perfect for protecting flesh from extremes of temperature. But she knew this chill would not be easily assuaged and she was so tired.

She had cleared the taller dunes a mile back and now laboured across the flat expanse forming the border with the badlands. She was keenly aware of the complete lack of cover, taking only scant comfort from the fading light and the empty desert revealed by her frequent backward glances. *Could have lost him in the dunes,* she thought, knowing it a desperate appeal for luck.

She stumbled to a halt as the half-sun finally appeared on the western horizon. Her shadow stretched away across the sands, an unmistakable marker to any pair of eyes, but it had to be risked now. Despite the gloves her hands still shook as she opened the box to extract the vial of Blue. The tremble grew worse as she fumbled with the stopper, almost dropping it and choking down shout of panic as the precious crimson drops retreated from the lip of the vial. She cast one final glance at the way she had come, seeing only her footprints in the carpet of deepening red, then poured the remaining Blue into her mouth.

For an unblessed the taste of Blue was bitter, vile even, leading to an instant, often unbearable headache and nausea. For a Blood-blessed, however, it was always a profound experience. The acrid taste faded as the trance took hold, normal vision segueing into the mists of memory and imagination. Losing oneself in the swirl could be blissful and Ethelynne's early lessons at the Academy had been rich in warnings regarding addiction, but today the fear and panic made it a dark trance, the mists storm clouds amid which recent events flashed like lightening. Fortunately, Madame Bondersil had evidently been awaiting this moment and the warm concern in her greeting was enough to calm the impending storm.

Ethelynne. What has happened?

Dead they're all dead apart from Wittler and he's trying to kill me...

Calm. Focus. Ethelynne felt the storm abate further as Madame Bondersil's thoughts flowed into her, replacing panic with sober reflection. *Tell me.*

The Crater, Ethelynne replied. *We reached the Crater.* She paused to refocus as the upsurge of memories threatened to reawaken the storm though Madame Bondersil was quick to interpret the images.

You found a White? she asked, her thoughts conveying a sense of amazement Ethelynne had thought beneath her.

Yes... No. We found bones, a skeleton. Too large for a Black. It had to be a White... And an egg. I have it.

The others? What happened to them?

Clatterstock, the Harvester, he thought the bones might contain marrow, so he broke one, powdered it... The powder did something to them... Something that made them fear, and hate, and kill... Bluesilk killed the Crawdens, Clatterstock killed her... Wittler killed him.

But not you?

No. It had no effect on me. When the killing began I took the egg and ran... Wittler is coming for me, Madame... He's tried twice now... He said something to me, when it happened, just after he shot Clatterstock... 'You know what I saw.'

And do you?

No. I saw nothing but madness.

Where are you?

On the Iron Sands, near the badlands.

A pause, Madame Bondersil's thoughts now forming their own storm. Ethelynne found a crumb of comfort in the deep affection she saw amongst the roiling frustration. *You have blood left?*

Ethelynne replied with an image of the vials, concentrating on the empty Blue and the meagre stock of Black.

Madame Bondersil's storm became more concentrated, flashing as it shifted through the memories Ethelynne had shared of the journey, settling on something from just a week ago, something from the river. *What is the first thing I taught you?* the tutor asked.

Her memories calmed, forming into an image of a little girl in a new dress, a dress Ethelynne's mother had spent a month's wages to buy. The little girl stood among a dozen other children of the same age, all with their hands outstretched, displaying the patch of white skin on their palms. Not burnt like the thousands of other children tested that year, their parents bound by law to present them to the local harvester and watch as he used a long glass pipette to drop a single bead of undiluted blood into their hands. Most screamed and cried as the blood left a dark, black mark, but some, only a very few, stood and stared in wide eyed wonder as the bead seeped into their skin and turned it white.

Blue for the mind, the children chanted in unison. *Green for the body. Red for the fire. Black for the push.*

Red for the fire, Madame Bondersil's thought was implacable, emphatic, the accompanying images unnervingly clear. *Now you need to get moving.*

Despite their coarse manners and coarser language, Ethelynne still found reason to like each of the Sandrunners. Clatterstock was a wall of green-leather criss-crossed by belts festooned with knives. His face was a slab of stubbly granite with thin lips that parted to reveal a smile that was three parts gold to one part teeth. She liked him for his knowledge; a lifetime harvesting blood made him an expert in their quarry.

"You ever see a wild one, little miss?" he asked two days out from Carvenport. The inland road they followed wound through dense bush country that would soon transform into thick jungle where contractors still came to hunt for Greens, though they were fewer in number every year. She was obliged to travel on the supply wagon with Clatterstock, sitting next to him for many an uncomfortable hour as the oxen hauled them over countless ruts. "A real live wild one," he went on, leaning close, a glint in his eye she might have taken for a leer but for the humour she heard in his voice. "Not those sickly, tooth-pulled things in the breeding pens."

She gave an honest shake of her head, provoking a laugh as he drew back, snapping reins on ox rump. "Well, that's one thing we'll fix for sure. You mind me well, little miss. When it comes to the blood, it's all me. You watch all you want, but you leave the bloodin' to me. First time you gaze into the eyes of a wild one, you'll know what hate looks like."

Unlike Clatterstock, who carried just a repeating carbine, Bluesilk had guns aplenty. Petite and buxom with a thick mass of blonde locks tied into a shaggy ponytail, she wore a pair of six-shot repeaters on her hips with a third under her arm. The arsenal was completed by the shotgun strapped across her back. Next to Wittler, Ethelynne found her perhaps the easiest to like. At night, when done cleaning her guns, she would sit cross-legged, one hand holding a small compact up to her face whilst she applied various powders and paints to eyelids, cheeks and lips.

"Where's your warpaint, love?" she asked Ethelynne one evening, eyes fixed on her mirror and a broad-headed brush leaving a faint red blush on her cheeks. They had come to a small trading post, a collection of huts and storehouses with a long pier extending out into the broad, rapid waters of the Greychurn River, their route to the badlands and beyond.

"We weren't permitted make-up in the academy," Ethelynne told the gun-hand. "It was said to be unseemly."

"Y'mean they told you it'd make you look a whore, right?"

Ethelynne blushed and looked away.

"You keep on this track, girl," Bluesilk went on, "and you'll find there's much worse people than whores in this world."

Ethelynne's eyes went to the holstered six-shooters lying atop Bluesilk's shotgun. "Will you teach me to shoot?"

"Shit, no!"Bluesilk gave an appalled laugh. "That ain't proper for a girl like you. Besides it ain't your role in this grand company. You're here for the Spoiled. Those I don't put a bullet through, that is." She looked up from her mirror to offer a half-smile, waving her brush in invitation. "You come sit by me though, and I'll put some rosiness on those cheeks."

So she didn't learn to shoot, not from Bluesilk and not from the Crawden brothers. Like Wittler, they both carried long-rifles in addition to the pistols on their hips. "Brother One, this young lady would like to fire my rifle," the younger Crawden had said to his sibling, mock indignation on his face. He was by far the better looking of the two, clean shaven where his brother was bearded, and with a tendency towards mockery she might have taken exception to but for the evident regard in his gaze. "Surely she must know this is a weapon of great delicacy, only to be operated by the most expert hands."

"Be nice, now, Brother Two," the elder Crawden advised before offering Ethelynne an apologetic smile. "Long-rifle'll take your shoulder off, miss. 'Sides, it ain't…"

"My role," Ethelynne finished. "I know."

They were on the river now, the wagon's cargo unloaded onto a large flat-bottomed barge the day before. The trading post's owner, a man near as broad as Clatterstock but with a genuinely lustful leer to him, had grown angry when Wittler refused a contract to spend a week hunting Greens. "Going for Red, this trip," he said. "Black if I can get it."

"My ass you is," the trader replied. "You goin' t'the Iron Sands again. Didn't lose enough good people last time, huh? Spoiled've got your scent now, Wittler. They won't be best pleased t'see ya."

Ethelynne had noted how the trader's fierceness dissipated and his face grew pale under Wittler's silent and prolonged gaze. "Grateful if you'd have a care for our animals," Wittler said eventually, tossing the trader a purse. "We'll be needing the barge."

Brother Two found her at the prow of the barge as they came to the point where Wittler had chosen to moor up, a shallow cove where the canyon walls descended to a gentle slope. They had cleared the jungle four days back, the Greychurn now winding its way through high, curving walls of pinkish sandstone.

"You wanna learn a thing, miss?" Brother Two said, putting an arm around her shoulders, light enough not to cause offence as he turned her towards the southern horizon. "See those peaks? Tell me what you see."

He held up a spyglass which she duly took and trained on the distant heights ahead. She stared at the peaks for a time, seeing only rock, though it was oddly coloured, mottled all over as if pock-marked. "What is that?" she asked.

"Red Hive," Brother Two said. "Their spit's loaded with enough bile to eat the rock. Wait a mite longer and you'll see."

She did and was soon rewarded by the sight of a dark shape emerging from one of the marks in the stone. It seemed tiny from this distance but she had seen enough of them in the pens to recognise the shape, and knew it was as big as a horse. She watched it crawl from the hole and onto a ledge, wings spreading to catch the warmth of the rising sun.

She heard a metallic snick and turned to find Brother Two loading his long-rifle, sliding the cartridge into the chamber and working the lever to close it. "Need Green to kill a Red," he said with a wink, taking a flask from his belt and lifting it to his lips. The amount he drank was more than strictly necessary for his purposes, but she knew Green had other effects on the unblessed beyond enhanced senses. He lowered the flask, licking his lip and issuing a slight groan. "That's a fine blend, I must say. Clatterstock is an artist." With that he raised the long-rifle and fired with only the barest pause to aim.

The range was considerable so she had time to raise the spyglass and find the Red again before the bullet struck home, except it didn't. She saw the Red flinch as the bullet smacked into its rocky perch, mouth gaping and head lowering in an instant threat posture. The beast was too far away to make out its eyes but Ethelynne had no doubt of its ability to discern the source of its distress.

"You missed," she told Brother Two, a somewhat redundant statement as the Red had now taken to the air, wings sweeping as it gained height, growing in size until it filled the lens of the spyglass.

"Shitdammit!" Brother Two hissed, feverishly working to reload the long-rifle, cartridges scattering across the deck as he fumbled, swearing even louder.

A high, peeling cry echoes along the canyons, the Red flattening its wings as it flew lower, less than two hundred feet away. The scream sounded again as it neared, mouth gaping to reveal rows of razor teeth, and its eyes... *First time you gaze into the eyes of a wild one, you'll know what hate looks like.*

She tossed the spyglass aside and reached for the box on her belt, extracting the Black and thumbing the stopper free, raising it to her mouth...

A single rifle shot sounded behind them, the drake's scream choking off as it veered away twenty feet short of the barge. It twisted in the air, flailing wings raising water from the river, before colliding with the slope ahead. The drake slid down the rock and screamed again, the cry plaintive now, desperate. Its claws scrabbled on the sandstone until they found purchase and it began to scramble up, blood trailing across the rock, wings spreading in preparation to fly. Another rifle shot sounded and a cloud of blood erupted from the drake's skull. It collapsed onto the slope, tail and wings twitching as it slid towards the water.

Ethelynne's gaze went to the starboard rail where Wittler stood, smoking long-rifle in hand. He turned to her and she saw judgement in his narrowed eyes, perhaps also disappointment, before they tracked to Brother Two. "And the purpose of this?" he asked.

The younger Crawden blanched a little under the scrutiny but quickly rallied to offer a sheepish grin. "The young miss wanted to learn a thing..."

"The young miss is not your concern," Wittler told him, each word spoken with considerable precision. He jerked his head at the dead drake on the slope. "Three cartridges to take this thing down and we ain't got time to harvest a single drop."

"Any cost can come from our share, Cap'n," Brother One said, moving between Wittler and Brother Two. His stance was respectful, but also firmly defensive. "Besides, there'll still be blood in the heart for when we make our way back. Ain't a total loss."

"You let me assess the profit and loss for this company, Craw." Wittler's gaze narrowed further, his face showing none of the affable surety Ethelynne had become accustomed to. "Your brother's here because you vouched for him. Best if he doesn't give me further cause to regret deferring to your judgement."

"He surely won't, Cap'n. My word on it." The Elder Crawden took hold of his brother's arm and led him to the stern, pausing to offer a respectful nod to Ethelynne. Wittler lingered a moment, his gaze now free of judgement and a certain warmth returning to his voice. "Careful with that, Miss Ethy." He pointed to the unstoppered vial of Black in her hand. "We'll need every drop before long."

She watched him return to the tiller, calling to Clatterstock to make ready with the anchor. As the barge drew closer to the bank Ethelynne's gaze was drawn again to the Red. It had stopped twitching now, its precious blood flowing thick enough to leave a dark stain in the river's flow.

She drank half the remaining Green on reaching the Badlands, staggering a little as the effects took hold. Green was second only to Red as the Ironship Syndicate's most valued export, a greatly prized medicine among the unblessed, curing infection better than any physic human hands could concoct. But for a Blood-blessed it was both panacea and ultimate tonic, banishing her exhaustion and filling strained muscles and nerves with renewed vigour. Ethelynne drew breath as she straightened from a sagging crouch, deep and long, the air sweet despite the lingering tang of the Iron Sands. She cast a final glance at the red desert, experiencing a momentary satisfaction at its emptiness before her newly keen eyes picked out a plume of gunsmoke rising less than a mile away.

What at the odds he'd miss three times? There was no boom from the rifle, the distance was too great for that, just the whine of the bullet as she threw herself flat. It impacted on one of the narrow conical tors twenty feet ahead, chalky rock exploding into a pale white powder.

Ethelynne surged to her feet and sprinted forward, faster than any unblessed could ever run, the confused, jagged maze of the badlands closing in around her. She kept running, pace only slightly slowed, hurdling boulders and leaping to bound from the surrounding rock, hurling herself onwards, following the marks left by Wittler's charcoal. The lessons in Green had always been her greatest joy back at the academy, outperforming all the other students as she raced around the cavernous gymnasium. There was no exhilaration now, just the fear and her thudding heart, and the lesson learned long ago. *Red for the fire...*

"Never been so cold my whole life," Brother Two said, handsome face drawn in misery as he shuffled closer to the glowing circle Ethelynne had conjured in the sand. "Thought the wind over the southern seas was the coldest thing a man could feel, but it's got nothing on this."

"You've sailed the southern seas?" Ethelynne asked.

"Surely, Miss Ethy. Sailor on a Blue-hunter for more'n six years. Think Reds're big, wait'll you see a Blue..."

"Quiet," Wittler said, voice soft as he rose to a crouch, eyes scanning the darkened dunes beyond their camp. Ethelynne noted he had drawn his six-shooter. A double-snick came from her right and she turned to see Bluesilk similarly crouched, a pistol in each hand. They had cleared the badlands the day before, Wittler leading the way through the twisted labyrinth of chalk and granite. He set a punishing pace, pausing only to check his ancient map and scratch a black mark on one of the conical tors with a stick of charcoal.

"Don't wanna lose your way in here," Clatterstock said, sweating more profusely than the others though he showed no sign of slowing. "'Specially if the Spoiled come callin'."

Ethelynne had been obliged to take her first taste of Green in order to keep up, just enough to make her legs move at a decent pace, though even then she found the going hard. It took almost a full day to traverse the Badlands, whereupon Wittler allowed a pause to survey the vast redness of the Iron Sands.

"No sign, Cap'n," Bluesilk said, sweeping her eyeglass across the dunes. "Maybe they'll leave us be this trip." Ethelynne detected a note of forced optimism in gun-hand's voice, something Wittler evidently saw no need to succour.

"They'll be along," he said. "Spoiled don't forget a scent, nor turn from a feud when there's still blood to be settled."

Ethelynne watched him sniff the air now, seeing a grim acceptance settle on his face. She caught it then; an acrid stain on the easterly wind, redolent of corrupted flesh and stale blood. *They drink it like wine,* Clatterstock had told her back on the wagon. *Untreated, undiluted. And somehow, they stay alive. They was here long before us, so I guess they had time to learn many a thing. Never learned to fear though. Must've left near a score lyin' on the sands last trip, but still they kept on comin'.*

Wittler briefly scanned the camp, checking to ensure they had all drawn weapons, then moved to Ethelynne's side. "Well, here's where you earn your share, Miss Ethy," he told her in a whisper. "You remember what I told you?"

She nodded, finding she had to swallow before she could voice a response. "The arrows."

"That's right. You leave the killing to us. But keep those arrows off." He paused to peer deeper into the dark and she fancied she saw a smile play on his lips. "Need us some light too, if you could oblige."

She reached for her box and extracted the Red and the Black, surprised to find her hands weren't shaking. She removed the stoppers from both vials and drank, Red and Black mingling on her tongue in bitter concord before she swallowed it down, feeling the power building inside, a fierce intoxicating rush. "How far out?" she asked Wittler, raising herself up.

"Thirty yards should do it."

She sought out a patch of sand at the specified range and concentrated. Some Blood-blessed were given to theatrics when utilising their talents, their hands describing elaborate gestures as they intoned cryptic phrases in ancient languages. But that was all farce. The only tools a Blood-blessed needed were a disciplined mind and a decade or more of practice.

Ethelynne summoned the Red, feeling the power surge and the air between her and the patch of sand thicken with heat. She had taken a large gulp and the results were immediate, the sand taking on a fierce glow. She stood and turned in a slow circle, the glow spreading and following her gaze until the camp sat surrounded by a ring of melting iron, the dunes beyond lit by a soft yellow light. She heard Brother Two give a low whistle of admiration and forced the resultant smile from her lips. *Emotion is the enemy of focus,* Madame Bondersil had said more times than Ethelynne could count.

For a second nothing happened, the newly lit desert silent and empty, then came a faint hiss of something small and fast cutting the air. Ethelynne instantly switched to the Black, instinct finding the arrow before her eyes did. *Black for the push.* She caught it a foot short of her chest, watching it quiver as she held it in place. The head was fashioned from crudely shaped iron, the shaft a length of whittled bone and the fletching a ragged tail of dried grass. She blinked and broke it in two, letting it fall to the sand as a great hiss rose from the surrounding dunes.

"Best hunker down!" Wittler called to her but she ignored him, moving to the centre of the camp and raising her gaze skyward. The arrows fell in a black hail, perhaps a hundred arcing down out of the dark. She let them get within ten feet before unleashing the Black, sending out a single pulse of power, the arrows scattered and shredded like chaff.

"Hoo-yah!" Brother Two whooped. "How'd ya like that, y'stinky bastards?"

She saw them then, low black shapes beyond the circle's glow to the south, scattering dust as they charged, the light catching on spearpoints and hatchet blades. The Crawdens' long-rifles fired simultaneously, two shapes falling, the others coming on without pause. Bluesilk began to fire when they reached the circle, standing and blazing away with both pistols, more shapes twisting and falling, the rest leaping the circle amid a chorus of inhuman snarls. Ethelynne could see their faces now, dark and scaly with spines protruding from forehead and jaw, their eyes bright yellow, slitted and full of hate, just like the Red back at the river.

"Guard Miss Ethy!" Wittler yelled, rushing to Ethelynne's side and loosing off a rapid salvo with his revolver, two Spoiled falling dead as they reached the edge of the camp. The rest of the company followed suit, Bluesilk crouching as she replaced the cylinders in her pistols with a swiftness that seemed incredible, the Crawdens blasting away with their revolvers whilst Clatterstock emptied his repeating carbine with practised efficiency.

A lull descended as the Spoiled drew back, lingering in the shadows beyond the diminishing glow of the circle, the air now filled with their guttural snarls. Ethelynne scanned the surrounding sands, snaring the intermittent arrows launched by the Spoiled and snapping them before they could reach the company, the Black diminishing with every catch. The chorus of snarls increased in pitch, building by the second, a discordant but definite cadence becoming discernible among the babble, almost like a chant.

"Shit," she heard Clatterstock growl. "Death song."

"If you got anything left, Miss Ethy," Wittler said. "Now would be about the time."

She reached for the vial of Black once more, drinking deep, leaving only one last drop. "You need to be quick," she said. "I won't be able to hold them all for long."

The snarling chant rose to a crescendo and the Spoiled came surging from the dark, yellow eyes gleaming and malformed lips drawn back from wicked sharp teeth. She stopped them ten feet short, summoning the Black to snare each one, some caught in mid-air with club raised.

"Aimed shots!" Wittler said, raising his pistol.

It took maybe five minutes but it seemed an age, Ethelynne feeling the Black ebb away like water from a leaky cistern as the Sandrunners methodically put a bullet into each and every frozen Spoiled. When it was done, and she had let them fall, they counted eighty-six bodies on the sand.

"Looks like we bagged us a whole tribe, Cap'n," Brother One said, drawing his knife and crouching beside a body. "Ironship pays cash-money for every Spoiled head."

"Leave it," Wittler told him, casting a disinterested gaze over the corpses before turning to the south. "Got us a White to find."

She used up the Green before getting clear of the Badlands, feeling the last of it drain away as she leapt to propel herself onward with a shove against one of the tors, landing hard on suddenly weak legs. She fell face first and lay still for a time, willing herself to move, but finding only the strength to keep breathing. "Black..." she murmured, lips dry against the stony ground. "Black for the push... Red for... Red..."

Her eyes were already half-closed when she heard it, echoing through the Badlands, rich and vibrant in its utter madness. "You know what I saw, Miss Ethy!" Wittler screamed, voice growing louder with every word. "You know what it showed me! I ain't gonna burn! You hear me, girl? I AIN'T GONNA BURN!"

Ethelynne abandoned all pretence of focus and let the terror seep into her, filling her with a single desperate urge; *stay alive.*

She yelled with the effort of raising herself up, wept as she gained her feet, stumbling on and voicing curses so foul she didn't realise she knew them, regaining focus, mind fixed on a single goal. *There'll still be blood in the heart...*

Ethelynne had been hearing or reading about the Crater all her life, the centre of the Red Sands, site of a calamity great enough to turn an iron-rich mountain range into a desert and, some said, provide a birthing ground for the fabled White Drake. In the event she found it a disappointment, just a circular gouge in the red wastes about sixty feet wide and ten deep. No great colony of Whites nursing nests full of precious eggs, no treasure to reward their perilous quest.

"You, uh, sure this is it, Cap'n?" Clatterstock ventured after they had clambered down the steep but not unassailable wall to the Crater floor.

Wittler ignored him, eyes locked on the ground as he roamed about.

"I mean to say," the harvester went on. "The map is plenty old. Could be there's other craters to the south…"

Wittler stopped and held up a hand, waving him to silence, eyes now fixed on something next to his boot. Abruptly he went to his haunches and began to scrape away at the sand with his hands, Ethelynne hearing a laugh of unalloyed triumphed as the dust rose around him. After several minutes digging he rose and stood back, the others coming to his side to peer down at his find. It was maybe six feet in length, longer and broader than either a Red or a Black, and more bulbous, perhaps to accommodate a larger brain.

"Contractors," Wittler said in a formal tone. "I give you the skull of the White Drake."

It took a full day to dig it out. They had no spades and were obliged to rely on hands and knives to scrape away the soil, but by nightfall they had revealed a complete skeleton some thirty feet long, sixty including the tail. It snaked around the body in a tight protective arc of revealed vertebrae, and there, nestled, between its two great forearms, a single white egg.

"We're gonna be so damn rich," Brother Two breathed, then laughed as he lunged for Ethelynne, lifting her up and whirling her around. She found she couldn't contain a giggle when he set her down, sank to one knee and took her hand to formally propose marriage.

"You're only after my money," she laughed, gently but firmly disentangling her hand.

Clatterstock stroked his thickening beard as he ran a hand along one of the great ribs. "Don't look so old," he mused. "Old bone turns to rock after a time. Could be there's still some marrow to be had here."

"Marrow?" Ethelynne enquired.

"Surely, Miss Ethy. Grind up drake bones and the powder's still of use. Not so potent as blood but it'll fetch a fair price. I'd hazard this here beauty will fetch a sight more."

"Just one," Wittler said. "The smallest. Wanna keep her as intact as we can."

"Certainly, Cap'n." After some pondering the harvester chose one of the claw bones, only as long as Ethelynne's forearm.

"Well now," he said, laying the bone on a leather ground-sheet and hefting his hammer. "Gather round and watch the show…"

She had feared it might not be there, scavenged to nothing by its own kind or slipped into the river and carried away. But there it was, the skin already peeling and shrouded in flies, but still wonderfully, actually there. She slid down the slope, grunting as she collided with the Red's corpse, the flies voicing an angry buzz as they rose from their meal. She hauled herself over its thick neck, crouching next to the sternum and fumbling for her box.

"ETHYYYY!" The voice was hoarse, the madness even more evident in its roaring croak. And also close. *Too damn close.*

Ethelynne lifted the vial of Black and tipped the last remaining drop into her mouth. She let it burn its way down, staring at the patch of desiccated skin on the Red's chest. *Focus.*

"You… You stop that now!"A hoarse yell and a shot. A pistol this time, meaning he was finally out of long-rifle shells. She heard the bullet impact somewhere on the drake's corpse but kept her gaze firmly locked on its chest, summoning the Black and using it all up in a single frantic spasm. *Black for the push… and also the pull.*

The Red's chest exploded in a fountain of half-rotted flesh and shattered bone, Ethelynne opening her arms to receive the gift that burst forth.

"STOP THAT!" Another shot, landing somewhere in the river judging by the splash. Ethelynne looked up now, seeing him at the crest of the slope. His hat was gone as was his duster, his shirt and pants ragged and torn. He moved towards her, gun-arm outstretched and pistol wavering as he staggered like a drunkard but with an odd, desperate appeal in his gaze.

"You know what I saw," he croaked, taking another shuffling step closer. "You know… I gotta…"

Ethelynne raised the Red's heart, throwing her head back and mouth wide as she squeezed, and drank.

For an unblessed the slightest taste of undiluted drake blood is invariably fatal. The Blood-blessed are more resistant to its effects but do not enjoy complete immunity, survival being dependant on the quantity imbibed. Ethelynne choked down two full mouthfuls before the fiery agony forced her to stop, leaving her collapsed against the Red's flanks, heaving and retching.

"Won't save ya'!" Wittler yelled. "Think you gonna burn me now? You show one inch o'that pretty head, I blow it off, ya hear?" A snick as he cocked his pistol. "Just one inch…"

Ethelynne convulsed and vomited a good supply of blood before managing to choke down her gorge. She shrugged off her pack, blinking sweat from her eyes as she ripped away the ties to reveal the egg. *Cold,* she thought, pulling it free of the pack, laying it down and scuttling back. *Waiting for the waking fire.*

Focus was beyond her now, the pain raging from throat to belly too intense for anything other than a single, explosive release of heat. She had seen it many times in the breeding pens, an endlessly fascinating spectacle, the brood drakes breathing fire on their eggs when they judged the time right. She had loved to watch them hatch, though it was always somewhat sad, for the hatchlings were immediately taken away, leaving their mothers to voice their distress in long, keening screeches.

The fire raged for only a few seconds, Ethelynne reeling and huddling from the heat of it, more intense than anything she had conjured before. When it faded she looked for the egg, finding it blackened and cracked, a faint glow pulsing inside.

"Stop!" Wittler came reeling into view, eyes wide as they tracked from her to the egg, then back to her. His mouth twisted into what might have been a smile, the lips cracked and bleeding as he snickered in triumph as he raised his pistol.

He pulled the trigger, Ethelynne shrinking back, eyes closed tight in expectation, but hearing only the click of a hammer meeting an empty chamber.

Wittler stared at the revolver in baffled consternation for a moment, then tossed it aside. "Got other options," he said, reaching for the knife on his belt and starting forward.

Ethelynne's toe delivered a gentle nudge to the egg and it rolled away, coming to a halt at Wittler's feet. He stared at it, all vestige of triumph vanished from his face. "Not..." he said, weeping now. "Not gonna b —"

The egg exploded in a blaze of combusting gas, the shell, harder than any stone, transformed into shrapnel by the force of the blast. It shredded Wittler's legs below the knees and sheared away much of his right arm, leaving him a gibbering red mess, his remaining hand slapping feebly on the sandstone slope as flames licked over his flesh.

Very slowly, Ethelynne got to her feet, every breath hurting as she dragged air down a ravaged throat. A deep, worrying pain lingered in her belly but her limbs still worked enough for her to limp towards Wittler, and the small White drake crouched amid the remnants of the egg.

It stared up at her with bright, slitted emerald eyes, mouth opening to issue a faint hiss. Although a new born, Ethelynne knew on meeting those eyes she gazed upon something ancient, something that understood. *It knows what I am*, she thought, her gaze going to Wittler as his scorched, lipless mouth issued a final, rattling gasp and he lay still, flames dying to embers on his blackened flesh. *I ain't gonna burn...*

She looked again at the White, watching it cock its head in apparent curiosity, wings spreading into an experimental flap. "The future," she said. "That's what lies in your blood."

The White hopped forward, wings flapping with greater force, a screech issuing from its mouth followed by a gout of yellow flame. It met her gaze a final time with its terrible knowing eyes, then turned about and leapt nimbly onto Wittler's corpse, head bobbing as it began to feed.

Ethelynne turned away and hobbled to the barge. It took a while to haul up the anchor, but when she did the current began to take the craft downstream. It would follow the river south then west, skirting the badlands and winding back into the jungle where, she knew from Clatterstock, another trading post waited. She allowed herself one last look at the White. It sat with head raised, serpentine neck bulging as it

Anthony Ryan

swallowed a chunk of Wittler's flesh, then gave an appreciative squawk before returning to its meal, paying her no mind at all as the barge drifted on and she saw it no more.

Smokestack Lightning

Gavin G. Smith

Mississippi River, 1875

Sabin Revere stretched out and laced his fingers behind his head. He was lying on the bed in the lavishly appointed cabin on the Texas Deck of the paddle steamer the *Pride of Jupiter*. The elf was watching his lover as 'she' spun around the room. She was beautiful, but as attractive as the body was, the beauty was behind the violet coloured eyes. As the warm afterglow of their lovemaking faded, the way she looked just made him sad.

"Well?" she asked, raising her arms and turning around for him. "You didn't say anything when you saw me."

"I had little chance," Sabin said smiling. "You all but leapt on me."

"I did leap on you. I know you like variety."

Sabin forced a smile. "You are always beautiful, no matter your form," he said. He took a packet of cards from the bedside table and started shuffling it one handed. Her arms dropped.

"What is it?" she asked. Sabin did not answer. She lay on the bed next to him. "What?" more softly now. Sabin did not look at the beautiful blonde haired elven women now lying naked next to him. Suddenly Sabin was very much aware of the humidity, the motion of the river craft, the vibration of the throbbing engines that powered the three hundred foot paddle steamer, and the sound of the paddle blades, or buckets, dipping into the shallow turgid river. He felt a hand on his arm.

"I think someone lies dead," Sabin said and cursed himself inwardly for saying it. She rolled off the bed and went to the mirror on the dresser and sat down.

"She was not a very nice person," she told him. "And you know I have to hide." Sabin said nothing for a moment. He just kept on shuffling the cards.

"What name will you give yourself?" Sabin asked. She told him the name grinning, grinning into the mirror.

"The gods will curse you," Sabin said shaking his head.

"Sigrid Freysdottir?" It was clear that Renoir Bourbonne had not quite meant it to sound like a question. Sabin wondered if the owner of the *Pride of Jupiter*'s scepticism came from his own name. He was clearly trying to imply a connection to the Bourbon dynasty. The Confederate State's southern gentry may not have been actual blooded aristocracy in the eyes of European old families, that didn't stop them behaving as such in the new world. Even so, 'Sigrid' implying that she was descended from one of the progenitors of the entire elven race before they had been banished from *Álfheimr*, was pretty bold. Though Bourbonne obviously followed the Olympian pantheon. The elven tycoon, like the majority of highborn elves, had long since turned his back on the Aesir and the Vanir for more civilised gods. Sigrid's Norwegian accent, real, and the easily assumed bearing of an European aristocrat, fake, made the charade a little easier to sell. Sigrid just smiled as Renoir leaned down and kissed the back of her lace covered hand.

The elven tycoon had shoulder length silver blonde hair and was tall, with high cheek bones that made his face look somewhat angular, as had most of their race. It was difficult for elves to go to seed, they tended not to age or grow fat, but there was a softening around the otherwise angular lines of Bourbonne's cheek bones that suggested the tycoon enjoyed indulging his appetites. He wore a light grey summer suit with a long jacket, and loose bow tie that Sabin decided was only a few steps away from a ruff.

Bourbonne wasn't heeled. He didn't need to carry a gun, visibly anyway. On one side of him stood the tall figure of something that had once been a man. It was dressed in the black Confederate uniform of one of the Cerberus units. The tight skin stretched over emaciated flesh, the black eyes, and the sewn-together lips told Sabin that the revenant had probably been raised by Bloody Bill Anderson himself. Nobody had been able to work out where the Confederate guerilla fighter and high priest of Hades had found so many hydra teeth to sew into his raised men's mouths. The dead gunfighter had a Le Mat pistol at each hip. Sabin really didn't want to tangle with the revenant. If he had to it would mean that their plan had already gone very badly wrong.

"This boat is beautiful, sir," Sigrid said. Bourbonne beamed and she was right. The paddle steamer's saloon was as plush and well-appointed as any fine hotel, well any fine hotel in the New World. There was just a little too much gilt and ostentation on display for Sabin's taste. "Like a floating Versaile." Bourbonne's smile faltered. *Too much*, Sabin thought. Bourbonne was doubtless the younger son of a lesser family, but to accrue this much wealth and power in the Confederate States he would be no fool.

"And you, sir?" Bourbonne asked.

"Sabin Revere," Sabin said. "A pleasure." Swapping his cane from his right to his left, Sabin proffered his hand. Bourbonne took it. His grip was strong, assured, it was not the soft grip of a pampered aristocrat.

"English?" Bourbonne asked.

"Indeed!" Sabin said, smiling.

"May I introduce you to the star of the show?" Bourbonne asked, the smile back on his face now. His Creole drawl was probably an affectation that he had become used to, Sabin decided. Bourbonne turned to the massive figure stood at his other shoulder.

"This is Spiculus," Bourbonne said. The ogre was eight foot of muscle piled on muscle wearing only a *subligaculum*. His deep brown, almost black skin told of the slave's African origins and glistened from where he had been oiled. His eyes were a light brown colour beneath a heavy ridge of bone. Sabin was surprised by the intelligence he saw in those eyes, but then he found that what he thought he knew about the various races often proved to be nonsense upon meeting said races. The ogre's heavy jaw jutted forward, though his bottom incisors protruded only a little. Large, curled, ram-like horns grew from either side of thethick skull. Sigrid stared up at the ogre pretending to be entranced, at least Sabin hoped she was pretending. She reached up to touch one of his pectoral muscles.

"Miss..." Bourbonne warned. Sigrid stayed her hand but did not retract it.

"Sigrid, please," she said. Spiculus had shown absolutely no sign that he was even aware of their presence.

"Siculus has been oiled for the games. I would hate for you to get it on your gloves and perhaps stain that pretty dress," the tycoon said. Sigrid smiled at him and lowered her hand.

123

"Slavery, gladitorial combat, such things would never be allowed back home," she turned to look at the revenant, "even necromancy is frowned upon, you truly are very daring Mr Bourbonne. Like the emperors of Rome." Bourbonne's smile wasn't quite making it to his eyes.

"Well some of these boys just don't want to stop serving their country," he told Sigrid. Sigrid opened her mouth to say something else.

"River pirates?" Sabin blurted. Bourbonne turned to look at him, one eyebrow raised quizzically. A state of war between the Confederate States of America and the Union was still in effect, but major hostilities had stopped more than ten years ago. Now most of the fighting tended to come down to government supported cross border brigandage. "This man Murray?"

"No man," Bourbonne spat. "He's a godsdamned orc. This is what happens when you let slave stock think they are the same as civilised races. He's no pirate either." The tycoon's accent was slipping slightly but Sabin couldn't quite trace it. "He's a union privateer. The Mississippi has a lot of places to hide, but he can't hide forever. You saw the ironclad escort?" Sabin had seen the squat, angular, low form of the *CSS Redeemer* gunboat, bristling with cannon that was escorting them up the river. "Orcs are a cowardly and low people, as are the race traitors that run the Union. They would not dare attack a fully armed ironclad, we are perfectly safe."

"Well I'm certainly pleased to hear it," Sabin said.

"Now if you'll excuse me, I have more guests to greet before the games begin," Bourbonne said.

"Godsdammned whoreson," Sigrid said through gritted teeth as Sabin all but led her away.

"Will you calm down," he hissed but he understood why 'she' was upset. Sigrid knew what it was to be hunted for the colour of your skin. Still, Bourbonne was about to become considerably poorer.

Sabin wasn't trying to lose exactly, though he certainly didn't want to be winning with such totality. The people he was playing were making it difficult to do otherwise, however. There were four of them, he suspected they were related. They were well dressed but their manners spoke of a rougher upbringing. Close to where Sigrid was leaning on the bar, smoking a cigarette in a holder, sat a fifth cousin or brother. He wore the grey dress uniform of a Confederate officer.

"You're winning a lot, English," one of the cousins sitting at the table said. He'd heard the others address him as Jimmy. He was the biggest, and the oldest looking with the exception of officer at the bar. His broken teeth, broad shoulders and powerful build running to fat suggested a dockside thug to Sabin. He had lived in enough port cities to know the type. The four of them had sat down at the table with the view to working together to fleece the 'fancypants' foreigner. They were lamentably bad at doing so.

"Sorry?" Sabin suggested absently. Both himself and Sigrid had been checking out the other guests in the saloon and Bourbonne's security. There were a number of obvious gunmen. Older gentlemen, mainly human, though a couple of dwarves and a half elf. They wore their guns as if they knew what they were doing, and many of them bore scars; that, and the way the surveyed the room suggested that they were ex-military.

"Are you getting smart with me?" Broken-tooth Jimmy demanded.

"Hmm?" Sabin asked, turning back to the angry man he was playing cards with. "No, I'm trying to avoid any sort of smartness in this game. My deal?" He collected the cards and started to shuffle, continuing to look around the room. He felt someone grab his wrist. He was aware of the fifth brother/cousin at the bar taking an interest. At the same time he was aware at the periphery of Sigrid ferreting around in her purse. Sabin looked down at the thick fingers that had grabbed the cuff of his shirt.

"I don't think you should deal," Broken-tooth Jimmy said.

"Fordhams," Sabin said evenly. "Of Saville Row. That's in London." He peeled Jimmy's finger from his cuff.

"I don't give a good godsdamn. I think we'd all be a lot happier if we done the dealing," Jimmy spat. Sabin shrugged and handed him the pack and resolved to do his best to lose the next few hands.

"Hey, English," the Confederate officer said from the bar as Jimmy shuffled the deck. He had relaxed a little when Sabin had handed over the cards. Sabin sighed and turned to face him, made sure that the confederate officer could see the two .45 calibre, silver-plated, pearl handled, single action, quickdraw model Colt Army revolvers in the crossdraw holster he wore over his crimson waistcoat.

"Either Sabin, or Mr Revere, please. And you are?"

"The name's Major Tobin Larouxe, reckon you've heard of me," the Confederate officer said.

"Sorry, no," Sabin said. "But then I am not from here." He saw the human's face harden.

"I was wondering something," the man growled. "When's England going to get round to recognising the CSA?"

Sabin stared at him. He could see Sigrid trying to stifle a smile.

"Well funnily enough I was discussing that very matter with Mr Disrelli only yesterday."

Tobin Larouxe was on his feet. "Are you making fun of me?" he snapped.

"Well I'm trying not to but you're making it very difficult."

"You better watch yourself, English," Broken-tooth Jimmy said. "You think those fancy guns scare us?"

Sabin sighed. "I've no idea. Perhaps we should go our seperate ways?"

"First you owe me an apology," Tobin Larouxe said. Sabin sighed.

"I'm terribly sorry," Sabin offerred. For a moment Larouxe seemed taken aback by the apology. Then his eyes narrowed.

"You funning me again, boy?" Larouxe demanded.

"Ain't healthy to go funning Tobin like that," Broken-tooth Jimmy said. There were nods of agreement from the other brother/cousins.

"Fine, you tell me exactly what it is that you want from me so that I may extricate myself from this situation," Sabin said. He wasn't certain but he was pretty sure that Sigrid was trying to stifle a smile at his predicament.

"He's yeller," one of the younger members of the Larouxe clan said. Sabin turned to look at him.

"Is that it, boy, you yeller?" Tobin Larouxe demanded.

"Let's say yes," Sabin and stood up, reaching for his winnings. A number of the obviously wealthy guests in the salon were paying attention to the altercation, as where a number of the guards, but it was clear that nobody was going to intercede.

"Now just a second," Broken-tooth Jimmy said. "You cheated us." The rest of the Larouxe clan were nodding in agreement. "You just leave all that there."

"Fine," Sabin said and turned to move away from the table.

"You really are a coward ain'tcha boy?" Broken-tooth Jimmy said. There was laughter from the other Larouxe family members at the table. It was the word boy that made him stop.

"No," Sabin said. "I was a boy before your first ancestor had coitus with the diseased slug and begat your fetid line, and given your collective stupidity I feel that it behooves me to explain that you have just been insulted." He was aware of Sigrid slumping as the words came out of his mouth.

"Why you...!" Tobin was already drawing the .44 at his hip. Sabin acted instinctively. He drew one of the Siblings from its quick release sheath at his back and sent the throwing axe tumbling through the air. There was a gunshot. *Guns! I have guns!* Sabin thought too late. It felt like a hammer blow in his side, then burning. Sabin grabbed for his cane. Broken-tooth Jimmy was reaching for his pistol, the rest of his clan were doing likewise. Sabin drew the rapier blade from the sword cane and plunged it into Jimmy's chest. There was another gunshot. The youngest Larouxe, the one who had called him yellow, had his pistol in his hand but he also had a red spot in the centre of his forehead. The back of his head and his hat were missing. Tobin Larouxe was staggering backwards, a smoking pistol in one hand, the throwing axe embedded in his head. Sabin finally had the presence of mind to draw his two Colts. The hard metallic clicks as his thumbs pulled back the hammers on the twin revolvers brought the two remaining Larouxes up short. They froze. Broken-tooth Jimmy sat down hard and coughed blood down himself, the rapier still imbedded in his chest. Tobin Larouxe toppled over. Sigrid walked forward her derringer still smoking.

"Are we learning about the difference in the ballistic properties of a bullet, compared to flying ironmongery?" Sigrid asked.

"I forgot," Sabin said apologetically. His side felt curiously numb and wet. He had the strong urge to sit down.

"Two hundred and fifty years since you started using firearms," Sigrid said looking around. Sabin was aware that a number of the guards had their hands close to their weapons but none of them had drawn. There was the sound of clapping as Bourbonne made his way through the crowd towards them the revenant at his side.

"Well it seems like the games have started early." The elven tycoon stood over Tobin Larouxe's body and looked down at the axe embedded in the human's head. "And someone invited a Viking." He turned to one of his guards. "Remove the bodies and get this scum off my boat." Several of the guards moved to grab the two remaining living Larouxe brothers/cousins. They started whimpering as they were hauled away. They didn't seem keen to be left stranded so far from New Orleans and out amongst the bayous. "Please accept my apologies for this terrible lapse in hospitality." Sabin heard screaming followed by splashes from outside the saloon. "But let me assure you that they will have a very difficult journey home." Sabin sat down hard and touched his side. His hand came away wet and red. "But Mr Revere you are shot." He beckoned over one of the slaves who had been serving some of the other guests in the saloon. "Boy, take Mr Revere here to see Doc Cole." The slave bowed. Bourbonne turned to Sigrid. "My dear would you do me the honour of being my personal guest, at least until Mr Revere has been patched up? The games proper will surely begin soon, and I should hate for you to miss anything."

The slave led him out of the saloon and along the deck towards the aft of the paddle steamer. Outside the thick wet air seemed to deaden the sound of the two massive side wheels that propelled the boat. From either side of the wide muddy river great leaning pond cypresses and southern live oaks dripping with Spanish moss seemed to bend towards the paddle steamer, reaching for him. The yellowing, gibbous moon was going some way towards making the shadows of the trees look animated as well. On the other hand Sabin was aware that he'd lost a lot of blood. He was leaning heavily on the slave who was half carrying him, half dragging him down the passage that ran alongside the saloon. He heard a splash and was aware rather than saw shadows moving in the water. They passed one of the huge, creaking, side wheels. There were torches burning at the rear of the *Pride of Jupiter*. Sternwheelers were more practical on the Mississippi than side-wheelers but the rear of the *Pride of Jupiter* was a flatbed. That was where the games took place. The guests watched from the overlooking balcony on the Texas Deck. There were already guards in place, hard-faced men and women, again mostly human, bearing Winchester lever-action rifles. Sabin wasn't sure if it was the flickering red light from the torches or the blood he was dripping onto already bloodied boards that made floating gladiatorial arena appear so hellish.

One of the guards, a wild eyed, red-haired human woman, pulled open the thick iron-reinforced door to the slave quarters for them. There was a moment of panic as Sabin suddenly thought that Bourbonne was on to him and had decided to make him a slave but the fact that he was still armed, went some way towards reassuring him that this was not the case.

There were two guards inside the slave quarters. Both of them were carrying coach guns, double-barrelled 10-gauge shotguns. Cages ran down either side of the slave quarters. On one side it was mostly humans of African descent, eying him sullenly as he was dragged in. On the other side the cage held a number of orcs sat on benches. They looked, fit, healthy, well fed, and scarred, presumably from previous games. As fierce as the orcs in their cage looked, they were all giving Spiculus a lot of room. The huge ogre was sitting on the bench close to the door of the cage, staring into space. He did not even glance Sabin's way.

Between the door and the cage on one side of the room, but out of reach of the bars, lay a collection of various melee weapons and pieces of archaic armour. On the other side was a stained wooden table with a half empty bottle of whiskey on it.

"What the hell you bringing a white man in here for?" one of the guards snapped at the slave carrying Sabin. The elf felt the man tense. "I'll have your skin stripped down to the bone..."

"You hold your peace, Carter, any swamp-spawned halfwit can see he's been shot. Do you know another sawbones on this boat?" The man sitting at the table leaned into the dim lantern light. He was a fleshy man, with a thick white beard covering the lower part of a jowly face, his eyes were bloodshot and the bags underneath them made him look as if his entire face was drooping. He wore a sweat-stained white linen suit, and had an old cap and ball revolver riding his hip that looked big enough to hole the ironclad escorting the *Pride of Jupiter*.

"You watch your mouth, Doc!" the guard, Carter, snapped back.

"Go tell it to Caesar you don't like how I talk," Doc said before turning to the slave. "Get him on the table, Joe, let's have a look." The slave helped Sabin up onto the table.

"Are you a priest of Asclepius?" Sabin asked hopefully. The

human just laughed and showed him some forceps.

"I'm here for the slaves, we don't even got no opium. This is really going to hurt. Joe put that bit in his mouth, can't have his screams disturbing the passengers now."

Sabin had spat out the foul tasting bit so he could get some screaming done only to have Joe hold his hand over the elf's mouth. Then, mercifully, he'd passed out. When he came to his moaning was largely reflex. He actually didn't feel too bad all things considered.

"Thought I heard gunplay earlier," Doc said from the chair next to him. A glass appeared floating above his face. "Figured you deserve this." Sabin reached up and took the glass from the old human. "Heard you did for Tobin and Jimmy Larouxe?"

"Tobin almost did for me," Sabin said. His side felt a little hot, but there was no pain. He sat up, dangling his legs over the side of the table, and looked down at his ruined waistcoat. There was a poultice over the wound. He didn't have to concentrate to see the spark of magic in the poultice. The warm feeling would be the healing magic working on the wound. "It was worth killing him for what he did to my shirt and waistcoat." Doc's expression remained grim despite the attempt at levity. He knocked back the whiskey and poured another glass. Sabin steeled himself and took a sip of the whiskey expecting it to be disgusting. Instead he was pleasantly surprised to find that it was good Scotch. "So you're a doctor?" Doc nodded. "No magic?" Doc nodded again. "The poultice?"

"I get them from a woman who works out the back of one of the Basin Street whorehouses. Half negro, and half Choctaw Indian, some say she got nunnehi blood in her, others say her grandmother was descended from Anansi hisself. She was supposed to have been a whore once, but if she was it was a long time ago because Granma Spider is old and as ugly as sin itself. She makes the poultice, collects webs and makes her sacrifices in the St. Louis necropolis when there's no moon. Even the ghouls leave her alone. She says there some black dirt from the Nile itself in there. I don't know about that but it works. You'll scar for a while but I know that doesn't last long on you elven types." Sabin frowned when he heard the word scar. Elves hated any blemishes on their skin, in the same way they hated all ugliness. He sat up on the table and looked around, taking another sip of the Scotch.

"Good whiskey," the elf said. He guessed they could get hold of it now the blockade was over.

"Yeah well, my services are pretty cheap these days." Doc said quietly.

"The poultices must cost a bit, though?" Sabin enquired. Doc didn't say anything, he just looked down. The elf looked over at the slaves. One of the orcs was glaring at him but looked away when Sabin caught his eye. "I guess Bourbonne doesn't want to waste valuable slave stock."

"Who, Caesar?" the Doc said bitterly. "He doesn't give a good godsdamn. He considers himself a sportsman. Spiculus is his most valuable fighter but if he loses, he loses." Suddenly the doc was staring at Sabin. "It's not a waste of slave stock, sir. It's a waste of life, I don't care which god you follow." Sabin found himself nodding. He tried not to care. It was easier that way. He had understood Sigrid's anger as an abstract, but now, in this room that smelled of sweat, human filth and old blood, and would soon presumably smell much worse when Doc was up to his elbows in the broken bodies of the wounded gladiators, those that hadn't just been fed to the alligators, he could feel the corruption of the place seeping into him like the humidity that soaked his clothes. Now it was Sabin that looked away from Doc's fierce gaze. He took his pocket watch out and flipped it open, cursing himself when he saw the time. They were approaching the deeper part of the river. He could hear feet on the balcony that overlooked the gladiatorial area. The balcony was directly above the slave quarters.

"That's a fine watch," Doc said. "Hephaestian manufacture isn't it?" Sabin snapped the pocket watch shut. "Normally two of them isn't there? Both perfectly synchronised?" The elf smiled as he tucked the pocket watch back into the pocket of his ruined waistcoat. Doc had clearly been around.

"It's a fake," Sabin said. "You won't tell the dandies upstairs, will you?" Doc didn't answer. He looked unconvinced. Sabin pushed himself off the dried blood-stained table. "Thank you very much for your ministrations doctor but if you'll excuse me I must go and tend to my wardrobe before the festivities begin." Then he turned to the slaves in their pens. "Those who are about to die: I salute you." He offered the gladiators an exaggerated bow before turning and leaving the slaves' quarters.

Sabin could tell by Sigrid's body language that she would like nothing more than to plunge a dagger into Bourbonne's neck and shower in the arterial spray. Instead she was clapping politely as the elven tycoon, his hand around her waist, cheered along with the rest of the crowd, the games having apparently started whilst he had been changing. Sabin had left the poultice on, however, despite it smelling a little unpleasant. One of the guards tapped Bourbonne on the shoulder as Sabin approached. Bourbonne glanced behind him and saw Sabin, his arm had disappeared from around Sigrid's waist by the time he had joined them. Sigrid flashed Sabin a look of desperation.

The elf looked down into the flatbed at the rear of the *Pride of Jupiter*. Spiculus, equipped as a *retarius*, armed with net, trident and a weapon that looked like a dagger whose blade had been replaced by four spikes, was fighting three of the other slaves: two of the Africans and one orc. One of the Africans was equipped as *murmillo*, with a stylised fish on the crest of his helmet. He wore an arm guard and carried a *gladius* short sword and a long oblong shield. The second African was equipped as a *cestus*. He wore a pair of *scizores:* vambraces that ended in protruding half-moon blades. The final gladiator, the orc, was armed as a *scissor*. He carried a pair of *gladia*, their blades connected by a hinge. It didn't look a very practical weapon.

Bourbonne looked Sabin up and down. "Pleased to see you could join us again," the latter day *lanista* said and offered the other elf a cigar. Sabin declined and Bourbonne lit one for himself. Spiculus was standing in the centre of the other three gladiators as they looked for an opening. Sabin noted that there were crosses on either side of the river where escaped slaves, many of them having been tarred and feathered first, had been crucified. He guessed that Bourbonne had timed the games this way to prevent armed slaves from getting any ideas.

"Well it's what we came for," Sabin said and forced a smile. "I apologise for my part in the fracas in the saloon."

The scissor attacked Spiculus' back. The huge ogre spun out of the way, displaying surprising grace and obvious training. The orc cried out as the net enveloped him. Sabin couldn't quite work out why until he saw the barbed hooks on the inside of the net bite into the orc's flesh. Bourbonne clenched the cigar between his teeth as he clapped, the rest of the cloud joining in as did Sabin and Sigrid. Like most elves

Sabin had an instinctive dislike of orcs but he didn't think that this one had been given much of a chance. The other two gladiators saw an opportunity and attacked. The cestus leapt high into the air, hoping to drive one of his crescent shaped blades into the huge ogre's head, the *murmillo* charged forward. It was over very quickly. Spiculus kicked the net-trapped orc over the back of the paddle steamer and into the river. He thrust out the trident, impaling the *cestus* in mid-air. The *murmillo* stabbed out with his *gladius* and Spiculus swept the short sword's blade aside with his *manica*, the arm guard that covered his left arm. There was screaming and thrashing from the back of the boat. Sabin knew that it took a lot to make an orc scream. He saw that Spiculus's right foot was standing on the rope attached to the thrown net, which was used to reel entrapped gladiators towards the trident. Spiculus brought his left leg up and one massive foot stepped on the *murmillo* driving him to the ground. The ogre dropped the trident with the impaled *cestus* on the end of it, drew the four-spiked dagger and drove it into the *murmillo*, even as the other gladiator was trying to get up. The slave spat blood, kicked and was still. The *cestus* was trying to crawl away from Spiculus. The ogre almost fell over as the rope attached to the net was yanked hard. The ogre reached down and grabbed it with both hands and pulled. Many in the crowd actually screamed and stepped back from the balcony as Spiculus pulled the torn, bleeding net out of the muddy river, a huge alligator attached to it, the orc, still struggling and alive even as it was being eaten. The guards moved back from the rear of the boat, levelling their Winchesters at the monstrous reptile. Spiculus let go of the rope and let the net drop into the water. The ogre's facial expression had barely changed. He walked to the cestus who was still trying to pull the trident out of his chest and looked up at Bourbonne. There was booing from the crowd. Bourbonne took a drag on his cigar and then gave the thumbs down.

Sabin turned away and looked up at the paddle steamer's smokestacks. He saw the sparks shoot out of the chimneys and then float away in the thick, humid air. He heard cheering and then a splash, he assumed that the *cestus* had been flung overboard. Sabin made himself turn back. He could see the black forms in the river following the boat. Sabin forced himself to smile and clap. He noticed Bourbonne looking at Sigrid. She hadn't screamed, or cheered, or clapped. She was just staring down at the blood-stained deck, the smell of ruptured and evacuated bowels mixing with the humid rot of the surrounding swamp. Sabin caught her as she fainted.

"I'm terribly sorry," Sabin said.

"I could have a slave..." a concerned Bourbonne started.

"She'll be fine. I think the spectacle is all a bit too much for her rarefied, northern-European sensibilities. I have smelling salts and a good bottle of brandy back in the cabin."

"Shame for y'all to miss the rest of the fights, that was just a warm up."

"It is, and we're unlikely to see the likes of this again but I'm afraid that certain proprieties must be observed," Sabin said, with a bit of effort. Sigrid was starting to feel heavy in his arms.

"Oh indeed, please let me know if either of you need anything," Bourbonne said casting a long, lingering look at Sigrid that made Sabin want to shoot him there and then. The elf turned around and carried Sigrid away.

"Well how was I?" Sigrid asked as she quickly changed out of her dress and into more masculine clothing that was easier for her to move around in.

"I'll be honest," Sabin said as he checked the contents of his bag and then slung it over his shoulder. "You've had better performances." Sigrid pouted. "It's to your credit though." *Particularly where you come from.* He nodded towards the rear of the boat. "That's sickness." Sigrid nodded and looked away from him. He noticed that she was putting pamphlets into her own bag. "What are those?"

"Underground Railroad. Even out here there's people who will help," she told him. He suspected that she half expected an argument but he just nodded. Freeing the slaves during a rest between the bouts would act as the diversion they needed.

Sabin's three barrelled, 12-gauge shotgun was hanging from a sling under his arm, tucked inside and almost concealed by his long suit jacket. He broke the weapon to check its load, flicked it shut and let it hang down on its sling. He checked the watch Red had given him again.

"How long?" Sigrid asked.

"Just under five minutes." He used a match to light the oddly clear candle and took out the secret that he had written on the piece of paper. He closed his eyes and told Jana, goddess of secrets, the boon he wanted of her. Then he burnt the paper. That wasn't the sacrifice. The sacrifice had been carrying the secret around with him written down, risking discovery. It was a powerful secret as well: who, and more importantly what Sigrid actually was. He would only know if the magic worked when he tried use it, however.

On the other side of the room Sigrid was asking her own two-faced goddess for a boon. Cold emanated from his lover and Sabin stepped back from her. He felt the same instinctive dread he always felt when she called upon her matron goddess. When she had finished she looked paler, her features pinched, crueller somehow, and she exhaled her breath in a cold mist, despite the humidity.

"Ready?" Sabin asked. Sigrid just nodded. He tucked his pointed ears up under his hat.

The magic of Jana's blessing would not render him invisible. As far as Sabin knew that was beyond the capability of even the most powerful gods-blessed wielder of magic. Instead it guided him to move when no one was looking, it encouraged the shadows to embrace him, it whispered convincing lies to the minds of those who did see him, making them think they had seen someone else.

He tipped his hat to the elderly man he passed in the corridor, the man barely glanced at him. Sabin made his way forward on the Texas Deck between the two rows of cabins. He found the cabin that Red, the disgraced priest of Hephaestus, had highlighted on the map. Sabin glanced around and then listened at the door. When he was reasonably sure that there was nobody in the room he slipped the skeleton key out of his bag. There was a sound like knuckles cracking as the key, made from the bones of a hanged but once very successful London pickpocket, reformed itself to fit in the cabin's lock. Sabin drew one of his .45s and let himself into the cabin.

The cabin was empty and had been left in something of a mess by its inhabitants. Sabin looked up at the ceiling. Bourbonne's own private stateroom was immediately above. Sabin took the dynamite and the glue out of his bag.

Sabin checked the synchronised Hephaestian watch, lit the long fuses that Red had carefully cut for him, and left the room, hoping that its inhabitants didn't come back before the dynamite exploded. It had gone quiet at the rear of the ship, he guessed they were between bouts. One of the slaves pushed past, barely noticing him.

Sabin moved quickly, going out onto the deck. Just behind him he could see the low angular shape of the CSS Redeemer, hear the chugging of the ironclad gunboat's engines. If they got involved then it could all go bad very quickly but if all went according to plan then this would look like a boiler explosion and the boilers on paddle steamers exploded all the time. In theory they should be very far away before anyone realised otherwise.

The guard patrolling the deck ignored Sabin as he opened the door to the engine room and clambered part of the way down the stairs pausing only to pull the black neckerchief up over the bottom of his face. There were some actions, after all, that were just too blatant for even the goddess of secrets to hide. He brought the three barrelled shotgun to his shoulder and went down the remaining stairs and into the roar of the pounding, steam-powered pistons that drove the two massive side wheels.

He was standing on a metal catwalk between the pistons. He could see the glow from the slave-fed firebox that heated the boilers. There were a number of dwarven engineers, second-class citizens in the CSA but freemen, supervising the slaves as they shovelled coal to feed the *Pride of Jupiter's* steam engines, all six of them. All were surprised by Sabin's sudden shotgun-wielding appearance.

One of the soot and oil-stained dwarves had complained about having to do 'slave's work' when Sabin had put them to work to clear part coal beds. Sabin had explained the dwarf's choices, using the business end of his shotgun as emphasis. He glanced nervously at the watch again. Sabin suspected that he probably should have got the slaves to help shovel coal but he hadn't quite been able to bring himself to do that.

He felt something bump the ship. It didn't feel all that different to the numerous times that the paddle steamer had hit logs. Then it was followed by a disconcerting grinding noise. The dwarves were looking up nervously at Sabin. The slaves didn't look too happy either. There was a thump. It came from directly beneath the paddle steamer.

"What in the hell have you done?" the belligerent dwarf he'd threatened with a shotgun earlier demanded over the thunder of the engines.

"Okay that's enough. Get out of there," Sabin told them, gesturing with the shotgun. He turned to the slaves. "When this happens all hell will break loose. Stick with the other slaves they'll know how to get north." The slaves nodded.

"You an abolitionist?" the verbose dwarf demanded. *Nothing so grand*, Sabin thought. "If the slave catchers don't nail you up the Klan will."

"I'm just a thief, sir," Sabin told him. The dwarf opened his mouth to retort but screamed instead as a spinning, steam-powered, saw blade, accompanied by a horrific whining noise, burst through the wooden hull of the paddle-steamer from below. The blade cut a circle out of the deck.

"Is that one of them submarines beneath us?" the dwarven engineer yelled at Sabin.

"Sort of," Sabin muttered.

"We'll sink!" the dwarf screamed, the rest of the terrified-looking engineers and slaves nodding in agreement.

"Not immediately, there's a seal... It's complicated," Sabin told them, by which he meant he didn't fully understand it himself. "Just don't panic."

"Something just cut a hole in the bit between the boat and the water! It's kind of hard not to panic!"

The circle of wood had dropped down a few feet but no water had flooded in. There was a lot of swearing coming from underneath the cut out piece of hull.

"Get that out of there, now!" Sabin snapped, gesturing with the shotgun. "And believe me you'll want to do it quickly." The slaves and the dwarven engineers rushed to comply. The removed piece of hull revealed a leaking, accordion skirt of rubber and iron surrounding a pile of wet sandbags atop the carapace-like copper-plated wooden hull of some kind of craft. The steam saw mechanism was mounted on a circular rail.

"It worked!" the hunchbacked, ginger-bearded, grimy-looking dwarf shouted from a hatch in the top of the craft. He was wearing heavy leather aprons, thick leather gloves, a pair of protective goggles that somehow magnified his rheumy-looking eyes, and what appeared to be an armoured bowler hat. Sabin stared at the dwarf. "I showed them bastards in Charleston I could do it!"

"What do you mean it worked?" Sabin demanded angrily. "You mean there was some doubt in your mind?" The elf considered turning the shotgun on Red and giving the dwarf all three barrels. The only problem was that neither he, nor Sigrid, had any idea how to pilot *Hephaestus's Crab* (Sabin had tried to talk him out of the name).

"Where's Odedra?" Red asked looking around. "Time's a'wastin'." Sabin couldn't believe that the dwarf had just used Sigrid's real name like that. Though it was a good question.

"She'll be here in a moment," he said, not entirely convinced himself.

"She?" Red asked confused.

"How well did you cut those fuses?" Sabin asked showing Red his watch. The dwarf opened his mouth to answer. "Get out of the damned hole!" Sabin shouted.

"Oh right," Red said and climbed out of the hole cut through the hull and into the engine room. He did so with some difficulty due to his deformity, the result of voluntary exposure to the powerful forge magic of his twisted patron god. Sabin helped drag him away from the hole, holding the shotgun with one hand, covering the slaves and the engineers.

"Get back!" he snapped at them, herding them away from the *Crab*, dragging Red. "Later you and I are going to discuss appropriate times for experimentation."

"But I'm a genius, you see the weight of the *Pride of Jupiter* is actually helping to maintain the seal, and I've mounted rollers on the top of the..." This last was drowned out by the sound of the explosion. First the dynamite glued to the ceiling of the cabin Sabin had broken into went off. Then the circle of dynamite on the floor of the same cabin went off a moment later. A hole appeared in the roof of the engine room, the explosion's partially tamped pressure wave knocking them back a little and rattling teeth, and a heavy iron safe fell through the hole and onto the sandbags on top of the submarine. Sabin already had the bag of grave dirt in his hands. He had a moment to recognise the Hermetic, high magic symbols engraved into the iron before the lemures, shades of the unquiet dead necromantically bound to the safe as guardians, swarmed all around, trying to tug the life and vitality out of him. Sabin flung the grave dirt over the safe. The dirt had been taken, in exchange for offerings, from the graves of those deemed to be

Union heroes. It had then been blessed by servants of Charon, and coins had been sacrificed to the Ferryman's sub-church, so that the lemures could be guided to Hades. The shades faded to nothing. Those of the slaves and dwarves who weren't too terrified to do so started to pray to their gods. Sabin heard the first screams, cries of alarm, a bell ringing, and over all of it the unmistakeable sound of gunfire.

"Well shit," he muttered.

Sabin stepped out onto the deck. He had left Red supervising the prisoners to lowering the safe into the *Crab* at gunpoint. Sabin was aware of the *CSS Redeemer* steaming up alongside the *Pride of Jupiter* to offer assistance. He knew that they didn't have a great deal of time. The engine room would be one of the first places that Bourbonne's people would look for the source of the explosion. Fortunately most of the panic was going on in the saloon and balcony above, as the rear lower deck of the paddle steamer was mostly for the slaves. Blood ran down the deck from the gladiatorial arena. There were more gunshots. They sounded as if they were coming from the slave quarters. Sabin rounded the corner onto the blood-slick gladiatorial area. Two guards, rifles at the ready, crouched by the thick door to the quarters, a third lay on the deck missing a face. As he appeared they turned, detecting movement. The muzzle flash lit up the humid night, the thunder of the shotgun echoed once, twice amongst the cypress trees that lined the banks. The two guards stumbled back, falling to the deck. A bullet whistled past Sabin's neck, catching his hair, he swore as he felt the heat of the bullets passing and spun around. There were uniformed Confederate riflemen on the deck of the *Redeemer* firing at him. Sabin cried out as splinters from a bullet impact opened up his cheek. He yanked the door to the slave quarters open and threw himself inside.

It took him a moment to take in the situation. Two dead guards. Doc either dead or senseless on the floor next to his table, which was dripping with fresh blood. The remaining slaves were out of the cages and gathering the guards' weapons as well as the gladiatorial weapons. Spiculus had Sigrid by the neck, her feet a good four feet off the floor.

"Let her go now!" Sabin said, pointing the shotgun at the ogre. The escaped slaves all turned to stare at him. This would get messy if they rushed him. One of the African-descended human slaves levelled a guard's coach gun at him. "I'll spread your brains all over the ceiling if you don't let her down right now!"

Sigrid held up her hand, gesturing to Sabin not to fire. Sabin heard footsteps behind him and moved out of the way as the door swung open. The orc fired one of the stolen coach guns and the first guard was blown backwards through the door and into the guard behind him. The orc took a shotgun blast to the chest for his troubles. Sabin squeezed the trigger on his shotgun. The pellets, at point blank range, took most of the top of another guard's head off. A pistol fired and another guard dropped. Sabin let the empty shotgun drop on its sling and fast drew one of the Colt Armys, fanning the hammer, firing the revolver in quick succession three times. A fourth guard staggered back and fell to the ground. No more were in evidence. Sabin drew the other .45 and cocked both the revolvers with his thumbs, pointing one at Spiculus and another in the general direction of the slaves.

"Let her go please!" Sabin was all but begging. "I know you might not think it, I know you can't trust someone with skin this colour, but we fight each other and the guards and we'll all get killed." Then he noticed that Sigrid, who was still being held up by Spiculus was holding her .41 calibre Colt Lightning pistol in her right hand. She'd shot one of the guards whilst Spiculus had been strangling her. The ogre lowered her to the floor almost gently and then let her go. Sigrid massaged her neck.

"I had it handled," she managed hoarsely after several attempts.

"Oh I'm sorry, honey," Sabin snapped as he holstered one of the Colts so he could reload the other. "This isn't a rescue, we're just running a little behind and I thought I'd come and ask you to hurry up."

The big ogre was just staring down at the much smaller elven woman. The other slaves seemed to be looking at Spiculus for leadership despite the fact they had been due for slaughter at his hands up until a few minutes ago. Sigrid recovered her shotgun and handed Spiculus some pamphlets.

"Can any of you read?" A couple of the slaves nodded. "This has got directions to find people who can help you, but you can't let it fall into anyone else's hands, so remember what you need and then destroy it, okay. Take the other slaves with you if you can." The big ogre just looked at her.

"It's okay, take your time," Sabin said, reloading the shotgun with three new shells and then snapping it shut. He was sure they were blown. Bourbonne's people had to be in the engine room by now.

"Spiculus?" Sigrid asked.

"Dijon," the big ogre said, his voice was surprisingly high pitched.

"Tebrin," Sigrid said, telling the ogre her real name. Sabin stared at her.

"Why don't you just take out an advert in the Picayune?" the male elf demanded.

"Like the mustard?" Sigrid asked Dijon, ignoring Sabin.

"Like the place in France," Doc said. Sabin felt the barrel of the cap-and-ball pistol against his head, heard the hammer pulled back. Sigrid was already moving. "Darlin' I will turn his head into a doughnut if you don't get still real quick." Sigrid froze.

"A what?" she asked.

"It's an American thing, fried dough... never mind it has a hole in the middle," Sabin tried to explain. The ogre turned to face the doctor. Sabin kept on glancing at the door but he couldn't hear if anyone was outside over the sounds of panic and the constant bell ringing. He thought he heard someone shouting orders in the distance, however. A few of the slaves were moving, the guard's revolvers in hand, trying to get a clear shot at Doc. Sabin wasn't sure he liked that as an idea either.

"This your doing?" Doc asked.

"Yes," Sabin said.

"You're not abolitionists, are you? You're common crooks," Doc said.

"There's nothing common about us, darling," Sigrid said. "And so you know, anything happens to him I'll make you suffer before you die." Doc nodded in understanding.

"Freeing the slaves was just a happy aside," Sabin said.

"A diversion you mean?" Doc asked.

"Well it's not turning out so well."

"So innocent people get put in danger so you can get richer?"

"The only innocent people on this boat didn't have any choice in coming aboard," Sigrid spat.

"And their wives and their kids?" Doc asked. Sabin wondered when he'd stopped caring about things like this. He just stared at the door, wondering when the next armed guard would come through it. Was Red already dead?

"Come on, Doc, you don't seem the type to condone this," Sabin said.

"Ever wondered what happens to these boys you're freeing when the slave catchers and the bounty hunters catch up with them?" Doc asked. "Or did you just make that decision for them yourself?"

Sabin opened his mouth to reply and then closed it again.

"That's not a good reason for inaction," Sigrid pointed out.

"I will leave many slave catchers dead in my wake, more of them than the slaves I killed," Dijon said quietly. The orcs and the Africans were nodding in agreement. "They will not take me again."

Sabin breathed a sigh of relief as Doc lowered the hammer on the pistol and removed the barrel from the elf's head. The old human went back to the blood-stained table and poured himself another glass of whiskey and knocked it back.

"We're not all like this you know," he said. "Go on, get out of here."

They went along the other side of the paddle steamer this time, staying away from the approaching *CSS Redeemer* and its riflemen. It sounded as if the passengers were being kept in the saloon, guarded by the majority of the gunmen and women to keep them safe from the slaves whilst they determined if the *Pride of Jupiter* was on fire, or sinking. Sabin and Sigrid reached the door to the engine room.

"They have to have gone down there by now," Sabin said. Sigrid nodded but they had little choice. Morally freeing the slaves had been a good idea, practically he was less sure. "Still, no good deed goes unpunished."

"It wasn't a good deed. It was supposed to be a diversion, remember," Sigrid muttered. Sabin wasn't quite sure how to respond so he turned the lever on the engine room's door and pushed it open. The pair of them were down the steps quickly, shotguns at the ready. They found a vastly overconfident Bourbonne with a long nosed, Colt Bluntline Special clapped to Red's head. The grimy, hunchbacked dwarf was down on his knees looking sorry for himself. The elven tycoon looked angry. The revenant was stood next to Bourbonne. The engineers and the slaves were nowhere to be seen.

"Oh you're gonna' pay," Bourbonne said, shouting to be heard over the roar of the engines, his accent slipping a little. "Put the shotguns down, now!"

"After you've told us we're going to pay?" Sabin said. "That would seem unwise."

"Okay," Sigrid said and put her shotgun down on the metal catwalk.

"You too!" Bourbonne all but screamed at him.

"You need to remember something," Sabin told him.

"What's that?" Bourbonne demanded.

"You shoot the dwarf and your little empire here, sinks."

"You'd best do like your lady friend did!" Bourbonne screamed. He didn't seem particularly rational, which would explain why he wasn't down here with his remaining gunmen. He was taking this personally. Besides, he'd probably underestimated Sigrid.

"She only put the shotgun down so she could do this," Sabin said. Sigrid fast drew the Colt Lightning, fanned the hammer to cock it, and fired from the hip. The revenant went for both his Le Mat revolvers, he was fast but Sabin already had his shotgun in his hands. The elf fired, moving sideways. Bourbonne cried out as Sigrid's shot caught him in the shoulder. A cloud of dust and black river sand exploded out of the back of the revenant as Sabin's shotgun blast hit it. Red cried out as a stray pellet grazed the side of his head. Bourbonne was moving, running for cover behind some of the engine room's machinery. Sigrid cocked the Lightning and took a moment to aim before firing the revolver again. There was a cry from Bourbonne and he went down behind one of the massive pistons. Sabin was moving sideways as he fired the second barrel of his shotgun. The revenant seemed to jump back in another explosion of black sand and dust but he was still on his feet, aiming one of the .42 revolver/20-gauge shotgun hybrid pistols at Sabin and the other at Sigrid. Muzzle flashes lit up the engine room's interior as the revenant fired at the same time as Sabin. There was a horrible scraping noise and the paddle steamer rocked as though it had collided with something. Sabin was aware of water spraying out of the hole where the *Crab* had breached the paddle steamer's flat bottom. Sabin's shotgun blast caught the revenant in the upper arm, reducing his black trench coat to frayed tatters as it marched towards them firing. The revenant's shot sparked off machinery next to where Sabin's head had been. Sabin ran down the narrow catwalk between two of the massive pistons. He was aware of Sigrid doing something similar on the other side of the engine room. The revenant reached the catwalk junction and fired his pistols at each of them just as Sabin reached the corner closest to the hull. He cried out as one of the .42 calibre bullets creased his shoulder, forcing him to drop the empty shotgun and sending him staggering into the hull. He threw himself around the corner, drawing the two Colt Armys. The revenant was following him. Sabin sped up. The unliving might have been fast on the draw but it moved as if it was in no hurry, and he didn't think it was terribly bright. He ran back to the central catwalk and circled behind the revenant. The unliving realised what he was doing and started to turn. Sabin thumbed the handles on the Colts, firing one and then the other, advancing on the revenant, aiming for its head, or more specifically its mouth. The unliving staggered with every shot but it still advanced on Sabin, raising the two Le Mats, flipping the lever on the hammer with its thumb and firing the central 20-gauge shotgun barrels at near point blank range. Sabin cried out as buckshot caught him in the upper right hand side of his chest, and tore off the left hand side of his face. He dropped both of the empty revolvers, his right arm useless now. Somehow through the pain he had the presence of mind to draw one of the Siblings with his left arm and hammer it into the revenant's right-hand wrist. The hand axe drove the undead's hand against the machinery and nearly severed it from the wrist. The revenant hit Sabin in the face with the butt of the Le Mat revolver in its other hand, breaking the elf's nose, making him feel instantly nauseous and causing him to see flashes of light. Sabin sat down hard. The revenant worked the lever on the big revolver's hammer again and lowered the weapon to finish off the elf. The shotgun blast nearly decapitated the revenant, disintegrating its jaw, sending the reanimating hydra's tooth flying across the engine room. The headless revenant sank to its knees. Sigrid was standing behind it, her retrieved shotgun smoking.

"Are you dead?" she asked as Sabin slumped down onto the catwalk. He had certainly had enough of getting shot.

"No, I'm just a little tired," Sabin told her.

Sigrid helped him retrieve his various weapons and supported him back towards the hole where the *Crab* had 'docked' with the *Pride of Jupiter*. Red was there. He had retrieved his pistol and was gingerly dabbing his ear with a now bloody finger.

"You shot me!" the dwarf cried. Then he looked at Sigrid. "When did you get all purty and femaleafied?" he asked.

"I've always been purty... pretty," Sigrid told him.

"Just get into the submarine," Sabin snapped at Red. There wasn't a great deal of water leaking in through the seal but there was more than enough to make the elf nervous.

"Actually I call it a perambulating..."

"Red!" Sabin shouted. *Oh excellent, now I'm shouting out our names,* Sabin thought.

"Bourbonne?" Sigrid asked.

Red pointed to the corner by the boiler. "He's still alive, some of the piss and vinegar seems to have leaked out of him though, not to mention his blood."

Sigrid waited until Red had climbed down into the *Crab*.

"Just kill him and let's be gone," Sabin said. 'Sigrid' looked at him. The anger was back.

"He's the kind of elf..." she started.

"We don't have time," Sabin told her. He was leaning against one of the supports trying not to bleed to death. Sigrid didn't answer him. Instead she drew a small knife and cut a flap in her stolen skin. Just enough so that he would be able to see the skin underneath. Sabin was shaking his head.

"What if they get a necromancer to look in his eyes to find his killer?" Sabin asked. Sigrid turned and walked away from him towards where the wounded Bourbonne lay. She knelt down over him. Sabin could hear her talking but couldn't make out the words.

"No! You can't be...!" Bourbonne screamed, real terror in his words. "You were wiped out thousands of years ago! They'll..." A gunshot cut short his final words.

"What do you mean we're sinking into the mud?" Sabin demanded. He was lying on an uncomfortable wooden bench as 'Sigrid' cleaned and dressed his wounds. She had a bandage wrapped around her own face.

"Well as it transpired riverboats are quite heavy!" Red said somewhat testily as he frantically worked levers. All that could be seen through the two circular bolt holes was muddy water, but they had felt the *Pride of Jupiter* land on them after they broke the seal and flooded the paddle steamer's engine room. They had also felt the *Crab's* legs sink deeper into the Mississippi mud. The idea had been that the *Pride of Jupiter* would roll off the *Crab* using the rollers protruding from the top of the strange underwater vehicle. That had sort of worked. The paddle steamer was sinking just behind their current position but in doing so the weight had caused the river-crawling *Crab* to get stuck.

"And that's only occurring to you now?" Sabin screamed at the dwarf.

"Have you any idea the miracles I have performed here?" Red demanded.

"Have you any idea what's going to happen the moment the *Redeemer* works out what happened?" Sabin countered.

"Just so I understand, the plan to get us out of this is to scream at each other?" Sigrid enquired.

"We're going to run out of air soon. We'll have to surface. Surrender to the *Redeemer*," Red said. "At least I've proved it can work. Now the naval office will have to listen to me!"

Sigrid had to hold the furious Sabin down.

Red had extended the legs and popped the hatch. Sigrid had helped Sabin out of the craft and the three of them stood on the carapace-like hull, those that could holding their hands up as the gunboat steamed towards them, cannons covering the *Crab*, sailors with rifles levelled at them on the armour-plated deck.

The first cannon round almost blew them off the top of the *Crab*. Sigrid grabbed Sabin and dragged him down onto the *Crab's* armoured carapace, using the folded accordion skirt as cover. Shrapnel flew past them, raining down on the river, as shell after shell impacted into the *Redeemer*.

Ears ringing, Sabin finally risked looking over the lip of the seal's folded rubber and iron skirt. The *Redeemer* was sinking, joining the *Pride of Jupiter*, the top of which was still protruding out of the river just behind them. There were sailors in the water, swimming for the riverbank.

Another ironclad, a Union Monitor class, was steaming towards them, having presumably just rounded the bend to the north of their current position. It was flying a blood red flag with an hourglass on it. A pirate flag, and it seemed that time had indeed run out for the *Redeemer*. The Monitor class ironclad was making straight for the *Crab*.

There was a strange figure standing on the prow holding a 10-gauge shotgun at port. He was a grizzly-bearded orc, with prominent protruding lower canines. He had an eye patch on but it was pushed up onto his forehead under a ludicrous leather tricorn hat, both his eyes looked perfectly healthy. He did however have an iron peg leg, which ended in a mace-like ball. The iron peg was painted red but the paint was flaking off in many places. Sabin assumed that it was Captain 'Bloody-Leg' Murray, the infamous Union privateer.

The ironclad manoeuvred expertly alongside the *Crab*.

"I ran into some survivors from the *Pride of Jupiter* early this morning," Murray said. "Imagine my disappointment when I heard the paddle steamer I was intent on raiding had sunk. One of Bourbonne's men had an interesting story to tell, however, after some persuading." Sabin started to sag. He knew what was coming. It had all been for nothing. He could see Sigrid coming to the same conclusion. Red just looked frightened. "Seems y'all saved me some trouble. Just how much do you think is in the safe?"

Oak

Lou Morgan

The cottage didn't look as though it had been built so much as dropped from a great height onto a patch of land at the edge of the village. It slumped in several different directions at once, the edges of the thatched roof dipping almost to touch the grass bank behind it as though the bundles of reeds were trying to reroot themselves in the earth. It was the only home for a day's walk in any direction without a horseshoe beside the window, and the only one whose door had no lock. It was not the kind of house that needed either: nobody called at that cottage lightly.

From the relative safety of the meadow path, Bron, Bors and Gwen eyed it warily. They knew better than to run up to the door, or to peer through the small window into the darkness, or even to try and scrump one of the apples growing on the slightly drunk-looking tree in the garden. Not, Gwen thought, that her grandmother would even think of it as a garden; maybe there were useful plants in there, somewhere. Maybe there were herbs for headaches and flavours for possets; berries that would stain lips and fingers and cloth... but from where she stood, all she could see was a tangle of grass and thorns.

The problem was that somewhere in there, under the tangle, was Bron's father's knife.

It was his own fault. If he hadn't lost his temper, he wouldn't have thrown the knife. They wouldn't have watched it sail like a swallow through the air, looping over and over and over itself, blade tumbling over handle all the way back down – into the middle of the thorns. Of course, if Bron's aim with a bow were any better, then he might actually have hit the rabbit he'd been aiming at in the meadow, and then he wouldn't have had anything to lose his temper *about*. And instead of throwing the knife he would have been kneeling on the grass of the meadow, using the blade to skin the rabbit he'd just shot.

But there was no point in wishing time undone, because if Bron wasn't home with his father's knife by sundown, *he* would be the one getting skinned.

Bron sniffed and wiped his nose on the back of his hand. "I think you should fetch it, Bors."

"Why me?"

"Because you're the youngest. And I said so."

"I'm not going. Gwen's the one who scared the rabbit off. She should go." Bors poked at Gwen. She poked him back.

"I did no such thing." She pushed her hair out of her eyes. A gust of wind immediately swept it back over her face. "Besides, if you'd let me have the bow, I could have hit it."

Bron snorted. "Could not."

"Could."

"It's *my* bow, anyway."

"And it's your father's knife. Which *you* threw. So *you* get it."

They went back to watching the cottage. It didn't look menacing, exactly. It looked… empty. Unloved. Not like the homes in the middle of the village, where smoke curled up from the chimneys and people sat out in the last of the day's spring sunshine, plucking chickens or skinning rabbits for the pot (provided their aim had been better than Bron's…). This cottage didn't have the look of a home.

"I won't fetch it." Bron folded his arms across his chest the way he'd seen his father do it when he didn't want to talk about something any more.

Gwen rolled her eyes. "What will you be telling your father, then?"

"My father?"

"I mean: what are you going to tell him when you go home without his knife? Other than ask him not to beat you." The last part was meant lightly, but one look at Bron and Bors' faces told Gwen that their father wouldn't think twice about taking a switch to either boy – or both. She wished she could unsay it.

But she still wasn't going to be the one who fetched the knife.

"They say a witch used to live there. She would catch children and skin them and hang them up in the smoke from her fire to cook. Just like *pigs*," whispered Bors, suddenly sounding younger than his nine summers. '*They*' actually meant Aelfric, one of the older boys who took pleasure in telling the younger children the most frightening stories they could imagine. There was usually a witch involved somewhere. Gwen half-wondered what Aelfric would do if he ever actually met the kind of witch he liked to tell stories about. It almost certainly involved crying.

"There's no witch living there," she said, hoping to calm Bors. "I don't think anyone at all lives there. Not any more."

"On the contrary!" said a strange voice from behind them.

Bors let out a high-pitched yelp, while Bron tried to make it look like his startled twitch had been part of a cough - and Gwen found herself turning to look at the owner of the new voice, which sounded like shadows and edges and secrets.

It was a man, a young man, barely older than Bron. He had dark hair that tumbled to his shoulders – and which appeared to have several twigs and grass stalks caught in it. His eyes were cornflower blue at the edges, but darkened at the centre to the shade of the millpond in midwinter. His tunic wasn't so different from theirs: muddy-coloured wool, tied at the waist with a belt... but his belt was leather, and hung with a row of little pouches that bounced off his hips and off one another as he moved, and the tunic had a large, thick leather patch stitched onto the left shoulder. His boots were covered in dust, and he leaned on a staff. He had obviously been watching and listening to them argue for some time.

Bron was the first to recover, planting his feet and looking the stranger up and down even as Gwen ushered Bors behind her. All of them had heard the whispers passed between the adults before the fire at night when they thought the children were asleep. There were unfriendly soldiers on the roads, moving from village to village across the kingdom. No one knew what they would do next: sometimes they passed through with barely a second glance; sometimes they burned every building in the village to the ground. Sometimes they would smile at the people they passed; sometimes they would... do something *else*.

But this man didn't look much like a soldier. For a start, he had no sword or axe. No shield. No helm. He looked more like a pilgrim than anything else: a man who had been on the road a long time. As the children eyed him, there was a fluttering overhead and a small falcon swooped down to land on his shoulder. It shook itself, then blinked at them from its perch. Bors peered out from behind Gwen to get a better look, the threat of a stranger forgotten.

"Is he tame?" he asked.

The stranger smiled. "Tame? No. Not tame. You can't tame birds. You can only teach them that they can trust you. Whether or not they do... That's up to them." He wriggled his fingers into one of the pouches hanging from his waist and pulled out something small, feeding it to the bird – who snatched the offering and swallowed greedily. The stranger rubbed his fingertips on the edge of his tunic. "So then, my friends. What is it about my garden that interests you?"

"Your garden?" asked Gwen.

"Mine, yes."

"But... it looks abandoned."

He followed her gaze towards the tangle of green and brown branches and frowned. "I've been away longer than I had intended."

"How come I've never seen you before?" Bron asked, his hands settling on his hips.

"It was a *lot* longer than I had intended." The man smiled at them, and nodded what looked like a goodbye, stepping past them and into the knee-high grass. "Ah." He pointed to a spot just in front of his boots – right where they had been looking. "Is this what you were looking for?"

There was the knife, sticking straight up from the soil.

Bron mumbled something and moved forward, intending to take the knife from the man... but no sooner had he taken a step towards the garden than he found himself back behind the others with his hand firmly closed around the handle of his father's knife as though he had never thrown it at all.

Gwen tried to forget about the man with the falcon, but he wasn't easily forgotten. He hadn't given them his name, and when she asked who lived in the cottage on the edge of the village, no one seemed to know the answer. Her grandmother looked up from her stitching and said that perhaps she remembered there being a man who had lived there, but that was a long time ago, and he had been old when she was still young – younger than Gwen was now... And before Gwen knew it, *she* was the one doing the sewing while her grandmother talked. It was a trick she never quite understood, but her grandmother was the mistress of it.

As the weeks slid by, and summer became autumn, autumn

became winter – and there was news. Soldiers had been sighted two villages west: barely a day's ride away. A couple on foot, leading a horse laden with what must have been all they had left, stopped for water in the village, and the story they told turned the air colder than the frost had. A dozen men, all mounted, all with swords and axes, cutting down anyone who happened across their path. Broken skulls, severed limbs; men and women hung from the branches of thorn trees. One homestead where the inhabitants had put up a fight and been left handless, footless, helpless. A warning not to stand against them. "The new king's ravagers," the travellers called them – and before they left, the woman looked hard at Gwen. "You hear hoof beats, you hide, girl. You *hide*."

But where was there to hide? The soldiers were spreading across the land like a pox, an infection of the body. Nowhere was safe, and soon enough there would not be a single village that had not felt the new king stamp his rule and seal it with blood. Wrapping her shawl more tightly around her shoulders, Gwen walked out into the dusk, following the path towards the meadows – now cold-baked into stillness and sleeping under a hard frost. There would be no stars tonight, the sky was a sheet of grey. Without thinking about why, or about what she was walking away from or towards, Gwen walked. And with every step of the way, she heard phantom horses in the distance.

The world darkened about her. The wind pulled at her hair, at her clothes. It pushed her this way and that, like another body leaning against her own and trying to steer her with its will. The further out she walked, the stronger the wind became – until simply putting one foot ahead of the other was a battle, to walk an arrow's length a war. But when she tried to turn back, the wind grew stronger still. It doubled and redoubled in strength until she was bowed over against it just to stand in one place. A vicious, sudden gust whipped her hair into her eyes so hard that tears spilled down her cheeks – snatched away by the gale. Another ripped her shawl from her grasp and carried it off into the air.

And then, ahead of her, she saw a light. Faint and flickering, but real. A single lantern in a window. If she could get to it, perhaps she could shelter there until the wind dropped…

No sooner had she thought this than the wind died to little more than a breeze that smelled of applewood smoke, leaving her cowering at nothing and feeling foolish. It was strange, yes, and more than a little suspicious, but shelter was shelter.

She hadn't realised how far along the path she had walked, because when she raised her hand to knock at the door she recognised it. She was at the door of the little cottage that belonged to the man with the falcon. If the sky had been lighter, she might have turned around as soon as she realised; as it was, the knuckles of her hand paused an inch from the door... and again, a gust of wind swirled about her, pushing her hand against the knotted wood. The door swung open, and at first all she could see was feathers: wings beating a hand's breadth from her face, then eyes – sharp and dark – and a beak. And then a human face. A man's face with eyes that were both the softness of summer and the hardness of winter at once.

"Strange weather for a walk," he said, standing aside to give her room to pass. Inside, the single room was warm and faintly smoky from the fire in the hearth. Bundles of leaves hung from the beams to dry. A stool sat upside down on the hearth rug, its feet pointing up to the roof, and a heap of sheepskins were piled untidily in the corner. The light that she had seen from outside was not a lantern, as she had thought, but a single candle in a wooden cup. Gwen hesitated on the threshold... and one more time the wind rose up behind her and pushed her gently inside. Her eyes adjusted to the light and the smoke hanging in swags through the room, swirling in the movement from the falcon's wings as it flew from its master's shoulder to a perch on the far side of the cottage. Gwen's eyes followed the bird as it landed and shook out its feathers, settling down to preen.

"It's... a tree."

Because it was. There was, in the corner of the cottage, a tree growing, the trunk knotted and gnarled. Branches spread through the beams – some of them *were* the beams. And despite the winter, despite the cold and the frosts, it was in full leaf. Gwen had never seen the like.

"How?"

"I needed somewhere to put the bird." He looked thoughtfully at the tree. There was a frying pan hanging from one of the lower branches. "And somewhere to hang the skillet."

"Oh."

"Sit, please. You should sit." He gestured to the upside-down stool, then seemed to wonder why she wasn't sitting on it. He cocked his head on one side, looked at it a moment longer… and then hurried across and turned it the right way up.

Gwen sat. She wasn't sure what else she should do. She watched him sweep the skillet down from the tree. On a higher branch, the falcon tugged at its feathers with its beak. White down fell to the ground.

"You aren't a witch, then," said Gwen, uncomfortable on the stool.

"I might be." He was setting the skillet on a rack over the fire, a thick cloth wrapped around its handle. "What do you think?"

"I think it's not something to take lightly. There's still plenty who would see a witch burned on the strength of hearsay."

"The flames of hearsay, you mean," he said with a snort. "Gossip will burn a man faster than fire." He appeared to be looking for something around the hearth.

"Gossip is one thing, but the stories…"

"Oh, stories. Stories are never about what they're *about*. Stories are always about something else. It's misdirection, you see – making you think to look one way…" The fire suddenly flared, the flames reaching high into the chimney, and Gwen jumped. He carried on, oblivious: "While they do something else. May I?" He stepped away from the hearth and reached for her – and pulled an egg from behind her ear. Gwen opened her mouth and closed it again, silently, as he cracked the egg over the pan. It sizzled and spat on the hot metal.

"Misdirection." He grinned, and turned his hand to show her the second egg he had palmed, spinning it out with his fingers so that if she had not already seen it with her own eyes, she would have believed he had magicked it out of the air. He cracked that one onto the pan too, and began to talk again – more to himself, she thought, than to her – his voice rising and falling like the smoke. "No, a story is about the teller and about the listener. Never the story. Here." He passed her a wooden spoon and bowl and tipped the eggs off the pan into it. She stared at the bowl, then looked back up at him.

"Eat," he said. "I promise it won't enchant you. They're just eggs."

"Why?"

"Why are they eggs? What sort of question is that? Why is the sky the sky?"

"I mean – why are you giving them to me?"

"Why not?" He leaned against the tree, absently stroking the falcon – which scowled at him. "Why did you walk out of the village? Why did you walk this way, this hour? Why?"

Gwen ate a spoonful of egg.

"Why did the wind pick up? Why would it let you walk neither forward, nor back? Why did it bring you to knock at *my* door?"

Gwen put the spoon down as the back of her neck prickled.

"Why would I have a tree, a growing tree – quite out of season – in my home? And why would I let you see it? Why would I *bring* you to see it?" With a swift sweep of his leg, he was kneeling before her. "If I had not – if I had not brought you here, shown you these things; kept you here with wind and with words, you would have met the soldiers riding hard for your village even now. You would have met them alone, in the fields, with no one to hear or to help you." His eyes the colour of storms locked on to hers, and somehow the strength of his gaze held her where she sat – more than arms could have, or hands pressing on her shoulders. Even more than the distant, unmistakable sound of hoofbeats on the suddenly-still dusk air.

The bowl fell from her fingers, tumbling to the floor and splintering into two pieces. "Soldiers."

"You hear hoofbeats, you hide, girl. You hide"

The man straightened, rising to his full height – and to Gwen, he looked taller than he had been before, his shoulders broader. "The new king likes to tell stories, you see. He tells stories of witchcraft, of poisonous devils hiding in hedgerows. He tells of an evil that will ensnare the unwary, the unwitting and the unwise. He tells of a land that needs to be conquered – and once conquered, kept." He held out his arm and whistled once, and his falcon skipped across the air of the room to land on his shoulder. "And all this time, while he tells you what he would have you believe, you look."

"The wrong way," Gwen whispered.

"Now you see it," he said. And she did.

The man with the falcon was not a young man; it puzzled her that she could ever have thought it. He was a man in the middle years of his life: tall and strong, his shoulders straight and broad. His dark hair still passed his shoulders, but now it was streaked with grey like an old dog's. There were lines around his eyes and scars that criss-crossed his face. The tunic he wore was no longer threadbare and his boots no longer scuffed. Instead, the cloth was a dark green that shimmered as though woven through with moonlight, and the leather of his boots was dark and soft as the spring soil. A sword hung from his belt, blazing in the light of the fire – and when he laid his hand on a branch of the strange tree that grew in the corner, it shrank to a single staff topped with leaves. And Gwen understood who he was.

"You did all this for me?"

"Not at all. But does it matter why I did this? Or simply that I did?" He stretched his hand towards the door and flicked his wrist. "I was away too long. And now I must put that right, however I can." The door swung open, and the falcon launched itself from his shoulder and out into the fading light. The sound of horses was clearer than ever. These were not the phantom hooves that Gwen had imagined chasing her through the wind. These were real horses, bearing real men, real swords; real harm and real death. And as Gwen stood and watched, Merlin strode out to meet them with a smile on his face.

Unlike Gwen, the soldiers did not know the paths and trackways between the meadow and the village. They were unsure in the dusk, and their horses slowed from gallop to walk. Several of them carried burning torches to light their way in the gathering dark, the flames reflecting in the metal of their helms and giving them the look of men who had ridden straight from hell itself. Their voices, unfriendly and unfamiliar, were clear in the quiet – even if Gwen couldn't understand their words. One of them laughed: a hard sound that came from the back of his throat. A cruel sound that quickly died when he saw the man standing in their path. Merlin, leaning on his staff with a falcon on his shoulder, smiling up at them.

Up on their horses, the soldiers towered over him. They shouted at him – telling him to clear the path or to bow, no doubt. And still Merlin smiled. The man who had laughed tugged on the reins of his horse, pulling its head up as the others moved aside, and he dug his heels into its flanks. From the shadows of the doorway, Gwen saw blood where metal cut into flesh as the soldier spurred his horse on, straight ahead.

157

Merlin did not move. He remained, leaning on his staff in the middle of the path as horse and rider bore down on him.

Merlin stared at the charging warhorse and did not move - until he did. There was a sound like the sky splitting as the falcon took to the air, wings beating as it soared upward, and Merlin swung his staff under his arm and took a single step back. At the moment the horse was upon him, he lifted a hand and caught its bridle, and Gwen was afraid. Three summers ago she had seen a man dragged by a horse, his legs trampled beneath it until there was nothing left of them but mangled shreds. And yet, despite the speed and strength of the charger and the cruelty of its rider, as Merlin's fingers wrapped around the bridle, the horse slowed. Then stopped. It turned its head first one way, then another – as though seeing for the first time. Its mane began to ripple; to curl and lengthen. And all at once, every buckle, every strap and rope fastened across its body came apart. Saddle, bridle, reins and rider tumbled down. Gwen covered her mouth with her hands in horror as the other horses wheeled, their riders equal parts shocked and angered... and none more so than their leader, the man who had tried to ride Merlin down. He sprang to his feet – as much as a man in a full mail coat can – and ripped his helm from his head. His hair, cropped savagely short, glistened with sweat in the light from the torches and the shadows writhed across the contours of his face as he pointed at Merlin and shouted in the invaders' tongue.

Merlin smiled sweetly at him and swung his staff back out from beneath his arm, planting it hard against the earth. "Welcome," he said, and dropped into a mocking bow that only enraged the soldier more. The man threw himself at Merlin – his hands outstretched – only to be knocked sideways by the end of the staff.

There was a cry from one of the other soldiers, and then another: surprise at first, then fear. For their horses had changed too, and now they found their legs bound to the sides of their horses by curling manes that wound about them like vines, leaving them unable to spur or to dismount. The hooves of their mounts had sunk deep into the earth of the path like roots. Leaves sprouted from the ends of their tails while tiny white flowers speckled their manes. Overhead, the falcon wheeled through a sky filling with stars as the clouds pulled apart.

Another crack like thunder came as the soldier stumbled to his saddle, fingers fumbling with something tied to it. Merlin followed, his staff held lightly, the smile still on his face.

"Odo!" The shout came from one of the men on the horses. "Odo!"

He was calling the name as a warning.

Odo looked up just as Merlin swung his staff – his own arm rising to meet the strike. Blocking the staff was a tremendous club cut from a tree limb, as long as man's arm and capped with iron. The staff should have shattered – would have, if it had belonged to any other man – but like the one who carried it, the staff was older and stronger than it seemed.

As Odo clambered to his feet, Merlin struck again – and again his blow was knocked away. They fell to circling one another, their feet constantly moving over the uneven ground. One stepped, feinted… then the other, both men watching for the other's weakness, neither showing theirs. Mumbling from the others – now bound to their horses – as though they were praying for something. Freedom, victory, protection… Gwen wondered why they thought they deserved them more than her village, or the village before it. She should run, she knew it. Should head for the village, should warn them, should raise what was left of the fyrd, should tell them… What? That the Bastard's men were coming, yes… but that *Merlin* had protected her from them? At best they would laugh and call her a fool; at worst they would ask why the soldiers had spared her, call her a traitor.

The sound of wood splitting bone brought her back from her thoughts, back to the doorway of the cottage. Still no one had seen her, still she stood pressed against the frame of the door with her fingers digging into the wood and splinters pushing under her fingernails. Merlin's blow had been knocked aside and Odo had landed one of his own: his club smashing into Merlin's left arm. Merlin made no sound – other than to whistle once, sharp and clear – to the sky. The bird answered immediately, swooping down to sink its claws into the cropped hair that covered Odo's scalp. Blood streamed down his face, painting it redder still in the torchlight and blinding him. He swung wildly about with the club but Merlin outstepped him, landing blow after blow with his own staff.

The punishment for attacking the new king's soldiers was mutilation, death, both. A village could not disguise a dozen bodies – and bodies they would have to be, or more men would come. They would come, and the retribution would be brutal. And just as Gwen had understood who Merlin was at the last moment, she understood what he meant to do. There would be no bodies. There could be no retribution.

Even as Odo fell forward, his face against the cold winter-hard earth. Even as the horses became ever less like horses and ever more like trees; as the vines and branches that had been their manes pushed their way into the mouths and throats of their riders, as fear became pain became silence became the creaking sounds of the forest. Corpses became copse; death became a living, swaying thing and the torches the men carried snuffed out one by one.

What remained of Odo let out a broken moan and, finally, Gwen stepped from the shelter of the doorway. A gust of wind caught her hair and she looked around to find the cottage gone. There was nothing there now but a grassy bank, and a three-legged stool. Merlin stood tall, his shattered arm hanging by his side and his hair thick with grey.

"I was never the story," he said quietly. "I was the misdirection."

He drove the end of his staff into the ground with such force that it shook the world, knocking Gwen off her feet. She scrambled back, her fingers finding purchase against the hard soil, as the tip of the staff shot upwards into the night sky, branches bursting out from its sides. The staff thickened, swelling until it came to resemble the trunk of an old oak – and even as the trunk opened and wrapped around him like a cloak, Merlin did not move. He did not move as the wood closed about him, his foot still resting on fallen Odo's back... and although she strained her eyes in the near-dark, all Gwen saw was an ancient oak tree standing proud of a copse, its gnarled roots spreading out across what had once been a path – and high in the branches, a small falcon perched, looking down at the world below.

It cried out – once.

And as she lay under the spreading branches of the oak, Gwen heard voices calling to one another; saw the far flicker of lanterns. The men of the village, come to stand against the soldiers – only to find themselves at the edge of a wood that had sprung from nowhere and an oak in full leaf despite the season, a single Norman helm lying on the ground beneath it.

Gwen's father reached her first, panic in his eyes. He knelt beside her, his hand on her shoulder. His gaze swept her, looking for any sign of damage. There was none. "What happened here?"

Gwen stared at him, at the trees, at Bron's pale face half-hidden behind the older men. Her fingers closed on the cold, smooth metal of the helm and she passed it to her father, then turned back to look at the spreading oak tree, which seemed to have grown even larger, even broader, even older – as though it had never not been there.

"The story. It changed."

And so had the world.

An Owl In Moonlight

Freda Warrington

The occasion of my sister Hetty's wedding to the Reverend William Musgrove was an amiable affair, thanks in large part to the abundance of champagne and sherry at the wedding breakfast. I say breakfast: in fact the affair began at noon and lasted well into the afternoon in our parents' spacious, if modestly appointed, drawing room.

My sister fairly glowed. Her new husband bore a beaming smile, and he made our aunts flush red with embarrassed yet delighted laughter at his jokes. Whoever guessed a reverend could be so – irreverent? I saw why Hetty had chosen him and I raised my glass to their happiness. Outside, a great red- and white-striped dirigible strained at its ropes, ready to carry them away to an undisclosed destination on their honeymoon. France, I hoped; anywhere dreamy and sunny and pleasing to them.

I, alas, was having a less comfortable time of it.

"Thomas, you are twenty-one years old!" Hetty said to me, teasing. "It would so please mother and father if you were to find a respectable young lady of your liking. I want you to be as happy as I am, my dear. Truly, you deserve it." And she kissed me sweetly on the cheek.

Now, I did not mind this from my beloved sister. However, from a flurry of aunts – both married and maiden – the endless refrain grew cloying.

"Thomas, you are twenty-one," they said, some in stern tones, others with a wink. "Are you *still* not yet courting? Surely the time is long overdue. There are so many sweet, respectable girls with whom you could settle down – but they won't wait forever." This was said in a warning tone, as if young ladies, like plums, might over-ripen in the autumn and be eaten by wasps. "The next time we hear wedding bells, they had better be pealing for you!"

And so it was that I edged through one tide of chattering relatives after another, until at last I washed up in a corner with Great-uncle

Bartholomew.

This was the metaphorical fate worse than death at all family gatherings. Those poor victims inadvertently trapped with Great-uncle Bartholomew had been known to fake a swoon or a violent stomach ailment in order to escape his overbearing presence. But he who engaged the redoubtable uncle's attention throughout the duration of the gathering would later be lauded as a kind of quiet war hero, or a captain who'd bravely gone down with his ship for the sake of the many.

Today, I decided to be that hero. For Hetty's sake.

Bartholomew was a tall, coarse fellow, with big face that suggested elements of dray-horse and ape in his ancestry. This animated visage was fleshy, full of lines, and blotched scarlet from champagne. His once-gingery hair was now mostly white, but still thick and curly, worn in long mutton-chop whiskers fashionable in his youth – although I doubted that so much unkempt hair had ever been "fashionable" in the strict sense. His waistcoat strained over an impressive paunch.

Capturing me with enthusiasm, he arranged chairs so that I was literally caged in a corner between fireplace and bookshelves. He drew up his seat opposite, plump legs spread wide apart, passed me a glass of wine, and leaned in with his bloodshot eyes gleaming.

A waft of alcohol-laden breath almost felled me, mitigated only by the fact that I had imbibed more liberally than is my usual habit. Especially at this hour of the day.

"Ah, dear boy. Nephew – name? Name?" He snapped his fingers, as if to jog his memory.

"Great-nephew, sir," I replied. "Thomas."

"Thomas!" he said heartily, although I'm fairly certain he had only a fuzzy recollection, in this sprawling family, of whose son I was. No matter. "For the love of heaven, call me Uncle! None of this 'Great' nonsense – I need no reminder of how deep into my dotage I am!"

"Surely not so old, sir," I replied. He spoke over me as if I were someone to talk *at*, rather than to.

"Splendid wedding, eh? What a spread! Splendid! Now if I could only remember the bride's name…"

"Hetty," said I. "My sister."

He was roaring with laughter or just… roaring. "Hetty! Wonderful girl! So many weddings, they all blend into one long… wedding! Ha!"

He took a big gulp of his drink – he was on brandy, I noticed, so I obligingly refilled his glass from a nearby decanter. Perhaps, if I were lucky, he would pass out.

He poked me in the chest with a plump finger. "You'll be next, young man!"

Oh, not again. Perhaps I *would* be next, but at present I was too busy studying law to concern myself with romance.

"But Uncle, you are a bachelor, are you not?" I said this light-heartedly. He was a man of cheerful disposition, I'll grant him that. One only had to mention that the sky was blue, or that a particular door had a particular style of doorknob, and he would hold forth all day on the subject.

However, when I uttered my rather too intrusive remark, he went silent.

Astonishing. This never happened, to my knowledge. I rubbed my left ear, wondering if I had momentarily gone deaf. Then, after a pause of a good five seconds, he started up again.

"Indeed, young man, a confirmed bachelor all my days." His voice went low and gruff. This surprised me, too, since his habit was to bellow. "And I know what everyone thinks: what woman would have a garrulous, fat old fool like me? But I tell you, Thomas, I was once young and handsome, with a fine figure like a willow lath and the modest income of a cloth merchant's son-and-heir to my name. I could have had my pick of gentlewomen. It was not for want of opportunity, I assure you."

"Why, then, did you deprive a lady of a fine husband?"

"Oh, I had my reasons. It's quite a story – and one I've never had the chance to tell. Damned annoying, that. I never get past the first few words and someone stops me in full flow, declaring they have some essential task to do or an important person to meet, or that dinner is served, or some such nonsense."

I cleared my throat. I swallowed hard. "I should like to hear your story, Uncle," said I.

"True love, dear boy." He leaned forward, hands braced on his knees, his face uncomfortably close to mine. "Love was my undoing. I fell desperately, hopelessly in love with a woman who could never be mine. After her – no one else ever could or would compare. After her, all other women were shadows."

"That's... terribly sad," I said in all sincerity. "It's tragic."

"She wasn't human, you see. She was one of the faerie folk. A goddess, in fact."

This was the point at which, I surmised, my uncle's captive audience would suddenly remember a pressing engagement or an imminent repast. However, I had committed myself to listening and, to be honest, I was rather intrigued. Who doesn't like a good fairy tale?

"A goddess?"

"And possibly a madwoman."

This addition was startling. He tapped me on the knee and sat back in his chair, apparently pleased to have shocked me.

"Mad?" I said.

"She was like no human woman I had ever met. More akin to a ghost, doomed to haunt the netherworld, incessantly seeking something she would never find. I tried to help her... I offered myself to her service, a knight swearing fealty to his queen... and I wonder how many others she has driven to distraction over the centuries? I wonder..."

As he went on, he spoke to the air above my head, absorbed in his narrative to the extent that he forgot I was there. I was glad of a little space to breathe. Now I was the one who sat forward, trying to catch his words over the general hubbub of the room.

Bartholomew walked across the meadows beneath the full moon, or rather wove his way from the local hostelry towards his father's house. All his drinking companions had scattered to their own homes along the lanes and now he was alone. The night was eerily bright to his bleary eyes. He barely felt the air's chill, but he drank in the cold air as if it were water to sober him.

Frost was forming on every leaf, twig and grass blade. He could see frost feathers growing into long spindly crystals as he went, the fields turning from grey to white until the whole world glittered.

Presently he noticed a small deer watching him from behind the trunk of an oak tree. Prettiest creature ever seen. A pure white doe.

Bartholomew moved very slowly so as not to frighten her away. The world spun gently around him like a spider's web, or a tunnel made of gleaming gossamer. Dizzy, he staggered. When he regained his balance, there was no doe beneath the tree.

In her place was a young woman.

He saw at once that she was not human. She was all in white fur with flowing pale hair, her heart-shaped face as pale as the moon, an aura flaring around her like snowy flames.

She was more than beautiful. She was lovely enough to put the angels to shame.

Bartholomew's instinct was to run, but his legs turned to rubber and he tripped, sprawling clumsily at her feet…

Feet? Was that an owl's claw peeping from beneath her hem?

He froze. Kindly she leaned down and helped him up, and the moment he looked into her shining eyes he was lost. Hers forever.

The universe seemed out of kilter, like a sinister reflection of itself, doused in a blue-violet hue against which she shone like pure light. A dim purplish corridor stretched behind her and he knew, with strange trance-like certainty, that she was standing on the threshold to the Otherworld. And so was he.

"Will you help me?" she asked. Her expression was sorrowful. She twisted her delicate bare hands together, fingers interlaced.

He couldn't speak.

"Don't be afraid," she said. "I am Estel. They call me the Lady of Stars, because I came into existence with the stars, and I was all alone for great gulfs of time… But I did not know I was alone until the Earth formed and I saw creatures begin to move upon its surface and the forests growing and falling and growing again…"

"My lady," he croaked. He was overwhelmed by a desire to fall at her feet and cry with joy. Of course he'd read fairy tales, and ancient myths of gods and goddesses and the Otherworld. Nothing could have prepared him for the overwhelming reality of meeting this deity. None of those legends had touched the truth.

A doe. A simple girl in white. Yet she was the unknown goddess who came before all others. He did not need to be convinced. One look at her and he *knew*.

"I need your help," she said again.

"My lady Estel, anything within my power I can do to help you, I shall do," he answered.

"I'm searching for my lover. The dear true love of my soul."

Her words gave him a jolt of disappointment – an irrational response, since he knew that she was far above him, too alien and magical ever to consider courtship from him, a mere commonplace human. This knowledge, however, did not dampen his longing to aid her.

There was such a thing as chivalry; an unconditional vow to help another out of pure love, with no hope of gain for oneself. He made this vow to himself on the spot, never to be broken.

"I – I have seen no one, my lady," he said. "I know these woods and meadows. I would have noticed a stranger. As for your consort, if he is a god who shines as you do – how could I possibly miss such a being?"

Estel dipped her head a little and clasped her hands in front of her. "You do not understand…"

"Bartholomew," he said as she paused, prompting him to give his name.

"I have been searching for thousands of years."

"Thousands…?"

What response could he make to this? Her presence was so gossamer-delicate that he feared she would vanish like frost if he blinked. And yet here she stood in front of him, so real and commanding that the rest of the world faded to nothing around her.

"I've hunted everywhere. All through the human world and all through the Spiral."

"The Spiral?"

"Some call it the Otherworld. Or the Land of Faerie, or the Aetherial realm. There exists more than the visible world, Bartholomew. There are many worlds, and I have sought my lover Kern in all of them."

"My lady Estel, perhaps you should grieve for him, and cease your search."

He thought this was quite a wise thing to say, but she looked unmoved. Not angry, not upset. Simply determined, her eyes burning like silver fire with her unshakeable obsession.

"I have found parts of him," she said. "A strand of hair. Two small bones from his foot. Leaves from his cloak."

She was, indeed, mad. An insane goddess!

"My lady, I don't…" He tried to say that this was no evidence at all that she'd found anything of significance, but the words would not come out.

"Kern was lord of the forest, in the early days when Aetherials first took on living forms. I, who had always been alone, fell in love with him the first moment we met. And for centuries we were happy. But a male called Perseid, a cold prince from Sibeyla, the realm of snow, formed a desire for me. He tricked Kern away from me and tore him to pieces and scattered him all across the realms. What am I to do, but go looking for all the pieces? If I can make him whole again, he may return to life. And if he does not, at least he will be where he belongs again. With me."

Bartholomew took in her words with a sense of wonder and despair. He recalled the story of Isis, who had gathered the scattered body parts of Osiris… but there had only been a few: fourteen or forty or thereabouts, according to which version you read. Leaves, hair strands, bones? How many bones were in the human body? Did an elfin body contain the same number?

"This is an impossible task," he said.

"Do not say 'impossible' to me," she answered coolly. "I have searched for countless aeons. I'll go on until time itself ends. You have not even begun."

"I wouldn't know where to…"

"I keep being drawn to this place. I'm sure there is something here. If you would only help me, perhaps you will find the fragment of Kern that I cannot. Will you try?"

His heart gave him no choice.

"Of course. But how will I know?"

"Oh, you'll know. Every piece is guarded. Every piece is inscribed."

She drew on the air with her finger, and the twinkling white image remained for a second before fading: a spiral shape.

"And did you undertake the quest?" I asked, pouring my uncle more brandy.

"Oh, yes, I searched!" he said fervently. "I explored the forest for days until my clothes were damp rags. Miracle I didn't freeze to death! At first the ground was like iron, but then the frost thawed and the earth turned to mud. I ate berries from the bushes, autumn berries so wrinkled and sour even the birds had left them. Looking back, I would appear to have lost my mind, but I couldn't stop. I was under a spell. I had to undertake the hunt for her sake. I'd made a vow. The Lady of Stars held me in thrall.

"Just as I was beginning to despair, I saw something.

"I was on the bank of a stream, a tall steep bank with soil exposed where part of it had fallen away into the water: a tangle of tree roots and ivy. The object I spied was only a pebble, but it drew my eye because it was pale and smooth, while all the other stones were rough and grey. I plucked it out. My fingernails were already torn and full of dirt, so I cared nothing for the grime.

"I rubbed it clean with a handkerchief and there it lay; not a pebble but a little bone the precise size and shape of a small finger joint. And on it was engraved a tiny rune, a spiral.

"I enjoyed a full two seconds of elation before a – a *thing* flew at me. It was like a small dragon, but I cannot dignify it with that description. No, it was too hideous: a flying reptile with wings and fangs and poisonous yellow eyes. It was no earthly animal! Then I knew I had found something of value, for what was this, if not the object's guardian?

"The monster came straight for my face, clawing at my eyes. It hissed. Its breath scorched my cheeks. I fell backwards and dropped the bone, but it would not cease the attack. Its whirring wings and dagger claws forced me down towards the water's edge. However, I seized a fallen branch and defended myself, like Saint George fighting the dragon. I was no soldier – but for Estel's sake I became a knight that day... and at last I struck that devilish, hissing thing out of the air. It fell, and landed in the stream, and moved no more."

I have of necessity condensed my uncle's account. The telling took three hours, and the battle between my uncle and the yellow-eyed demon-dragon was a veritable epic, with much interplay and climbing of trees, not to mention narrow brushes with death before he finally whacked it out of the sky.

"Then I went down the bank and waded into the current to retrieve the finger bone," Bartholomew continued, somewhat breathless by now. "Washed clean by the water, it was pure white, like a polished jewel. I have done it, I thought. I have found one little piece of her soulmate to give her hope! Alas...

"In due time I found my way back to the oak tree, but Estel was gone. I waited for hours, but she did not come back, not even when the moon rose again. Eventually I fell asleep, and was woken by my father and brother standing over me, scolding me for drinking too much ale and falling down insensible in a field in winter! To them, I had been gone for only one night. *One night.*"

I hardly dared suggest to my great-uncle that he might have dreamed the whole thing. In truth, it had been rather a fine tale, and I didn't want to break the magic. I thought it a shame that people did not listen more closely before dismissing him as a drunken old bore. For him – unless he was the most astonishingly accomplished liar ever born – these unearthly events had really happened.

"But where was Estel?" I asked.

"Gone," he said with heavy sadness. "Alas, I never saw my goddess again. Time after time I went out under the full moon, looking for her, to no avail. But I never stopped trying. And I never gave up the search for pieces of her lover, Kern. I devoted my life to her, and for nothing, but I don't regret one single moment of it. Not a moment, young Thomas."

His eyes half-closed. He looked exhausted and I thought he was near sleep.

There was a stir of movement around us, rousing him. The party was coming to an end. This meant that Hetty had already gone to change into her travelling attire, and that my encounter with Great-uncle Bartholomew could reach a natural conclusion.

"Thank you, dear boy," he said, seizing my hand between his large, over-hot paws. "Thank you for letting me tell my tale. I feel... unburdened."

He took something from his pocket and pressed it into my hand. I looked. It was a small slip of ivory that might indeed be a finger bone, inscribed with a tiny spiral.

By the time I started for home – at present, my student lodgings – dusk was falling.

We had waved Hetty and William goodbye and good luck as their airship rose gracefully into the blue afternoon sky, propellers whirring. Hetty wept and laughed, wafting her handkerchief at us. The craft looked, I thought, like a giant red-striped humbug as it drifted and dwindled away. I felt a little strange as she disappeared over the horizon, floating happily towards her new life. I was glad for her, but also sad, oddly melancholy. She would always be my sister, but everything had changed. She was a married woman now, a clergyman's wife, and perhaps, before long, mother to my nephews and nieces. What an extraordinary thought!

Would I become the eccentric uncle, entertaining them with supernatural tales?

Would I, one day, be flying off into the sunset with my dear heart's companion at my side, my new wife, whom I have not yet even met?

And so I slipped away and proceeded on foot along ten miles of cart-lanes that wound between hedges, through the woods and across open fields towards my lodgings in town. I could have stayed with Mama and Papa, but I wished to clear my head, rather than have them talking at me all evening. Although my desire to marry was unformed and hazy, I knew with absolute certainty that I did not want to turn into another Great-uncle Bartholomew in my old age: eccentric and lonely.

An owl watched me from an oak tree as I wandered along. The moon was caught in the branches. The great arching black sky seemed to be a face looking down, as if the night sky was in fact the visage of a goddess with the stars of the Milky Way braided into her hair.

This was a beautiful illusion, awe-inspiring and more than slightly alarming. My heart began to race and stumble. I swore I would never drink so much, nor walk alone at night, ever again. I felt the smooth shape of the finger bone in my pocket and rolled it between my thumb and forefinger, as if it were a talisman against danger.

I saw no doe, although it seemed to me that the owl took flight and brushed me with its wings – a flurry of pale, knife-edged feathers.

Then she stood before me.

A small, slender woman in white furs. She *glowed*. Like a dewy cobweb at dawn, like moonlight on snow, she shone with her own light.

Her sweet face was sombre, her eyes staring intently into mine. She was imperious and intimidating, yet vulnerable, soundlessly imploring me for help.

I fell to my knees.

"I've waited so long," she said, her voice soft, sad, infinitely patient. She held out her hand to me, palm facing upwards. "Did you find anything, anything at all to give me hope?"

Silent, I dropped the tiny cylinder of ivory into her hand.

She clasped it to her heart and closed her eyes, lips parted. "There is an Aetherial legend that every bone of Kern's body is a stitch that holds the Earth and the Spiral together. If ever I found the whole of him, the two worlds would tear apart. Would I chance that, to have my beloved one with me again?"

I found my voice with difficulty. And I dropped my gaze, for I knew that if I looked at her for one moment longer, my fate would be that of Bartholomew – always to search, never to know peace.

"I think you would chance anything to find him, my lady Estel."

"Ah well," she said softly. "It is only a tale."

CR80

"An Owl in Moonlight" is dedicated to Charlotte Burton and Thomas Firth.

Heaven Of Animals

John Hornor Jacobs

1

"Once we lived with common sense," Red Wolf said to the man on the horse next to him. He looked back over the rump of his mount at the herd. "Back then, it was necessary to live off the land. We respected the elements, and we understood that death was a harmonious part of life."

"Goddammit, Red, why do you have to talk like that?" Dap said, shielding his eyes from the morning sun with his hand. "You ain't even a real Indian, for christsakes. And we *are* forced to live off the land, if you haven't fucking noticed."

Red Wolf remained quiet, watching the herd. The two men sat on a small hill, looking down at a lush valley bisected by a stream. The herd milled nervously on the far side of the running water, lowing. The sound of moans came softly across the valley, along with the stench.

Dap shook his head and resettled his rifle across the pommel of his saddle. He raised binoculars and scanned the valley, panning his head back and forth.

"I'm rarer than an Indian, Dap," Red Wolf said. "I'm a *phony* Indian. The last of a dying breed."

"Ain't we all?" He sat straighter in his saddle. "Look over there, Red. Looks like we got a freshie."

A dead man shambled out of a stand of trees near a ruined farmhouse.

"He's gonna outpace the herd. That's trouble. And one of us is gonna have to go down there and lure them across the stream, looks like."

Red Wolf nodded. He twisted in his saddle and squinted at Dap.

"Because we killed everything that moved, we imagined ourselves safe from wolves. Now look."

"Yeah, I hear you, Hoss," Dap said, his voice thick with tobacco. "Who's gonna lure those revs?"

Red Wolf watched the larger man for a moment, took off his hat and wiped his pate with a handkerchief, then said, "I'll do it. You take out the freshie."

"Awright. I'll lure next time. You're a miserable shot anyway."

Red Wolf kicked his horse and rode down the hill, toward the stream. As he got closer, the revenant spotted him and changed course.

Swinging a leg off his horse, Dap dropped to the ground and laid his rifle across the saddle.

"Be still, girl. Be still." He squinted his left eye and tightened his finger on the trigger.

The sound of his shot echoed across the valley. The pinwheel of vultures following the herd fell away. Crows erupted from the copse of trees behind the dead man.

"Shit." He worked the bolt, sending a shell flying. His horse nickered. He could hear the herd lowing, coming across the valley, their moans louder now.

Looking over the saddle, he saw Red Wolf sitting on his horse, looking up the hill at him, face inscrutable. Having screwed up their courage – or hunger – the herd began moving across the stream. Off to the right, the dead man closed the distance between himself and Red Wolf faster than Dap expected.

He placed a hand on his horse to settle her.

"Whoa, girl. It's all right." He slid the 30.06 across the saddle again and sighted the revenant. Dap took a deep breath and held it.

Again the shot echoed loudly, the sound beating the air, then diminished. Dap smiled, looking at the motes of blood hanging in the morning light. He saw that Red Wolf held his pistol and waited, staring at the prone body of the freshie.

He waved at Red Wolf, beckoning. Red Wolf kicked his horse into motion and walked slowly back up the hill, leading the horde of zombies out of the stream.

"We're getting our common sense back," Red Wolf said, once at the crest of the hill. "Living with the wolves inside us has made us see."

"Dammit, Red," Dap said, spitting into the dust. "Why do you have to talk like that?"

2

In the afternoon, they came out of the valley and onto the interstate. Dap cut the barbed wire fence adjacent to I-40 with bolt-cutters and walked his horse through. Red Wolf followed, scanning the rise of interstate for any stray zombies. The herd moved easily through the fields, moaning and shambling, occasionally falling into irrigation ditches or getting separated by barbed wire. Dap sniped the laggers as best he could. The heavens darkened and the wind changed.

Dap looked up at the sky. "Couldn't you let us get one herd in without all the damned weather? Is that too much to ask?"

Red Wolf nodded. "We're all wreckage. Each one of us a collection of tissues, powered by a beating heart. But not them."

"What the hell is that supposed to mean?"

Red Wolf opened his mouth but Dap held up a hand and said, "Wait, don't tell me, Tonto. I'd rather not know." He paused. "You know how to ride before? Or you learn in the chain-link fields?"

"The fields."

"Huh."Dap spat. "You ride pretty damned good."

Thunder rumbled in the west.

He looked at the dark clouds moving in, a sour expression on his face.

"Shit. The wind at our back is gonna make this twice as hard," he said, wrinkling his nose. He turned and looked back at the herd making its way up the embankment and onto the interstate, two hundred yards distant. "Hard and fragrant. Okay, listen, Red. I gotta save ammo for sniping. But you got that pretty little pistol. And beaucoups of ammo. Without the revs able to smell us, it's gonna be hard to keep them on our tail unless we get closer to them, and I don't want to do that," he paused, looking at the smaller man. "Or we make a big ruckus. So I want you to shoot off that little noise-maker every few minutes until we get back to camp. All right?"

Red Wolf tilted his head and looked at Dap, unmoving, except for the shifting of his horse.

"We got ten more miles to get back to the races, and we can probably make that before dark if we hoof it, but the sound is gonna be drawing them from all over, not just the ones on our tail. There might be ones in front of us too, so stay alert."

He didn't wait for an answer. Tapping his horse with his spurs, Dap trotted ahead, moving between cars. Red Wolf looked after him, then raised his gun in the air, and fired. The undead behind them lowed. The wind blew the stench of the dead toward the men on horseback.

By the next exit, it began raining, coming down in fat, warm drops. A summer rain.

Dap picked off two corpses lumbering toward the approaching riders, shrugging themselves out of derelict cars. He fired three times.

"This rain's throwing off my aim," Dap said, sucking his teeth. He looked back toward the herd. "We're gonna have to let 'em get closer. See how they're all drifting apart? They can't smell us. This here rain is getting them all confused. Plus we're downwind. Damnation. Rein it in."

They stopped the mounts in the interstate, away from nearby cars. Rain dripped off of Red Wolf's hat and down his neck.

"Go ahead and fire that pop-gun, Red. Let 'em know we're here."

Red Wolf fired and then all fell silent, except for the patter of rain and the lowing of the zombies, who shambled toward the waiting men.

"So, whatd'ya do for a living, you know, before?"

"A teacher. A poet. I made a living with words."

Dap nodded and pulled a pack of Red-Man from his back pocket. He stuffed his cheek full of tobacco and chewed.

Red Wolf peered at Dap through the rain.

"Do you think I'm crazy, Dap?"

"Yep." He didn't even hesitate. "Crazier than a shit-house rat." He shook his head. "Hell, Red. We're all crazy. And why not? Everybody dies. Eventually. And becomes one of them. Makes me batty just thinkin' about it." He hooked a thumb at the herd behind him. "Inside everybody is one of them waiting to get out. 'Cuz of some virus or something."

"Lesch-Nyhan necrosis."

"That what they call it?"

"That's what they called it until the TV stations went off the air."

Red Wolf turned back to the herd. One of the zombies tripped on a piece of debris and spilled forward onto its face.

Dap laughed, a hard sound thickened with saliva.

"And you? What did you do before this?" Red Wolf turned to look at him, reseating himself in his saddle.

"Rancher." He shook his head. "Don't that beat all? It's the end of the world and I'm stuck doing the same damned thing I been doing for the last twenty years."

"We're just smoke, Dap. Smoke and flame and our lives move like water down a stream. If you can have any continuity between one moment and the next... Well... I envy you, sir."

"Smoke, huh?" He reached out an arm and pointed at the herd shambling forward. "And that? Their flames been snuffed out. But they're still burning. At least with hunger."

"They're pure. They exist, all their senses focused on one thing. They've rendered down all of human existence into hunger. Instincts, long forgotten, tamped down, bloom. They hunger. They rise."

"What's that? Poetry?"

Red Wolf nodded, then smiled. "I used to be in love with my own words. But I love other men's words as well."

Dap barked a laugh.

"If they're so pure, why'd you have your gun out to shoot the freshie at the stream? Huh?"

"I didn't want Dharma to get hurt."

"Dharma?"

"My horse."

"Jesus, you're a piece of work." He sniffed, gauging the distance between himself and the herd. "Come on, let's go. They've got our scent, the pure sons-a-bitches."

He tugged his reins, and walked his horse into a zombie.

The corpse threw its arms around the horse's neck and buried its face in the fur, black teeth snapping. The horse screamed, a high pitched whinny that made Dap freeze. Rearing, the horse pulled the corpse off its feet high into the air. Dap flipped backwards, somersaulting over the rump of his horse, landing face down on the asphalt of I-40. His chin banged hard against the pavement. He felt his teeth crack and tasted the salty well of blood springing in his mouth.

Red Wolf pointed his pistol at the zombie and fired, Dharma moving unchecked beneath him. Dap's horse screamed again, a red flower blooming on her neck. The horse jerked toward the median,

179

dragging the zombie – and Dap's gear – with it.

Dap pushed himself off of the ground, blood streaming from his mouth. He reached out and grabbed Red Wolf's reins, stilling the wild movement of the horse.

"Raise up," he said, the words strange and tasting foreign in the new configuration of his mouth. "I gotta get on. Herd's coming. Scoot forward and I'll swing behind."

"You're bleeding."

"Scoot up, goddammit. Herd's coming."

Dap swung behind Red Wolf, gripping the smaller man tight around the waist.

"Gimme the gun. You ride. Take it slow. Gimme the ammo."

Red Wolf handed back the pistol, then pawed at his waist. He unsnapped his fanny-pack and handed it back to Dap, who slung it over his shoulder like a bandolier. Ammunition spilled from the pack.

"Don't you zip up anything you stupid..."

He popped the clip, inspected it, and then slammed it back home.

The herd was thirty feet away. Dap's horse stopped screaming from the median.

"Shit. I can't believe you shot my horse."

Dap slid off Dharma easily, despite his injury, and dropped to his hands and knees, blood dripping from his mouth. He scooped up loose rounds from the asphalt, stuffing them into his pockets.

"Dap," Red Wolf said, voice still calm. "The zombie that got your horse is coming back."

"Damn." He turned on his knees, pistol out. The corpse lurched forward in the rain, his jaw working, horse blood down his front looking like black ink in the low light. A hoof must have caught the corpse's stomach or pelvis, tearing it open. The zombie appeared to have an enormous penis. Guts swung from its lower body cavity.

Dap fired. The zombie wheeled, intestines swinging, then righted itself. It moved forward again. Dap fired once more, and the corpse's head rocked back. It dropped to the pavement.

He swung behind Red Wolf.

"Go. Go." He popped the clip, and began digging bullets from his pockets. The herd was ten feet away, moaning.

Red Wolf spurred the horse forward, and Dharma responded, moving into a trot. With each bounce, Dap's mouth throbbed with pain.

"Move us away from the herd, but don't go too far. We still gotta bring these undead bastards home."

Dharma stopped fifty yards away from the herd. Dap reloaded the pistol, worked the action, then tucked it into his belt.

"Damn, that was close. I can still smell them on me."

"They fall, they die. Their instincts stir. They rise."

"Would you stop? My mouth hurts."

The herd of zombies moaned in the rain. Dap slumped against Red Wolf's back.

"Get us home, Red."

3

They brought the herd over the rise and in sight of the races just as the sky turned dark. A pillar of black smoke rose from the corpse fires. They rode past fields locked behind chain-link fences. In the fields, men and women with hoes trudged back to the dining hall, going through interconnected gates. They stopped and waved as the two men rode past, leading the mob of zombies. Dap waved them away, so as not to confuse the herd.

The halogen beacons burned like stars, the smoke from the corpse fires making the blue light waver. The mouth of the races stood open, waiting for the riders and herd to enter. The sound of a generator buzzed in the distance.

"Damnation, that looks good to me," Dap said, lisping slightly. He'd pulled the fragments of two shattered teeth as they led the herd of zombies back to the fort. If he didn't spit, his mouth filled with blood. "You ever been through the races before, Red?"

Red Wolf shook his head.

"We took the old cattle races and refitted them for the revs. When you bring cattle to slaughter, they don't like sharp turns, so you gotta lead them down these soft curved chutes – the races – so that they don't turn around and head back to the fields. Zombies act pretty much the same way, as long as you got the lure in place."

"What's the lure?"

"Us."

They walked Dharma into the race's mouth. She neighed and

danced sideways. Dap wrinkled his nose.

"Didn't use to smell like this. It smelt bad all right, but not like this. All the dead folks have left little pieces of themselves smeared all along the walls. Hold up. Let's let em catch up before we get out of sight."

Dap hopped down and spat blood.

"Might as well walk the rest of this." He patted Dharma on the rump, keeping his hand there as he walked around the horse. "Thanks, Red. For what you done."

"What?"

"Get me out of there. There I was drifting off, chatting up a storm, and you pulled my bacon out of the fire."

"I save you, I save myself. It's all connected."

"Yeah. I guess. But you did shoot my horse." He shook his head. "I'll tell you what. I won't tell anybody if you don't."

Dap smiled and patted Dharma's haunch again. The herd shambled into the circle of light thrown by the halogens. When they were thirty feet away, Dap said, "Okay, let's go." He took Dharma's rein and led her through.

They walked around the curve of the race where the wall became thick bars. Men in motorcycle gear and blank, reflective helmets waited with hooks, grapples, axes and long spears. One man stood away from the rest, hand on the lever of the gate. Seeing Dap and Red Wolf, he pulled the lever. The gate slid out with a hiss of air.

"Got about sixty behind us!" Blood sprayed as he yelled. "Get ready!"

They moved into the small holding pen. The man at the lever pushed it forward this time and the gate slid shut behind them.

One of the waiting men popped the visor on his helmet. He smiled.

"Just hang-out there for a second, Dap. We don't want the herd to get wind of someone else and bolt."

"Simmons, you goddamned fool. This ain't a game." Dap moved forward until he stood at the end of the pens. Black blood and pieces of rotting flesh caked the bars. An angry cloud of flies whirred and spun in the air as Dap approached. The moaning of the herd grew louder, and the waiting men began checking their gloves, refastening the velcro strips on their motorcycle armour.

Dap turned to another man and bellowed, "Miller, open up this murder-hole, for christssake!"

Miller, also blank visaged behind a motorcycle helmet, jumped toward the gate, surprised. Simmons raised his hand and he stopped.

"Just wait a second. Just a little bit more."

The zombies took the last turn of the race, shambling into view. Simmons slammed his visor down with a gauntleted hand, nodded at Miller, and together they pulled the pins on the gate, swinging it open.

Simmons slapped Dap on the shoulder as he stomped through, leading Dharma and Red Wolf.

"Great herd, Dap. At this rate, we'll have the state cleared out in... shit... maybe two hundred years," Simmons yelled behind his visor. "Go get a drink. You earned it." He turned to refasten the gate.

Red Wolf descended from Dharma slowly, stiffly. A young boy dashed forward and took the reins of the horse and Dap tousled his hair. "Make sure she gets some of the oats and a good brush down, Cory. That girl's done a day's work."

The boy grinned and led her away, through the second set of gates ringing the zombie races.

Behind him, the moaning increased. They turned to watch the slaughter.

Once the herd crowded the race gate, arms outstretched, clawing, moans and garbled sounds coming from undead throats, the lever-man opened the pneumatic gate. It lopped off a few arms as it retracted. The zombies surged forward. The spear men brought up their tools and began mechanically smashing skulls. Hook-men ducked and snagged zombies, grabbing rib-cages and drawing the bodies out from under the pen, toward the wagons. For a while, just the sound of moaning and the thunks of the spears and axes filled the air. The linemen began grunting in time with their swings. A few curses filled the air.

"We got a bloater!"

Dap winced as a ruptured body cavity bleated a liquid fart of putrid gas. He pulled a handkerchief from his back pocket and covered his nose and mouth.

"We used to let folks watch. But they'd always get real upset if they spied a loved one, a daughter, a wife in the herd. Usually try and rescue them, or bribe the linemen to let them go. They'd rather know that their sister's lurching around, hungry for the living, than dead.

Messed up world."

"Love doesn't end at death, Dap."

"Yeah? Well, neither does stupidity, I guess. They'd throw themselves at the bars and usually be reunited with their family. Maybe not like they'd expected, though."

He hocked up a bloody piece of phlegm, spat it into the races, then painfully withdrew his pouch of Red-Man and packed his cheek full.

"I gotta go talk to the council about my horse and get our money. Goddamn, I'm not looking forward to explaining this to the resource committee. I'll meetcha at the saloon, okay? You figured out where you're gonna bunk down yet?"

"They assigned me a tent in Lot 10, near the water tower. Not too far from the river."

"Huh. Screw that. I got a bunk in a trailer near the stables. You can settle down there, if you want."

Red Wolf nodded, took off his hat and rubbed his bald head. He stretched, raising his arms skyward then leaned forward, doubled over, arms hanging, and gripped his calves. He stayed like that for a long time.

"What in the wide world of sports are you doing?"

"Stretching. Dharma's pleasant companionship but I'm not used to the long hours."

"Shit, son. Don't do that in public. Christ. You're gonna embarrass me."

Red Wolf sat at a small wooden table near the front of the saloon. Two men played guitar on stools, by the bar. A passable imitation of Lynyrd Skynyrd filled the room. Men – rough men in motorcycle boots, dungarees, and work shirts – waved mimeographed rations at the young waitresses working the tables. A few women, older and scantily dressed, moved through the bar traffic, laughing and winking. A bartender poured whiskey and served warm beer to the men.

Dap pushed his way through the crowd to the table, palmed a waitress' rear as she passed and winked at her scowl. He flopped into the wooden chair and tossed a handful of rations at Red Wolf.

"Damn, that's like going to the principal's office."

"What?"

"The council. They reamed me good for losing a horse. Kept talking about field expansion and livestock conservation." He winked at Red Wolf. "I didn't say nothing about your aim. Or lack of it."

"I feel bad about it. But maybe it's my karma." He cocked his head. "Or yours."

Dap motioned to the waitress.

"What're you drinking?"

"Tea."

Dap looked at the bald man sitting next to him. He squinted his eyes.

"Listen, I know you're batshit and all, but you got to be kidding me. We've been out for near thirty-six hours, outriding God knows how far, and brought back that herd of revs. All you're drinking is tea?"

Red Wolf nodded, a small smile playing at his lips.

Dap shoved away from the table and stood. He went to the bar. The other man remained seated, watching the rough trade around him, and sipped his tea. Dap returned holding two beers in one fist and a bottle in the other. A pint of Jack Daniels.

"You said we're smoke and fire and water and all that other shit. Well, have a drink. Be pure and calm and... whatever else you need to be... but have a drink with me."

"I am drinking with you." He took a sip of his tea.

"No. A *drink*."

His voice soft in the clatter of the saloon, Red Wolf said "I don't need it, Dap. I'm content to have some tea and sit here with you. I've eaten dinner, now I'm watching all these good people enjoy themselves and I am content. What more is there?"

"A shitload. Drinking. Fucking. Fighting. Killing the revs. Riding."

"Ah." Red Wolf held up his hand and waved to the waitress. She pushed through the crowd.

"What'dya mean, 'ah'?"

"Getcha something, honey?"

"A bit more hot water, if you'd be so kind."

She giggled, a strange sound coming from her lined face.

"Sure thing, honey." She looked at Dap, frowning. "You want something?"

"Yeah," he grinned, "A coupla shotglasses and a whole lotta you."

She walked away, tray held high.

"What'dya mean, 'ah'?" He unscrewed the cap on the pint and took a sip, hissed, swallowed, then shook his head. He held his hand up to his jaw, stuck a large unwashed finger into his mouth and probed at his missing teeth. He winced. "I really miss ice."

"I meant 'ah,' riding."

"Yeah?"

"I asked what more is there. You said riding. I said 'ah'."

"Oh." He felt around his jaw, testing the limits of the damage.

"Exactly."

Dap stayed silent. He sipped at the beer until the waitress passed by again, plopping two shot-glasses unceremoniously on the table. One tipped over and spun around. He righted it and filled it with whiskey.

"So, what about fucking? That's bout as pure as it gets."

"Yes. Sometimes I want to have sex. But my wife is dead."

Dap looked at the waitresses. Tears formed in the corners of his eyes. One spilled down his cheek before he could wipe it away.

"Yeah." He sniffed, wiping his nose on his sleeve. "But she wouldn't mind. I mean, we're still here, ain't we? It's such a goddamned monster of a world. Would she deny you comfort when you can find it?"

"Is it comfort? Or is it forgetfulness? I don't want to forget her, and I don't want to replace her. And are we talking about your wife, or mine?" He drained the contents of his mug. "I do like the tea. And riding Dharma, as well."

Dap stared down into his shotglass for a bit, then held it over the beer and dropped it in. The warm beer frothed. He picked up the glass and downed the drink in one long pull from the mug.

"Ah."

"Ah."

"We've been offered another job. New horse for me, new guns. Motorcycle armour for both of us. A sweet job. Riding escort for a scavenging operation. We gotta find more chain-link for the fields. Gonna push all the way into West Little Rock if we can, hitting hardware, liquor and gunstores. While we're gone, they're gonna double the size of the races and be waiting for us to bring back the biggest herd of revs yet. Two horses to a man, no stopping."

He poured another shotglass full and dropped it into Red Wolf's beer. He pushed the mug toward his companion.

Red Wolf pushed it back.

"I'm willing. When do we leave?"

"Day after tomorrow."

Red Wolf nodded, once. Dap lifted the mug to his lips, tilted his head, and drank.

"Done," he said, slamming the mug back on the table.

4

Dap moaned. From horseback, he waved his hand at Red Wolf riding near him. The other man handed him the clear, two-litre soda bottle tied with twine.

Raising the bottle to his lips, he took a swig of the liquid, swished it around, then spat it out.

"Damn, Red, that's some nasty stuff."

"Doc said you need to wash your mouth with saline solution."

"It hurts."

"All pain is temporary."

Dap lifted the bottle and repeated the process again.

"So's all pleasure. My whole damned head feels like it's gonna explode."

"It's the infection. Or the hangover."

"If it exploded, it might make me feel better."

The wagon trundled behind them on silent rubber wheels, heavy with stale tobacco, pickles and cheap scotch whiskey. A five hundred pound bail of cattle fencing was the best they could find. They'd siphoned almost three hundred gallons of gasoline from a station near Perryville.

The horses drawing the wagon frothed at the mouth. They'd discovered a motorcycle shop after much effort, only to find it devoid of any riding gear save one Kevlar riding jacket, a pair of boots and a few helmets. An Indian souvenir shop provided thirty pounds of cured leather for clothing and further armouring, plus a large haul of still good pemmican.

Miller, Sunseri and Ransom rode bait while Dap and Red Wolf led the procession. Simmons sat high in a bucket seat, perched atop the plywood wagon, a shotgun across his knees.

Man-sized saplings and Johnson grass veined the highway. Cottonwoods and birch ran up against the road which resembled little more than a game-trail through the countryside.

"All stop!" Simmons called from his perch. "Herd's breaking up. It's just too big to stay together in these woods!" He spat over the rim of the wagon. "Dap, take Silent back there and help with the bait. I'll keep watch on our frontside."

"We can't stay sitting here too long. Hear that?"

The sound of the herd was a dull roar.

"We're drawing 'em in from all over! We got over three hundred now."

"The council didn't put you in charge of this foray. They put me. I'm not gonna place any man nor horse at risk, okay?"

Dap yanked on reins, pulling his mount's head toward the wagon, where Simmons sat staring at him. "I know the council wants us to do our best to clear out the state of what revs we can. But we can't stop now. Maybe nearer the Ponderosa we can rest again."

"It ain't resting Dap. At this point, the herd's hit the point of no return. We gotta bring 'em in. If we don't bring them into the races, they might just wander around in a cluster and hit one of the fenced-in fields. Those chain-link fences'll keep out the onesies or twosies, but they'll fold with a herd like this battering."

Dap rested his hand on his pistol-grip and kicked out his hip, thinking.

"Damnation. I hate to admit it, but you're probably right."

Simmons smiled. "Hell has frozen over."

"Why'd we name it after Bonanza?" Red Wolf cocked his head curiously.

Miller, who had moved up near the conversing men, snickered at the name.

Dap glared at the man. "Everybody thought it was funny. I loved that show. There's worse ways of naming a town."

Simmons adjusted his shotgun in his lap. "How'd you even see it? It was off the air when you were born in... What? '75? '80?"

"'71." He laughed, making a short barking sound. "I guess I'm just well preserved."

"Pickled is more like it."

"My dad had it on Betamax. Remember those? Shit, I wanted to be Hoss so bad."

"Yeah. I remember Betamax. They lost the format war with VHS."

The men fell silent, thinking.

Dap said, "I'm gonna dig up a DVD player or something and make 'em start having movie night back at town." He rubbed his jawline. "We need something. Something to remind us of...the good times. Of being normal."

"I think that's a good idea," Simmons said, looking off into the brush. "Except it might remind folks how far we've fallen. And finding gas for the gennies ain't as easy as it used to be. Despite this nice haul. Probably be a bonus waiting for us." He nodded at the men's smiles. "Heads up."

A pair of zombies crackled through the brush in front of them, pushing long grass and branches aside.

Miller withdrew a billy-club from his belt and Dap reached over and grabbed a baseball bat from the wagon bed.

"Back to business, gents."

Red Wolf and Dap rode bait. The stench from hundreds of walking dead behind them filled the air, even though they rode into the wind.

"God, this is a miserable damned detail," Dap said.

His companion nodded, rubbing Dharma's neck. The highway rose from the country surrounding it, giving the two a clear view of the area. The sun had begun to slide down the western vault of sky.

"You're taking this little jaunt calmly, Red. You hoarding Xanax?"

"No. Thinking."

"What gives?" He reined in, looking back over his horse's rump at the oncoming herd. The three hundred zombies had grown to four, easily. Their lowing swelled their ranks, drawing others from the surrounding countryside. The men were a hundred yards away. The mob of undead moved like some enormous, grey-green amoeba, sloughing off bits of itself and drawing them back in. The herd was sixty yards deep and spilled over the side of the highway, into the brush. They could hear the crack and snap of branches as the off-road revenants made their way toward them.

Dap turned to look at the wagon cresting the rise. Miller and Sunseri sat watching. Miller gave a little girl wave, high and mincing, made absurd by his heavy gloves.

"In the Smithsonian, there's a room they keep the bones of every tribe of Indian. They keep it perfectly cool, and dry, and the bones...they've analysed, weighed, and measured them. They've catalogued and cross-referenced them."

"Yeah? So?"

Red Wolf was quiet for a long while.

Finally, he said, "So. What were they looking for?"

Dap took a swig from the two litre bottle of saline, grimaced, swished the liquid in his mouth, and spat.

"No clue, Red. There's probably revs gnawing on them bones now, if they got stuck down there." His horse nickered, rearing its head. The herd approached. Dap inspected his rifle and nodded for Red Wolf to check the load on his pistol.

"So what happened, huh? For you to be so looney-tunes? They get... they get your family?"

Red Wolf said, "She went to the grocery and took the kids. Amy. Gretch."

"Oh. Shit."

"But they came back home, after." He looked away, shook his head.

"It's a goddamned monster of a world."

"It's humanity. But, in death, we remove our masks. Show our animal natures."

Dap spat again.

"That's horseshit. Your nature is your nature. Some folks are shitheads. Some are sweethearts. All this philosophizing ain't good for you."

They fell silent and watched as the herd drew closer, lowing heavily. Red Wolf tied a bandanna across his mouth and nose to keep the stench out. The herd had grown so large after swinging through west Little Rock that it was hard to see the rear of the mass from their vantage. A sea of reanimated dead, shambling forward.

"You see that, Red?"

He shook his head. Dap pointed.

"There. Near the front."

"No."

"The blond. Semi-fresh. Got a tennis ball stuck in her mouth with duct tape."

"Hm. That's strange."

"You said it, Tonto." He turned to scan the hills around them.

It sounded like a firecracker, whistling through the air. Dap felt a puff of wind across his cheek. Then the report of a rifle cracked from across the valley.

"What was that?"

"Shit, Red. Someone's shooting at us."

The sound came again, a whistle as the bullet sped through the air. Then, *crack*... A rifle's report.

Red Wolf's horse screamed and crashed to the ground.

"Get down!" Dap called to the men on the rise.

A horse from the wagon fell, and they heard another crack - the bullet from the unknown shooter travelled faster than the sound - drawing the other horse, locked in its traces, down with it, screaming. From the corner of his eye, Dap saw a puff of white in the trees, on the skirt of a large hill.

Another *crack*. No one fell.

"Over there!" he yelled, pointing to the stand of trees where he'd seen the smoke. "Ransom! Sunseri! Get over there! Get him."

The herd's lowing grew louder. Ransom wheeled his horse and rode hard for the woods. Sunseri split off to the side, intending to flank. But then his horse pitched over, rump flying high, and he flew through the air and hit the ground, headfirst.

Crack.

"He's shooting horses!" Dap's voice pitched upward.

Another whistle and report. Miller had dismounted and pulled his horse behind the wagon.

Simmons keeled over, landing with a thump, near a wagon wheel.

Crack.

Miller ran to where Simmons had fallen, going to his knees.

"Shit! He's wiping us out!"

Dap dropped from his horse and went over to where Red Wolf lay.

"You okay, Red?"

Red Wolf shook his head. "Got me through the leg when he shot Dharma. I think my foot's crushed, too. I can't get out."

Dap cursed, looked to check how far away the herd was, and

shoved at Dharma's back.

"Damn. We gotta get you out of there quick. I can't budge her."He glanced around. "Wait a sec." He grabbed his rifle, shoved the barrel as far underneath the horse as he could, grabbed the stock and lifted, veins popping in his arms.

Red Wolf groaned and pushed himself out from under Dharma. Dap helped him up, to a standing position. He looked at his rifle. The barrel was bent. He dropped it.

"Come on, we gotta go."

Another whistle and Dap felt something tug at his jacket.

Crack.

"Shit. He's shooting again. Why the hell is he shooting at us?"

The herd drew close. The dead woman with a tennis ball taped into her mouth led the mass of revenants.

Dap pushed Red Wolf up and onto his horse, then swung behind. Blood from Red Wolf's wound ran in streamers down his Kevlar leggings.

"We gotta get you away from the herd before we can check out that leg."

He turned his horse, holding Red Wolf upright, and rode for the wood where he saw the flash of white, where Ransom had ridden.

In moments, he was among the trees, working his way up a hill. Shots rang out behind him. He looked over his shoulder, and watched as undead swarmed Dharma and moved up the hill toward the wagon and Miller.

Dap heard yelling.

He rode into a small uneven clearing where Ransom held a boy of maybe twelve or thirteen, a hint of wispy beard on his chin. He was blond and grimy, dressed in clothes too small for his frame.

The boy thrashed in Ransom's grip. A rifle with an enormous scope lay on the ground.

"Here's the little sonofabitch. He's gone feral. He shot at me but I was too close for him to see through that scope. Little idiot could've popped me if he'd of just raised his head from the eye-piece. Bit me good when I caught him." He held up his hand. A bloody half-moon marred the webbing between thumb and index finger. "We should stake him and let the revs have him for dinner."

Red Wolf swayed in the saddle. Dap dismounted.

He approached the boy. "Why the hell were you shooting us? You killed two...three men. Horses. And the town needs those supplies. Why?"

The boy still thrashed, crying now. He said, "Momma. Momma."

Dap shook his head. "Bop him one to quiet him down."

"Wait." Red Wolf slumped off the horse, leaving a bloody smear behind. "Let him go."

"Sorry, Red, but I'm not gonna do that. This little bastard's gonna pay." Ransom held him tightly.

Red Wolf limped forward, removing his hat. Awkwardly, he went down on a knee.

"Is she blond?" he said, softly.

The boy stopped struggling and looked at Red Wolf, eyes large.

"She died and you didn't know what to do. You tried to keep her safe." Red Wolf swallowed and his face hitched in pain. "You thought maybe there'd be a cure."

The boy nodded. "Momma."

Dap scratched his head and looked at Ransom.

"So you tried to make her safe, yes? You put a tennis ball in her mouth to keep her from biting, but she got loose, didn't she?"

The boy nodded again. Dap cursed.

"Goddamnit." Dap turned away and kicked at the ground. He looked out at the herd. "That don't matter, Red. It's real nice you figured out what happened..." He pointed to the herd. It had turned and had begun making its way toward where they stood in the copse of trees. "But he killed our men. Our horses. If we haven't lost all that scavenge, it's gonna take some doing to get it back to the Ponderosa."

Red Wolf shook his head. "He's just upset and trying to save his mother."

Dap spat. "So what should we do, then, send him to a shrink? Oh, I forgot. Ain't no shrinks anymore." He looked at the boy and said, "Hey, kid, your mother's dead. She'll eat your sorry ass if she gets a chance."

"I told you before, Dap, love doesn't end at death." He turned to Ransom. "Let him go. We're men, not animals."

"No." Ransom shook the boy.

"Ransom, go ahead and stake him. We'll wait here for a while and once the herds get close enough, we'll flank 'em and see what's left of

Miller and Simmons. Then we'll lead the herd back to the races." He didn't look at Red Wolf, couldn't meet his eyes. But he said, "Red, we'd never be safe with him. He can't be trusted. He'll kill us in our sleep. All over a dead woman."

At the mention of his mother, the boy squirmed, twisting his body wildly. Ransom lost his grip, and the boy's hand suddenly sprouted a hunting knife. He drove it into Ransom's neck, above the collar of Kevlar. Ransom toppled over. The boy froze, his eyes going wide, as if in disbelief of what he had just done. He looked from Ransom's body to where Dap stood by Red Wolf. The moment lengthened, and then he moved, dashing away, into the trees. Dap began to run after him, but stopped.

He turned to Red Wolf, who was having trouble standing. He picked up the boy's discarded rifle.

"Damn it, Red. Let's get you up on the horse before Ransom goes revenant."

They were on the interstate, near the races, when Red Wolf slumped forward. He pitched onto the horse's neck, arms dangling to the sides. Dap had removed his belt and put a tourniquet on his Red Wolf's leg, but the Kevlar armour had hard plastic ridges, and getting the tourniquet tight enough was almost impossible without dismounting and disrobing Red Wolf. But Dap's horse moved too slow for stops, after a long days ride and bearing two men. The herd was twenty yards away. Close.

Dap said, "We got about thirty minutes, pard. Just hold on." He patted his back.

As best he could, Dap examined Red Wolf's wound. The blood had blackened on the ride, becoming crusty. It looked as if it had stopped bleeding. But Red Wolf still stirred.

"Get your rest, pard. We'll be drinking in a few."

The mass of zombies were close behind them. In the distance, the corpse-fires pillared smoke into the atmosphere, tall black columns. Ever burning, Dap used the corpse-fires as a homing beacon. Soon they'd be near the chain-link fields.

Looking over his horse's rump, he spied Miller and Ransom shambling along with the rest of the undead. Simmons and Sunseri were missing. Head trauma, maybe. The blond woman with the tennis ball in her mouth still led.

Dap looked at the fields surrounding the highway, searching for the boy. He was watching. Dap could feel it.

"I'm gonna make sure she's dead! Gonna grind her up! She's gonna burn!" His voice was sore from yelling. "I'm gonna spike her head myself!"

Silence, except for the lowing of the herd. Crows watched from dead power lines. Dap studied the treeline.

"I got your gun! I'm gonna shoot her with it!"

Red Wolf stirred, shaking his head.

Dap could feel his body in front of him twist, coming to life. He patted Red Wolf again.

"Look there, Red. There's the fires, and here in a few we'll be rolling into the races. Almost home. Just sit tight."

The horse nickered, tugging at the reins.

They rode on, between derelict cars. The fields passed slowly by, scraggly corn and wheat growing untended by the hands of man. The wind came down from the hilltops and rustled grass near the road. They passed over a bridge, water gurgling below.

The horse whinnied, rearing. A bloody hole showed in her mane where Red Wolf had chewed into her neck.

In a moment of dislocation, Dap once again flipped ass over head and landed on the interstate, catching himself with his hands. Red Wolf's body smacked into the pavement, two feet away, face first. The mare bolted, heading for home.

The thing that had once been Red Wolf began to rise.

The corpse turned and fastened its eyes on him.

Dap scrambled backwards, and pulled his pistol. He stood, panting, in the late afternoon light. Red Wolf lurched forward, raising arms. He moaned.

"Goddamnit, Red." He shook his head.

He drew back the hammer on his piece, with a click. He wiped his eyes with his palm, clearing the tears away.

"Now you sound like one of them."

He raised the gun and fired. The corpse of Red Wolf slumped to the ground. Crows erupted from the nearby trees.

Dap looked at the fields. He screamed, an inchoate, lost sound. He dropped the pistol.

"I'm a man, goddamit! I ain't an animal! *A man*!" He turned to the herd. "*A MAN!*"

He gasped for air. Tears streamed his face.

"It's a goddamned monster of a world," Dap said, softly.

Silence then, except for the caws of the carrion crows wheeling above the herd.

He turned and ran. The herd lowed, following.

THE IRON WOLVES: RETRIBUTION

Andy Remic

The creature was large, bulky, and shifted in the Stygian gloom of the icy mountain cave. Behind it came the whimpers of children, their noises timid, their screams and crying now spent as realisation and despair had taken firm root.

The beast shuffled, moving closer to the cave mouth where a cool blue light filtered through the peaks of surrounding mountains on radiating bands of winter sunlight. It was bigger than a horse, although with differing physical proportions; a different *build*. It was... *almost* a horse, but not, for no foal could have emerged so twisted, so deformed, and lived. Bulging lumps of distended muscle protruded from a compact, slightly curved torso, a body that appeared to have been broken, the bones then fused back together again. The body was a rich chestnut colour, uneven skin patched with horse hair in segments, as if it had suffered the effects of a forest fire. It limped forward on three legs; the fourth, the front right, did not touch the ground, for it was too short and bent sideways at an irregular angle. Thick hooves still wore iron shoes, scarred and chipped, and above the uneven barrel chest was the head – a great, misshapen bulk, with broken equine face, long and tapered, but with the mouth pulled back, jacked open too far and showing huge, yellow fangs. The eyes were unevenly placed in a lopsided skull, one yellow, one black and double the size of the other, rolling wildly in the socket and speckled with internal bleeding. From one side of the disproportionate head curved a serrated horn, easily the length of a rapier, but grown from yellow bone, like a stray fang which had punctured the skull and grown outwards. There were notches and nicks on the horn, where battle had scarred it.

That twisted horse head lowered, and turned, revealing the large black eye, and as it hobbled towards the cave entrance several large wounds could be seen on its flanks; great openings of crimson dripped tears of blood, pattering softly to the icy rock as if the whole body wept at its very existence.

Inside the cave children began to wail, as light revealed the beast; a terrible, mournful sound to match the wind singing down from the high mountain passes: a song of sadness; a song of desolation.

The beast settled down uncomfortably at the entrance, equine head resting on the ground and on one iron-shod hoof, like a hound guarding its master's home. The black lips pulled back, showing cracked and chipped fangs, and borne on a sigh, like the exhalation from a corpse, came one word...

"Narnok."

"Here's trouble, looking for trouble," growled Dek, the pit fighter, nodding over his tankard at the three large men who'd just entered The Fighting Cocks tavern. Lantern flames flickered at the draught from the outside storm, and through the framed portal Dek caught a glimpse of broiling skies and a jagged lightning strike.

Narnok the Axeman turned and stared, scratching his beard. His savage face, with its crisscross of white torture scars and one good eye, one milky eye, showed a considered lack of emotion. He shrugged and turned back, one fist clenching involuntarily as he grasped his tankard and took a hefty drink. He belched. "There's no trouble there, lad. Now, as I was saying, I'm still having these elf rat nightmares; they... they *invaded* my face and my mind with their dark magic." He took another drink and his fingers touched tenderly at his lips, although there were no wounds. He gave a shudder, remembering the horror. "Those bastards."

Trista leant forward, her long-fingered hand with its unblemished skin resting on Narnok's bear paw. "It'll get easier," she soothed, voice music, her eyes glittering as bright as the diamond bracelet on her wrist. Narnok stared at her, at her elegance, beauty, the painted lips and long, oiled blonde curls, the perfect teeth and regal, high cheekbones. "I promise, all things get easier, with the passage of time. And the elf rats are gone now, Narn; just like the mud-orcs before them."

"They'll be back," growled Narnok, face dark, eyebrows furrowed. "As you said, everything ends; everything falls apart."

Now Trista's face darkened. "For that, Narn, I was referring to *something else*. And you damn well know it." Trista had a... dark history.

Betrayed shortly after her wedding day, she had embarked on a slaughter of newlyweds, for in her shattered, twisted mind she was saving them an agony in the future by immortalising their love at the point of marriage – with death. She had been saved, finally, by Kiki, Captain of the Iron Wolves, who had once more given her a purpose in life when General Dalgoran decided to reform their squad. But still, the bad memories, of marriage and murder, lingered, like old smoke from a honey-leaf pipe.

"My apologies. I did not mean to offend. It's just, after the elf rats cast that spell on me, after I was… invaded by their *roots*, it has given me a different perspective on life."

"Oh, will you actually shut the fuck up about the bloody elf rats," snapped Dek. "You've become a real boring bastard, you know that? Whining on and on about the same horse shit, night after night. It's over. It's done. You survived." Dek cracked his knuckles. "Get over it, Narnok."

"Why, you cheeky little bastard. *You* weren't the poor victim who had roots growing through his flesh; have you no respect for a man's personal living nightmare? I've a good mind to teach you a fucking lesson."

"You reckon, do you?" snarled Dek, his temper rising. He lifted himself from his seat, fists clenched. He was powerfully muscled, with a shaved head and small, dark eyes. Both arms were bare, showing several freshly stitched wounds and a myriad of tattoos, some only half finished. "I keep hearing these threats, Axeman, but you never actually show me."

"I'll show you what it's like to lose a few fucking teeth," snarled Narnok, his own temper becoming inflamed. His eyes narrowed, and he licked his lips. "Like I did the last time."

"Yeah, I suppose you'll be moaning again that I fucked your wife next." Dek's eyes were gleaming.

"By the Seven Sisters, that's below the belt, Dek, and you know it! Apologise."

"No."

"Apologise!" roared Narnok, surging to his feet.

Dek rose to meet him. "I'll apologise when you stop whining like a pig with a spear up its arse."

"I'm taking bets!" yelled Weasel, pulling out a well-worn stub of a pencil and a small, tatty notebook. A little man, and friend to Dek, Weasel was always there whether the odds were good or not; he was renowned for his arithmetical dexterity.

Trista suddenly rose, snapping out two slender daggers, which she held to each man's throat. The big men were suddenly very still, anger subsiding like a spent wave.

"Gentlemen, your argument with one another is pointless," Trista smiled, and removed the daggers, nodding ahead, "when there are plenty of others willing to offer you conflict."

Dex and Narnok turned, and stared at the three newcomers.

"Trouble looking for trouble," muttered Dek. "I told you."

"Shut up," said Narnok, facing the three big men.

One took the lead, stepping forward. He wore his black hair long, braided with silver wire, and his face was broad, swarthy, eyes dark under brooding, shaggy brows. A short sword of black iron was sheathed on his back, and he carried himself with a poise, a balance, that marked him as a warrior.

"Narnok the Axeman?" he asked.

"Fuck off," said Narnok, hand on his knife. "I don't know you. I don't want to know you. Our conversation has ended." He began to turn.

"You are Narnok the Axeman, one of the... legendary Iron Wolves. You fought at Desekra, at the Pass of Splintered Bones against Orlana's mud-orcs, and with your companions..." he nodded at Dek and Trista, "... helped slay the Horse Lady."

"So?" snapped Narnok. "What are you, her mother?"

There came a ripple of laughter through The Fighting Cocks. They now had an audience.

The newcomer frowned, but fought to retain his composure. "My name is Zall Karn; I come from a small village north-east of Dakerath, at the foot of the Naldak Teeth. I have been sent here to ask for your help, Narnok of the Axe."

"Well, I don't do no favours," snapped Narnok, and turned his back on the stranger.

"There is a creature. A beast. One of Orlana's... *creations*. It has stolen our children, taken them up into the mountains, to its lair. We tracked it, hunted it down; but it slew six of our men. It's a ferocious beast. A killer. We only stopped when it threatened to kill all our little ones."

Narnok turned back, and read the anguish in the stranger's eyes. He shrugged. "Sorry, mate. Truly. I am sorry for your loss. But I ain't no fucking charity. Your problems are your own. Now let me finish my ale, or I'll have my friend Dek here put you on your fucking back." Narnok sat down and grasped his flagon, taking a hefty drink. Ale dribbled through his thick beard, staining his shirt.

"This creature," said Zall, his voice little more than a whisper of smoke which drifted through the tavern, curling like a snake eating its tail, "asked for you by name."

"Eh?" Narnok turned.

"Orlana's beast. It said it would release the children, but only if Narnok, one of the Iron Wolves, came to its lair."

Narnok shrugged. "As I said. I ain't no charity. The door's over there. Dek, mine's a whiskey, mate."

"I don't think you realise the gravity of the situation," said Zall.

Narnok ignored him. Dek glanced at Trista, who gave a little shrug and a half-smile. Her red dress shimmered as she moved, and she sat down, toying with her crystal flute of wine; but her eyes never left the three men, who were rooted to the spot, refusing to move.

This is going to turn ugly, she thought, and calmed her mind, readying for battle.

"Do you fight?" said Zall, suddenly. Narnok turned, and Dek looked up. "How about a wager? If I can put this one," he gestured casually at Dek with his thumb, "on his back, will you travel with us? Talk to this beast that seems to know your name?"

"What do I get if he wins?"

"I have a pouch of silver here." He palmed it, dropped it on the table with a solid *thunk*. "That should cover any breakages."

"Oi!" snapped Dek. "Don't be arranging shit when I'm stood bloody next to you, right?"

"Well, do you think you can beat him?"

Dek eyed Zall up and down. "In my sleep, mate."

"I'm taking bets!" shouted Weasel, chewing the end of his stubby pencil, and there was sudden activity as tables and chairs were dragged out of the way, wooden legs scraping the stone-paved floor to create a space at the centre of The Fighting Cock's main tavern room.

Dek removed his shirt, stretched out his back and shoulders, rolling his head with associated cracks of released tension. His physique was impressive, and damaged. Whilst athletic and well-muscled, he was a map of tattoos, scars and stitches.

Zall moved to a table, and his companions sat, taking the big man's cloak and shirt. Zall revealed a broad chest, thick with hair, and heavily muscled arms. In contrast, his body was clean, unlike Dek's, which almost represented an experimental cadaver from the medical hub at Vagan University.

Weasel, frantically scribbling, moved to the centre of the space and Dek and Zall approached one another.

"Right," snapped Weasel. "I want a clean fight. Well, kind of clean. No biting, eye-gouging or fish-hooking. When a fighter's down, the other backs off. You both understand?"

"Do we look like idiots?" snapped Dek, and Weasel paddled backwards, scribbling in his notebook, dark eyes glittering.

A rough circle had formed. Narnok sat, Trista standing behind him, both their eyes checking out Zall's two companions. If things went bad, they might have to move fast. Narnok made certain his double-headed axe was close by.

Dek approached leisurely, for he was an experienced pit fighter, and not one to rush in. He knew his limitations; there weren't many. Zall, also, weighed up Dek. He threw two straight rights, then a left hook which Dek took on his elbow, stepping in close and delivering a head butt that sent Zall staggering back, blood leaking from his nose.

"Just a warning," winked Dek, lifting his fists once more in a traditional pugilist's stance.

Zall mopped blood using the back of his hand, then grinned at Dek. "Your warning is well received."

He rushed in suddenly, grabbing Dek by the waist and powering him through the circle of people. They crashed into tables and chairs, sending them flying, but Dek rolled easily to one side, standing and whirling on Zall, who was already up, defence in place.

They moved back to centre of the circle.

"You'll be paying for all this shit," shouted Baderman, from behind the bar on which rested the gleaming, oiled stock of a Vagall & Vinters Model 3 crossbow. Just as a casual warning.

Dek waved the comment away, and charged Zall, and there came a flurry of punches, straights, hooks and uppercuts. Both men were fast, powerful, but Dek was experienced and caught Zall a tight fast right hook to the jaw, a left straight to the nose, then an overhead slam to the temple which put Zall down on one knee, head lowered, saliva drooling to the paving flags.

The game was over. Zall was out and done.

Dek gave a tight smile, and stepped in for the kill, but Zall looked up fast – like a striking snake – and delivered a short punch to Dek's balls that sent the pit fighter staggering back, face turning purple. Zall launched himself forward, and five punches put Dek on his back, where he lay stunned for a moment, before growling and rocking to his feet.

"I'm going to break out all your teeth for that, fucker," he snarled.

Zall spread his hands apart, and smiled. "But the wager is over. I won. I put you on your back. That was the deal."

Dek ran the words through his anger-fuelled mind, then turned and stared at Narnok, who leapt to his feet, stomping over to Dek.

"You bloody idiot! Look what you've done! I thought you said you could beat him…"

"Well, I didn't see you stepping into the ring!"

"Because you're the bloody pit fighter!"

Laughter had broken out, and the crowd moved in, surrounding Dek.

"You lost that fair and square," said one man.

"It's been near two years since I saw you hit the ground," said another, slapping Dek on the back.

"You've got to admit, he lured you in, then took out your bollocks," laughed a third.

Trista came over and, reaching up, put a hand on both Narnok's and Dek's shoulders. "Looks like we have a little journey to make." She smiled, sweetly, and moved on to the bar.

"We?" shouted Narnok, after her retreating red dress.

She looked back and gave a dazzling smile that had no place on the face of a killer. "Why of course, honeycake. We *are* The Iron Wolves, after all."

Snow was falling, the sky was bright, and Narnok had a bastard of a hangover. He glanced over to Dek, who'd just spoken and was staring expectantly, awaiting a reply. A cold wind gusted, rattling the leaves of the trees and bringing with it flurries of powdered snow.

"Eh?"

"I *said*, we should be there and back in three days. Gods, Narnok, you look like you drank the barrel."

Narnok groaned. "I think it was maybe two."

Their horses picked a modest pace down the forest trail, amidst a smattering of oak and ash, dotted with towering red pine and spruce that swayed in the breeze, higher needles whispering. Ahead rode Zall and his two companions, their moods grim. This wasn't a journey of leisure, but of desperation. It would seem their hope in Narnok was not high. They did not appear impressed by what they had witnessed.

"I still can't believe you lost the fight," moaned Narnok, scratching his thick beard. "Even *I* could have done better than that. By the Holy Mother, even *Trista* could have bested him!"

"I am actually listening to your conversation, you know," Trista said primly. She was riding a fifteen-hand grey, and had foregone the red dress in favour of canvas trews, leather boots and a thick wool coat of dark green. Her blonde curls were tied back, and she had a narrow rapier sheathed at her left hip, along with a vast assortment of hidden knives and throwing daggers, and an unstrung yew bow.

"Well Tris, all I'm doing is pointing out to this fight-losing oaf that you, even though you're a girl, could have decked that big bastard and we wouldn't be heading out into the wilds on some pointless mission." He grinned at her, showing a cracked tooth.

"First," observed Trista, "*even though I'm a girl,* I could have taken both of them out together." She smiled, a narrow slash of red. "And second, and more pointedly, both would have had their throats cut." Her face turned serious. "When I fight, I kill."

"Point taken, point taken," rumbled Narnok, looking sheepish.

They travelled through the day, along winding forest tracks that rose from the evergreens up a series of rolling hillsides, and past an abandoned village, the stone shells of former buildings, eerie and ghost-like in their silence.

Snow fell, lightly at first but increasing in intensity as the hillsides became more and more dotted with boulders, and they began to climb, horses labouring. The Naldak Teeth loomed close, dominating the sky, forbidding in their sheer bulk. These were peaks said to be haunted and, because there were generous paths around the foothills, nobody except convicted criminals and soldiers on the run felt the need to venture into the Naldaks. Nobody who was sane, at any rate.

Zall fell back to them as the sky darkened. "We're only an hour from my village. We can shelter there for the night, and head into the mountains at dawn. If that suits you?"

"Will there be food and ale?" snapped Narnok. He found that the older he got, the less he relied on formalities. Like simple manners.

"Hot fires, fresh baked bread, salt-cured pork and home-brewed ale."

"That would be good," said Narnok, nodding, his eyes hooded.

Trista cantered alongside him. "Are you well, honeycake? You seem... rude. Well, ruder than your usual self."

"I am pondering. On this creature, one of Orlana's *splice* by the sounds of it, which asks for me by name. Why? By all the demons of the Chaos Halls, *why* would it ask for *me*? This stinks worse than a ten-day dog corpse, Tris."

"This whole thing could be a trap, Axeman."

"Hmm. I think not. There are easier ways to assassinate an old soldier. No, I believe their story; I just can't fathom *why* this bastard would seek to talk to me, of all the grumpy old Wolves he could find."

"Maybe he doesn't want to talk. Maybe he sucks the marrow from old heroes' bones?"

Narnok fastened Trista with a hard stare, his one good eye narrowed, his milky eye, as usual, giving his face a harsh, unfriendly appearance. He looked less like a hero, more... mass-murderer.

"That isn't even funny."

The night passed without event, and Zall was good to his word. The village turned out to see Narnok, Dek and Trista arrive, lining the short, frozen-mud street, and Narnok wriggled uncomfortably under their sombre, sorrowful gazes. A village without children... A town where all sixteen little ones had been kidnapped by some terrible monstrosity. It sounded like a heroic song crooned by a bard who was earning his supper. Only now, *now* the pressure was on Narnok to save the day. Good old Narnok, hero of Desekra, a true and elite trained *Iron Wolf*. He'll save the day. He'll bring the children back. Only Narnok wasn't sure the villagers had any faith in the battered old soldier before them. He wasn't a pretty picture. And he stank like he'd drank half of

Vagandrak's distilleries.

The bread was warm, with fresh butter. The pork, a little over-salted, was succulent. The ale was weak, watered down to last the winter. But they did not complain. They welcomed the simple hospitality.

Zall's house was modest, but Trista was given her own room, and Dek and Narnok shared a second.

As they huddled down under rough, scratchy blankets, Dek blew out the candle.

"Dek?"

"Yeah?"

"Do you think we can rescue these children?"

"I'll die trying."

There was a long pause.

"Dek?"

"Yeah?"

"*Why?*"

Another long pause.

"It's just something we have to do, Narn. It's... the right thing to do. To protect those who need our protection. That's why I joined the army. That's why General Dalgoran picked us out as Iron Wolves. For the training, like. We were the right... breed."

"It could be argued that you abuse your skills in the pit. After all, that training wasn't meant for hurt against civilians. And you sure hurt plenty."

Dek smiled in the darkness. "Better a pit fighter than the master of a whorehouse. *The Pleasure Parlour,* wasn't it? Now *that* is abuse of one's former privilege." He was referring to Narnok's previous employment, until an over-enthusiastic member of a criminal syndicate brought Narnok's little empire crashing down.

Narnok considered this. "You're wrong, Dek. My whorehouse was a good place for the girls to work. Safe for them. I made sure of that."

"So you were offering a public service? Looking after the girls, so to speak?"

"Aye." Narnok yawned. "Aye. I suppose I was. Get some shut-eye, lad. We have a busy day tomorrow. Rescuing kiddies, and such-like."

"You know them splice take some fucking killing." Dek's voice was low, contemplative.

"Well, lad, we'd better do it right, then."

The horses managed the first thousand feet of the climb into the Naldak Teeth, and below them a world of folded white opened like a billowing satin cloak. The snow had stopped, but as they passed where the last straggled evergreens had given up the fight due to altitude, it came back with a fury, blasting them with a diagonal violence. By an oval of narrow standing stones they tethered the horses, then Zall and his men led the way up a steep path which snaked between two chimneys of teetering, towering rock. Ice had formed beautiful symmetry, a frozen waterfall; they climbed past this, emerging onto a narrow ledge.

"Look," said Dek, gesturing.

The world lay before them, a vision of sparkling crystal, a vast, pastel painting of subtle perfection.

"Let's get on to the beast," snapped Narnok, loosening his axe on his back. Twin blades gleamed, black and evil; soul-takers, widow-makers, bastard-slayers. "I ain't got all day."

Higher they climbed, until the ground suddenly levelled out between two walls of rock. A small valley opened before them. It was littered with rocks, and snow, and icicles as big as a man.

"The cave is at the end," said Zall. His demeanour oozed fear. It emanated from his core like smoke drifting from a volcano. He took a step back.

"Not coming with us?" rumbled Narnok, unkindly. His single eye glittered and, reaching back, he unsheathed his axe. The twin blades were rimed with ice. They gleamed, as if acknowledging the time had come, a time for slaughter.

"It asked for you," said Zall, and Narnok realised: the man had found his breaking point. Every man had one. For some it was the loss of limbs, or cancer. For this man, it was the possibility Narnok would fail. The chance he would not be able to rescue the children of the village.

"Stay here. I'll be back shortly," rumbled Narnok, and flashed a gap-toothed smile.

He set off, boots rattling rocks, and Dek and Trista padded along behind him.

He stopped. And turned.

"Yeah?"

"We're coming with you, obviously," said Trista.

Narnok shook his head. "No. This is… strange. This is just for me. I can sense it, in my bones."

"We're Wolves," said Dek. "If you face death, then by the Seven Sisters, we all fucking face it."

Narnok considered this; he gave them a hard smile. "So be it," he said.

They marched down the valley, a natural tomb created by the mountains. Huge rocks appeared as gravestones, their chiselled names and dates weathered by the elements over millennia. The wind howled between the rocks, low and mournful, the voice of widows, the voice of orphans.

"Great," muttered Narnok, and gave his axe several experimental swings. It whistled, like an old friend. An old lover. A girlfriend… *A doting wife. A betraying wife. A wife who'd hired a torturer to cut up his fucking face, burn out his eye with acid, just to find the…*

Money.

Ahhh. The money.

Narnok smiled, as the old violence settled into him. It spread through him, like blood through fresh spring water. It seeped through his bones and soul, and equilibrium found him, and he welcomed it, and he was ready for the art of killing. Ready for the death.

The valley ended at a series of caves. A soft, mournful song emerged. The mountain was singing for him.

"Creature!" bellowed Narnok, suddenly. "Show yourself! I am Narnok of the Axe, and you requested my presence. Well, I'm here, you bastard, and I'm ready. I want the children of the village now, or I'll…"

It came from the central cave, limping, its huge, distended head grinning at him with a maw that was beyond nightmare. The distorted equine head shook, the curved side-horn cutting a gleaming sigil of Equiem magick through the gloom of the mountain ravine. The beast was horrific, and it stank of putrefaction. Several large wounds in its flanks had started to rot. Narnok welcomed this. Hopefully, it would slow the bastard down.

Iron hooves struck sparks from the icy rocks, and the splice lowered its head, eyes looking up as its huge bulk, its solid cords of muscle, quivered in readiness to attack. It was huge, bent, broken and reformed; one of Orlana's twisted creations; one of Orlana's *meldings* of man and horse and dark, evil blood-oil magick.

Dek moved closer. There was a sliding of steel as he unsheathed his black iron short sword. Narnok was aware of Trista's bow in her hand. She could put down five shafts in the time it took the beast to attack... and yet. Yet still they stood, observing one another.

"I want the children," said Narnok, voice hard. *But fuck,* he thought, *that's one savage piece of twisted magick horse shit. The question is: Can we kill it?*

"Come... and get them," spoke the splice.

Narnok's face frowned, and the old anger came back. "Listen, bastard, release the kids. I am here. Release them, and then we will fight, and I'll settle whatever twisted retribution you have come here for."

"Of... course."

Narnok watched in absolute disbelief as the splice stepped to the side, and turning its great deformed horse head, said something to the darkness of the cave interior. The children ran forward, haggard, filth-smeared, many barefoot; crying, they sprinted down the valley, dodging rocks, their feet leaving imprints in the powdered snow.

At the end of the valley, Zall and the other men fell to their knees, weeping, their arms open to welcome back their children.

Narnok turned, and took a deep breath. "Now I kill you," he said, marching forward, knuckles white as he clenched his axe. *If I can.*

Trista notched an arrow, the string drawn back, fletch against her cheek. Her breath plumed in the chill air, like dragon smoke. Her grey eyes were emotionless.

The splice grunted, and blood pattered against the rock from an old, opened wound. Then it grinned at Narnok, with those great yellow fangs, those drooling black horse lips, and the eyes surveyed him unevenly and... Narnok shivered to the core of his soul.

"Don't you recognise me, Narn?" said the splice.

Narnok shivered. "No," he said.

"Come into my cave," said the beast.

Narnok stared at that massive creature, at the horn and the fangs, and the buckled iron hooves which had no doubt caved in a hundred skulls. He breathed deep the freezing mountain air.

"What? So you can eat my skull? No, I'll fight out here if it's all the same to you."

"On your wedding day, you wore… a white shirt, and a black suit. You… joked it was the funeral of your… single lifestyle."

Narnok blinked. "How could you know that?" he whispered.

"Look what… they did to me, Narnok. Look what that bitch did to me."

"Who are you?"

"I'm sorry. I'm so, so sorry… about… Xander. He destroyed your face. Your eye. Our… friendship." The beast's head lowered, the eyes lowered, and its muscles quivered. Then it turned, and limped into the cave; disappeared from sight.

"Who is it?" said Dek, voice low, his tone one of awe.

"It's Katuna," said Narnok, slowly. His mind was reeling. Emption swamped him; like nothing he had ever felt.

Dek frowned. "Katuna? Your wife? Your fucking *wife?*"

"Yes."

"So – why are you here?"

"I am here to kill her," said Narnok, and with axe in hand, strode into the cave.

Narnok was gone for an hour. When he emerged, axe blades stained with blood, his face was ashen, like a walking corpse.

Dek ran to him, and grabbed him before he fell to his knees. Then he held Narnok. Held him whilst the big warrior cried.

"She was beautiful," said Narnok, on the journey down the mountain. "Olive skin. Dark curls. And she loved me, by all the Gods; she loved me."

"Until she betrayed you."

"Yes, she betrayed me. But then…" Narnok gave a death's-head grin. "We all betray each other, don't we?" He rubbed his beard. Each step was a hallucination. Each weary footfall a disintegrated memory. "She hired Xander; to torture me. To get the money. My wealth, from the king! And she got it all. And through the money she made powerful contacts. And through these contacts, found her way to Zorkai, and Orlana, who was looking for subjects to… well, you know how the

Horse Lady created the splice. Dark magick. Evil, Equiem magick."

"She wanted you. At the end," said Trista, with understanding.

"Yes. To kill her. But more… she needed to apologise. To seek forgiveness."

"And you forgave her?"

"I forgave her," said Narnok.

Snow was tumbling once more as they reached the oval of tall standing stones. Narnok stroked the velvet snout of his mount, so beautiful, so affectionate. He patted her.

"What now?" asked Dek, carefully, his eyes meeting Narnok's iron gaze. "Should we leave you alone? With your memories?"

Narnok shook his head. And gave a genuine, friendly smile; a smile Dek had not seen alight the big man's face for… decades.

"Alone?" He laughed. "No. I'd like to get fucking drunk with my friends," he said.

About the Authors

Edward Cox is the author of novels *The Relic Guild* and *The Cathedral of Known Things* (both Gollancz), along with short stories, reviews and poetry that have appeared in various places throughout space and time. Currently living in the Essex countryside with his wife and daughter, Edward frequently has to fight off attacks by giant spiders.

Rowena Cory Daniells is the bestselling fantasy author of *King Rolen's Kin*, The Outcast Chronicles and *The Price of Fame* (paranormal crime). Rowena writes the kind of books that you curl up with on a rainy Saturday afternoon. She has a Masters in Arts Research and was an Associate Lecturer. Rowena has a very patient husband and six not so patient children. She has devoted five years to each of these martial arts: Tae Kwon Do, Aikido and Iaido, the art of the Samurai sword.

Stella Gemmell lives and writes in an old rectory in East Sussex. She has a degree in politics and is a journalist. She was married to David Gemmell and worked with him on his three Troy novels, completing the final book, *Troy: Fall of Kings*, following his death in 2006. Her first solo novel, *The City*, was published in 2013.

John Gwynne studied and lectured at Brighton University. He's been in a rock 'n' roll band, playing the double bass, travelled the USA and lived in Canada for a time. He is married with four children and lives in Eastbourne, running a small family business rejuvenating vintage furniture. His first novel, *Malice*, won the David Gemmell Morningstar award for best debut fantasy. His second, *Valour*, appeared in March 2014.

John Hornor Jacobs is the award-winning author of *Southern Gods*, *This Dark Earth*, the young adult Incarcerado series, and *The Incorruptibles*. Jacobs resides in the American South and spends his free time when not working on his next book thinking about working on his next book.

Mark Lawrence is the author of the Broken Empire trilogy starting with *Prince of Thorns*. His day job is as a research scientist tackling various issues associated with artificial intelligence. His proudest writing achievement was winning the David Gemmell Legend Award for his third book, *Emperor of Thorns*.

Lou Morgan is the author of the Blood and Feathers urban fantasy books about warring angels, and *Sleepless*, a YA horror involving a study aid that is too good to be true. Her short stories have previously appeared in anthologies from Solaris, Jurassic London, Alchemy Press, and PS Publishing, among others.

Anthony Ryan is the New York Times best-selling author of the Raven's Shadow epic fantasy novels and the Slab City Blues science fiction series. After a long career in the British Civil Service he took up writing full time after the success of his first novel *Blood Song*, Book One of the Raven's Shadow trilogy. He has a degree in history, and his interests include art, science and the unending quest for the perfect pint of real ale.

Andy Remic is the author of sixteen novels, the first published by Orbit Books in 2003, with his most recent books, *The Iron Wolves* and *The White Towers*, published by Angry Robot Books in 2014, which both feature the protagonists from "Retribution", his story in this volume. His novels have been translated into six languages. He also owns Anarchy Books and is a budding indie film director. His writing website can be found at www.andyremic.com, his filmmaking at www.anarchyfilms.co.uk. His new novel *The Dragon Engine* is out in 2015.

Gavin Smith is the John W. Campbell award nominated author of *Veteran*, *War in Heaven*, *Age of Scorpio*, and *A Quantum Mythology*. He also wrote the *Crysis: Escalation* short story collection, and co-wrote *Elite Dangerous: Wanted*, and *Empires: the First Battle*, with Stephen Deas. Of "Smokestack Lightning", he says: "I was very keen to try and write something that paid tribute to David Gemmell's obvious love of westerns, (though strictly speaking it's a high fantasy southern gothic), and the long-running connection between the western and fantasy genres."

Gav Thorpe has a long history with the Warhammer and Warhammer 40,000 universes, and has written many novels for the same. He is a New York Times best-selling author with the novella *The Lion*. His epic swords-and-sandals fantasy *Empire of the Blood* is available from Angry Robot. Gav has worked on numerous tabletop and video games as designer, writer and world creation consultant. He lives near Nottingham with his partner Kez and son Sammy.

Freda Warrington is the author of twenty-one fantasy novels, including the award-winning *Elfland*, from which this story borrows its mythology. Her alternative history of King Richard III, *The Court of The Midnight King* has just been reissued on Kindle, Audible, and in paperback. Titan Books are reissuing *A Taste of Blood Wine* and its sequels – a gothic yet sensual take on vampires, set in the 1920s – including a brand-new novel, *The Dark Arts of Blood*. More info on Freda's website: www.fredawarrington.com.

Released November 2015
From NewCon Press

Orcs:

Tales of Maras-Dantia

Stan Nicholls

A brand new collection of novellas, novelettes, and short stories, set in the internationally best–selling realm of the Orcs. Many of the stories are brand new and none have been previously collected.

Cover art by Fangorn.

What the critics have said of previous Orcs titles:

"Subverts traditional fantasy tropes by centring on the much-maligned orcs. It is quick, fast, dirty, very funny and often surreal." – *The Guardian*

"...a wonderful piece of storytelling; fast-paced with plenty of hairpin twists, crammed with loads of juicy battles and properly bad baddies."– *Tom Holt*

"Incorporating wall to wall action with undercurrents of dark humour… The heroes are orcs – though you wouldn't want to meet any of them on a dark night!"– *David Gemmell*

"The standard of prose is high... and the characterisation, both of individuals and races, is excellent."– *BSFA Vector magazine*

"This is high fantasy for readers who like their heroes ugly and their wizards weird."– *Jon Courtenay Grimwood in SFX magazine*

"Exciting and highly original."– *Waterstones online*

"Weirdly charming, fast-moving and freaky. Remember, buy now or beg for mercy later..."– *Tad Williams*

Tolkien will never seem the same to you again…

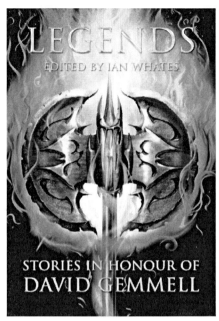

Cover art by Dominic Harman

LEGENDS
Stories in honour of
DAVID GEMMELL

Joe Abercrombie
James Barclay
Storm Constantine
Jonathan Green
Tanith Lee
Juliet E McKenna
Anne Nicholls
Stan Nicholls
Gaie Sebold
Jan Siegel
Adrian Tchaikovsky
Sandra Unerman
Ian Whates

Released in 2013, *Legends* is an anthology of all original stories written to honour the memory of one of Britain's greatest fantasy authors. Determined warriors, hideous creatures, wicked sorceries, tricksy villains and cunning lovers abound as fantasy's finest imaginations do their best... and their worst.

Produced in cooperation with the David Gemmell Awards, every copy sold raises money to support the awards.

Read the origins of James Barclays' famed *Ravens* mercenary band, enter Adrian Tchaikovsky's Realm of the Apt, follow warriors bent on vengeance and others seeking redemption, weep for the fallen, pity the lost, and cheer for the victors. Steel yourself, throw caution to the wind, and dare to enter the realm of *Legends*.

NEWCON PRESS

IMMANION PRESS
Speculative Fiction

The Moonshawl by Storm Constantine

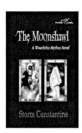

Ysbryd drwg… the bad ghost. Hired by Wyva, the phylarch of the Wyvachi tribe, Ysobi goes to Gwyllion to create a spiritual system based upon local folklore, but he soon discovers some of that folklore is out of bounds, taboo… Secrets lurk in the soil of Gwyllion, and the old house Meadow Mynd, home of the Wyvachi leaders. The house and the land are haunted. The fields are soaked in blood and echo with the cries of those who were slaughtered there, almost a century ago. Old hatreds and a thirst for vengeance have been awoken by the approaching coming of age of Wvya's son, Myvyen. If the harling is to survive, Ysobi must lay the ghosts to rest and scour the tainted soil of malice. But the ysbryd drwg is strong, built of a century of resentment and evil thoughts. Is it too powerful, even for a scholarly hienama with Ysobi's experience and skill? 'The Moonshawl' is a standalone supernatural story, set in the world of Storm Constantine's ground-breaking, science fantasy Wraeththu mythos. ISBN: 978-1-907737-62-6 £11.99, $20.99

Ghosteria 2: The Novel: Zircons May be Mistaken by Tanith Lee

Sometimes when people die, it comes as a great shock. Even to them…

A group of the dead linger here, in the yellow dwelling on the hill – once a castle, then a stately home, now falling into ruin. These ghosts drift and mingle, and brood on their lost lives. Death can be caused by so many things – war, pandemics, ordinary murder – even suicide or accident. Even time. But after death, surely, one could hope for peace? Not any more. For with 2020 the New Apocalypse began. Civilisation crashed, and outside this ancient building things terrible, predatory, mindless and unkillable roam and bellow.

Now all the lights have gone out for good –Where do you turn? ISBN: 978-1-907737-63-3 £9.99 $18.99

Immanion Press
http://www.immanion-press.com
info@immanion-press.com